THE BOOK OF ADAM

TOWN SECRETS

SCOTT GELOWITZ

For Jennifer,
Jessica, Zachary, Rachel and Rebecca.

You are my inspiration.

CONTENTS

ACKNOWLEDGMENTS

Thank you to my Family and Beta Reader team:

Charles and Anne Gelowitz,
Sheldon Gelowitz,
Cherie Frick,
Luke Frick,
Jennifer Gelowitz,
Kim Schaan,
and Kim Merasty.

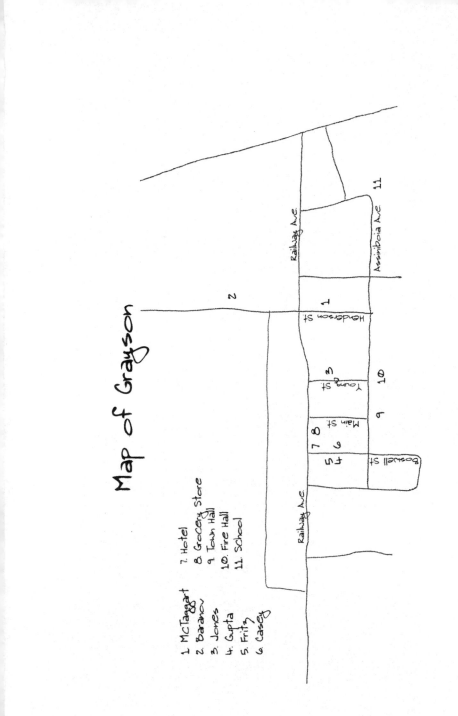

Map of Grayson

1. McTaggart
2. Baranov
3. Jones
4. Gupta
5. Fritz
6. Casey

7. Hotel
8. Grocery Store
9. Town Hall
10. Fire Hall
11. School

Railway Ave.

Railway Ave.

Henderson St

Young St

Main St

Boswell St

Assiniboia Ave.

CHAPTER ONE

The town of Grayson was buzzing with news, grim as it was.

"Did you hear? Something destroyed that town! There's not a soul left anywhere," said Aggie.

"Some of the buildings are still standing but not many," replied Martha, looking down toward her friend as they walked along Railway Avenue.

"Gives me the shivers, I'll tell you. I've met people from there before. Seemed like normal folks to me," said Aggie. Martha nodded in agreement.

"I sure hope they find out what happened. I feel like going on a long holiday 'til they figure it out. They're not that far away from here," replied Martha. Aggie shuddered.

The elderly ladies kept walking and talking until they turned the corner onto Main Street.

Although the sun was shining, it felt cool outside, especially for a summer day. The birds that usually filled the air with happy song seemed to sing sadly that morning.

Adam McTaggart sat on his bike in front of the grocery store, wondering when his friends would show up. He overheard Aggie and Martha talking as they walked past, ignoring him completely. *What did they say? A town was destroyed and the people are missing? Weird,* he thought.

James Jones the Third, (he preferred Jimmy), and Kevin Baranov rode up on their bikes. Jimmy had a puzzled look on his face.

"Hey," said Adam

"Hey," replied both Jimmy and Kevin.

"Did you hear about Langenburg?" asked Jimmy. "My parents couldn't stop talking about it this morning."

"I didn't know it was Langenburg, but I overheard Aggie and Martha talking about it when they walked by a few minutes ago," Adam replied, "I wasn't sure how much to believe. You know how those two can tell a story."

"Yeah, no kidding," chuckled Kevin. "My parents were acting pretty weird this morning too. I overheard the news on Dad's radio at breakfast, but they must have known about it earlier 'cause they were talking about Langenburg instead of listening. They never miss the news at our house."

The conversation stopped as a customer stepped out of the store carrying bags of groceries. The three boys waited in silence, looking around. When they were alone again, Adam spoke.

"What should we do now?" he asked.

Jimmy and Kevin looked at each other and shrugged.

"Let's see if Mark wants to do anything," said Adam.

"As long as we don't get seen by old George," said Kevin, "He freaks me out."

Jimmy laughed. "How come a big guy like you is scared of a little old man like George? He couldn't hurt you!"

"I'm not scared of him! He just creeps me out," replied Kevin.

The others smiled. They knew George was a little strange, but he wasn't dangerous.

"We'll ride around the block and coast into Mark's driveway from the other side," said Adam. "That way, we don't go past George's house so there's less chance he'll see us."

"We can try, but I think he can sense me coming," said Kevin. Adam and Jimmy chuckled.

It was a short ride to Mark's house, made slightly longer by the detour. As they approached, they could see the front of George's mobile home on the other side. Even though not much of it was visible, they could see things piled high in the front window. Adam couldn't imagine what the inside would be like.

As they pulled into Mark's driveway, George was nowhere to be seen. Even though he didn't admit it, Adam was relieved he didn't have to listen to George either.

Jimmy hopped off his bike and rang the doorbell while the other two stood a few steps behind him. Mark's dad answered the door and looked at the group.

"Hello boys, what are you up to today?" asked Gurpreet Gupta in his naturally low voice and rich East-Indian accent.

"Not too much, just hanging out," replied Jimmy. "We came to see if Mark wanted to come out with us today."

The door opened wide. "See you later Dad," said Mark as he squeezed his round belly between his father and the door frame.

"Just make sure you are home in time to eat, or your mother will be very very angry."

"Ok," Mark replied as he closed the door. "Let's go guys."

Mark grabbed his bike from beside the house as the others returned to theirs.

"HEY...YOU...KIDS...," came a yell from nearby. George jogged around the corner in a hurry to catch them.

Oh no, thought the group at the same time.

"Did you hear the news? The end of this town's coming! We're next! They're after the secret!"

"Hi Mr. Fritz," said Mark, seeming to have heard the warnings many times before.

"Mark, you and your friends need to get out of town! It's not safe here anymore. Just like I told you! They're coming for the secret," said George pointing at each of the boys.

"Who's coming?" asked Adam.

"...I don't know...but I know they're coming. Just listen to the news," said George

"Sure thing," replied Mark, trying to end the conversation and leave.

"Langenburg isn't the first place this happened to, you know. It's happened before...down east, on the coast... something's coming...," he repeated.

George stopped talking, having noticed Mark's dad appear in the window.

"You come over soon and I'll show you what I've found," George whispered, "You won't think I'm crazy then."

After a quick and almost frightened wave to Gurpreet, he turned and walked straight into his mobile home, locking the door behind him.

The boys looked at each other.

"I don't know about you guys, but this Langenburg thing has my parents pretty uptight," said Mark in a low voice, seeing his dad still in the window. He walked his bike toward the gas station and the others followed.

"Yeah, all of our parents are acting pretty strange," replied Kevin, with the other two boys nodding in agreement.

"Do you think George is onto something? I know I've always heard rumours about Grayson being different, but I never thought about it much," said Adam.

"I've heard a lot of his stories before, and they can be pretty convincing," said Mark. "When Dad makes me cut his grass and do odd jobs for him, I usually get stuck listening to his stories, like 'why no one from Grayson had to serve in either World War'. He has tons of stories about the founding families, hidden treasure, great evil destroying us all, and on and on. If it wasn't for his endless supply of chocolate bars and Root Beer, I wouldn't listen at all."

Kevin laughed. "You'd do anything for a free Root Beer, except work," he teased.

"You go listen to him for an hour and tell me it isn't work," Mark shot back.

"Anyway," Jimmy changed the subject as they walked, "what should we do today? It's the start of summer holidays and I'm already bored."

A car raced around the corner by the hotel, startling the boys and ending their conversation. It nearly slid into the pumps at the gas station before it recovered and sped past, pulling into the Gupta's driveway.

They watched as a man stepped out of the car and jogged up to the doorway.

"Isn't that Mr. Chen?" asked Kevin. "What's the big panic?"

The boys could hear a stressed conversation going on at the Gupta house.

"I should check it out," said Mark with a worried look on his face.

The group walked toward the Gupta house when they saw Gurpreet and Don Chen heading for the car.

"We have an issue at work. I'll be back later," Gurpreet called to Mark before jumping in the passenger seat. Don backed out of the driveway and sped past the boys, the engine roaring.

"What on earth could be such an emergency today?" asked Jimmy. "They work at the weather monitoring station. It's not like we get earthquakes here."

"I wonder if it has something to do with Langenburg," thought Adam aloud.

Had he known what was coming, Adam wouldn't have wasted the following few days in search of excitement with his friends. There would be plenty of excitement soon enough.

CHAPTER TWO

Adam woke up. Well, not exactly. He opened his eyes while lying in bed and looked at the clock. 6:34 am. Way too early to get up on a day he didn't have school. There was no going back to sleep though. His brain had started working and refused to return him to his dreams.

It had been a week since the news about Langenburg, and he hadn't thought about it until he woke that morning. It came to his mind in a vivid memory. Why would someone destroy an entire town, and just what happened to all the people? What if George was right and something *was* coming to Grayson? *Too early to think about that now*, he decided.

The sun shone through his bedroom window making it warm, even though it was early. It was a small room with few decorations, only things Adam had found or had built himself.

He sat up and looked around, then rolled out of bed to find clothes for the day. It was easy to choose a shirt as there were only two clean out of the five he owned. The jeans he had worn the day before weren't dirty, so he put them on over clean underwear. The rest of the previous day's clothes sat in a pile at the foot of his bed so he dropped them in the clothes hamper. That little bit of work would save him from hearing his mother complain later.

With careful steps he climbed down the narrow stairs. Having avoided all of the creaks, he turned into the cramped kitchen hoping to find something to satisfy his grumbling stomach. After searching through the cupboards for things he knew wouldn't be there, he settled for his usual piece of toast with a small bit of butter. *At least today I can have some milk,* he thought as he poured himself a glass.

Instead of sitting at the small kitchen table, Adam sat in one of the two living room chairs. They were the only furniture in the room except for the old television. The chair he chose was the older and uglier one, but it was the more comfortable of the two. His mother usually sat there, but she was still asleep, so Adam could enjoy it for the moment.

He finished eating, put his plate and glass in the sink and sat back down in the same chair, thinking about the day ahead. Kevin would meet him later, and they would decide what to do at that time.

Adam stared at the few pictures of his father on the mantle without really seeing them, mainly because there wasn't anything else to look at. If he turned on the TV and woke his mom, she would be furious.

He browsed each of the pictures, trying to remember his father, but the memories were weak. Edward had died when Adam was just two. Mary McTaggart was devastated, even though she said she had seen it coming. Years of drinking and smoking were bound to catch up with him, but a heart attack wasn't something anyone expected, especially since he was young and in good physical condition.

Something caught Adam's eye in a picture of Edward on the lowest shelf of the mantle. *Has that always been there?* thought Adam.

He moved and picked up the picture. It was a small portrait of Edward. The picture had been in the same place for as long as Adam could remember, but it seemed different somehow. On Edward's suit jacket was a lapel pin Adam hadn't noticed before. The pin was shaped like a bowtie and was easy to overlook. Deep in his mind Adam was sure he'd seen that shape around town before.

I wonder where that pin is? he thought. In days of boredom, he had gone through almost every drawer in the house, except for a few in Mary's bedroom, but had never seen it.

Adam heard movement upstairs, so he placed the picture back on the shelf and sat down in the other chair.

Mary made her way down the stairs and into the kitchen, triggering every creak along the way. She brewed herself a cup of coffee and sat in her living room chair.

"Good morning, Mom," said Adam.

Mary just looked at him and nodded slightly. Adam knew not to say much more until she had finished her first cup of coffee.

They sat in silence while Mary slowly sipped her black beverage, when Adam looked at the clock. It was 8:35 am. He must have stared at the picture for a lot longer than it seemed. It felt like a good time to be somewhere else.

He walked to the door, slipped on his runners and stepped outside. The morning air smelled of dew and grass clippings from their neighbour's lawn. The bright sun made him squint as he walked to the garage, but the warmth felt great.

Adam stepped through the side door of the small garage that sat near the back of the yard. It was nearly empty except for Adam's homemade bike, some old furniture, and a few tools he had either found or had been left there by the previous owner. His dad had left some tools behind, but Mary had sold anything of value long ago.

The garage was his refuge. Mary seldom bothered him when he was in it, unless she had chores for him, which seemed often. Most of the time, it was his own private space where he could do whatever he wanted.

The garage was where he discovered he had a talent for fixing mechanical things. He wasted hours pulling apart anything he could find and tried building other things from the parts, sometimes successfully. It was also where he built his bike from parts he collected at the dump, garage sales, and donations from his friends.

As he walked to the back of the garage, something in the corner caught his eye. A long time ago, that corner held a stove for winter heat. There had never been a stove there as long as Adam had been using the garage, and the only things left as evidence were the plugged chimney hole in the roof and the tin heat shield on the wall.

It was the heat shield that caught his eye. It covered a 2 square foot section on each side of the corner. The top edge of the left shield was hanging away from the wall a little. Being old and rusty it wasn't surprising, but Adam was concerned because his best hiding spot was behind the right heat shield. Years ago, the right side had come away from the wall, and he found that he could make it look like it was still secure with one well-placed nail. Most of the time, he had only few dollars in change hidden behind and nothing else.

He checked his hiding spot first, and after finding the money untouched he inspected the left side. It looked like the nail head rusted just enough for the tin to pop off, but he decided to check behind anyway.

He pulled the tin away from the wall and looked into the dimly lit space. To his surprise, something was there. He reached in and pulled out a large cardboard envelope. The envelope was a heavy one used to mail important documents and looked like it had been there for a while. It was addressed to Edward, but there was no return address.

The top was open, so Adam reached inside. He pulled out a small stack of papers and pictures. The picture on top was of a group of people standing in front of Town Hall. It must have been the Grand Opening, because they were all dressed in formal clothes and there were decorations hanging in the background. If it *was* the Grand Opening, the picture was from 1910. He had learned the year it was built while on a class trip a few years before. The date was carved into a brick near the main entrance.

Adam looked at the picture a little closer. Each of the people wore the same lapel pin as the one Edward wore in his portrait. Since he had just noticed the lapel pin earlier that morning, the ones in the Town Hall picture stood out. He would have overlooked them at any other time.

He set the pack of paper and pictures on the workbench nearby and looked back in the envelope, checking for anything he might have missed. As he angled the envelope toward the light of the lone window, something shiny flashed at the bottom. He reached in and pulled out a lapel pin, exactly the same as the ones they wore in the Town Hall picture.

The lapel pin was bowtie shaped, over an inch long and half an inch wide. A needle that was used to attach the pin to clothing ran the length of the back. The sharp end was held in place under a small metal latch, keeping it from poking whoever was handling it.

He felt a connection with it right away, sure that it *had* to have been his father's. Why else would it be hidden in their garage?

The crunch of gravel under bike tires snapped Adam back to reality. Someone was coming. Without thinking, he shoved everything back in the envelope and slipped it back where he found it.

The side door flew open and Kevin stuck his head inside.

"Waldron's been destroyed just like Langenburg," he said.

CHAPTER THREE

Adam was shocked by the news. Waldron was only 30 miles away.

"How do you know?" he asked Kevin.

"It was on the radio this morning when I got up. Mom and Dad were listening to it in the kitchen while I ate breakfast."

"What did it say?"

"Not much. There was a strange fog around the town, same as Langenburg. When it went away, the first people into Waldron couldn't find anyone. One guy reported that doors were ripped off their hinges and there was glass everywhere from all the broken windows. As soon as they got there, the police chased everyone away. They said they'll release news as soon as they know anything."

Adam looked at Kevin, thoughts running through his head.

"Do you really think we could be next?" he asked after a long pause.

"I don't know, but I'm starting to think George isn't as crazy as we thought. That's *really* painful to admit," said

Kevin looking somewhat sheepish.

Adam thought for a few moments. "We should talk to George," he said. "We've heard Mark's version of his stories, but I doubt Mark ever really listened."

"Yeah, he would've been stuffing his face the whole time or he wouldn't have been there at all!"

Adam laughed a little. "Should we ask Mark to come along?" he said.

"Naw, let's just leave him at home. He's heard it all before," said Kevin.

Adam nodded and picked up his bike, following Kevin outside. After manoeuvring it through the small side door they were on their way. It wasn't far from Adam's house to George's, but in Grayson no two points were far apart.

Arriving at George's, they parked their bikes and stepped up to his door. The screen door was barely hanging on and had more holes than screen. At one time it had been white, but the sun had faded it to a pale yellow.

Adam opened it and knocked. They could hear some rustling, then a far away voice from deep inside said, "Just a minute."

After a short wait the inner door opened slightly and George peeked out with one eye. After recognizing his company, the door opened enough to see his entire head.

"You heard about Waldron, didn't you?" said George.

The boys shook their heads in agreement.

"What do you want from me, then?"

"We just want to hear what you think is going on and make up our own minds," replied Kevin.

George stared at them, trying to read their faces. After a few moments, he must have decided they were trustworthy.

"Well, if you're willing to listen, come on in. Excuse the mess," he said, opening the door wide.

They followed George into his house. The place was dirty and packed with things from floor to ceiling in most places. Piles of newspapers and stacks of boxes were everywhere. If there was a method to the mess, neither boy could tell.

"So, what do you want to know?" asked George, leading them over a large box.

"Everything," replied Adam, following close behind. "What do you think is destroying towns, and why do you think we're next?"

George cleared some boxes away revealing an old love seat. He gestured for Kevin and Adam to sit. They did, even though the seat was dirty.

"Ok then. Where should I start?" George said to himself, pausing in thought. "So, as you know, the Town of Grayson was founded in 1908. Basic knowledge. And you also probably know that there were 6 different families that founded the town."

Adam and Kevin nodded in agreement.

"Didn't it ever seem strange to you that the founding families came from so many different places?"

Kevin looked like he was thinking really hard.

"Not really," said Adam, "but I never really thought about it."

"Yeah, to *you* it doesn't seem strange, but just think

about it. It was 1908. You had Russian, English, Irish, Indian, Chinese, and German men all coming here on the *same* train at the *same* time? I'm amazed they made it here without someone getting hurt, or even killed. And when they arrived, they worked together in peace, like old friends. Some of their home countries were at war with each other, and yet they all worked together without any major issues. That's what I find strange. There had to be something uniting them."

George shuffled through a pile of papers as he spoke.

"What else surprises me is why they would get off *here*? You have to remember, there was *nothing* here. No buildings, no roads, no rivers – nothing but sticks and prairie. At the time, it was hard to even *get* here." He pulled out a map of North America and held it in front of the boys.

"We're in the middle of North America, East to West, and far enough North. Pretty well the middle of nowhere, especially in 1908. Why *here?*" He pointed to the location of Grayson on the map.

Adam shifted uneasily. Maybe it was the information he was hearing, or maybe it was the forty year old love seat he was sitting on.

"They get out here, set up camp, and start working on building the town. They get a few houses up and soon bring their families and relatives to help build more. Within a couple of years, they've built some really impressive structures - Town Hall, the hotel, and a few others. After looking through most of the original buildings myself, I found this symbol somewhere in each one." George shuffled through a stack of papers as he spoke.

He found a couple of pictures and handed them to the boys.

Kevin didn't recognize the first one, but Adam did. It was a picture of the lapel pin he had just found, blown up from a smaller image. The word "League" was printed on a label in the picture. Adam hid his shock from the others.

The second picture showed the symbol carved into a piece of wood. It was labelled 'Hotel'.

"What is this? What does it mean?" asked Adam.

George thought for a moment. "I've been trying to find that out for years. *I* think it's the symbol of a secret group that the Founders belonged to. Whatever the organization is, it's what made them cooperate with each other instead of fighting. I have no idea what the purpose of the group was, but I have a couple of ideas. In all the research I've done I haven't even found a name for the group, besides the word "League" you see in that picture. Whatever it is, it's a well-guarded secret."

"But this is all over 100 years ago?" Kevin stated. "You still think this 'League' is operating here?"

"Yes, I do, but I think only a few people in town are members. I also think that they are guarding something – a treasure of sorts – but I don't know what."

"And this *treasure* is what someone was looking for in the other towns?" asked Adam, following George's logic.

"Right. I think the other towns are different branches or locations. Maybe the towns were hiding their own treasures as well, I'm not sure."

"Let's back up a second," said Kevin. "You think a bunch of people in town are part of this 'League'?"

"Yes and no. At one time I think everyone was part of the organization, but I don't think there are many members left. *I* think there's only one person who knows what the secret is, and maybe one person who knows how to find it as a backup. The less people that know about something, the easier it is to hide."

"Who do you think it is?" asked Adam.

"Well, I first thought it would be the Mayor, but that's too easy. He's too much of a politician. And he's kind-of stupid," said George without missing a beat.

The boys chuckled. They knew George was right. Mayor Jeff Wyndum's nickname since childhood was Windbag. The townspeople had voted him in as Mayor just to get him out of town on business trips. While he was gone they didn't have to listen to his stories, and when he got back he would at least have new ones to tell.

"So, I've narrowed it down to the Town Council, because they decide the direction the town takes as far as building and development. Just which ones are members, I don't know. As you know, we haven't had much development in a long time."

"Who else might know something about the symbol?" asked Adam.

George looked at him, paused, then said, "Well... your dad *was* at the top of my list....until....you know..."

It seemed to almost hurt George to speak about Ed McTaggart in front of Adam.

"There has to be others you suspect?" Adam asked again.

"Of course, I'm just not positive. My neighbour here," he pointed to the Gupta house, "is the grandson of one of the founders. He's the only one who stayed here while the rest of his family moved on, and he *is* the oldest son," replied George.

"Do you think he knows the secret?" asked Kevin.

"I've shown him the picture of that lapel pin before and asked him what it meant, but he just pretended he had never seen it before. The look on his face told a different story."

George glanced at the clock, nearly hidden behind a stack of magazines. "Ok boys, It's time for me to go. The bus is almost here and I'm getting out while I still can."

"You're leaving?" asked Kevin.

"Yep, and I think you should do the same."

Adam and Kevin made their way back to the door as George led the way.

"Thanks for talking to us," said Adam as they stepped out and took a deep breath of fresh air.

George looked side to side making sure no one was around.

"Like I said, get out of town for a while. Convince your parents to go on a vacation or something. Langenburg and Waldron happened exactly a week apart, so you don't have much time," said George. "Now go home." He pulled his head back into his house and slammed the door.

Kevin looked at Adam and shrugged his shoulders as they walked back to their bikes.

"What do you think?" asked Kevin.

"Follow me," said Adam without answering Kevin's question. "I have something to show you."

He hopped on his bike and led Kevin back to his

garage, saying nothing the entire way.

Adam jogged into the garage and took the pin from its hiding place, but left the pictures in the envelope. Kevin had stayed at the front of the garage, so Adam walked back to him, opening his hand as he got closer.

"Does this look familiar?"

Kevin's face showed the shock he felt. "That's the one from the picture George showed us! Where did you get it?"

Adam explained how he found the pin.

"What should we do with it now?" asked Kevin. "Should we ask your mom about it?"

"No. Definitely not." Adam knew that asking Mary would get the pin taken away and they'd be left without answers. "I'm not sure what to do. I think we should show it to Mark, though. Maybe he knows something more, being the oldest son of the oldest grandson of a founder."

"I doubt it, but another opinion couldn't hurt, even if it is *his,*" said Kevin.

They rode back to the Gupta house and rang the doorbell. Mark answered the door.

"Is your dad here?" asked Kevin.

Mark looked at them as if the question was strange.

"No, he's gone to work again."

Adam and Kevin looked at each other, and Mark picked up on the look.

"What's going on?" he asked.

"Come out and we'll tell you," said Adam.

Mark followed as they walked south from his house. They stopped in front of the old lumber yard and sat on the step of what used to be the office. No houses were nearby, so they could speak freely without being overheard.

Adam and Kevin filled Mark in on their visit with George.

"Thanks for not taking me, really. I've heard all those stories and seen his pictures a thousand times," said Mark.

"So, do you recognize this?" asked Adam as he brought out the pin and showed it to Mark.

Mark was clearly shocked. "No way! Where did you find this? Not from George?"

"No, Adam found it at home. It was his dad's. He even has a picture of his dad wearing it," said Kevin.

"Just look at it! It's the one in George's picture!" exclaimed Mark. "That makes me re-think all the stories he told me. I wish I would have listened more. What if there *is* a treasure here in Grayson?" He paused for a second, and the others could see another thought take over his face. "Whatever happened to the other towns *could* happen here!" he exclaimed.

Adam and Kevin nodded in agreement, having already thought the same.

Adam asked "Has your dad ever said anything to you about these stories?"

"Why would my dad have anything to say?" asked Mark.

"George seemed to think that because you are direct descendants of one of the Founders, your Dad would know about this pin and possibly even the secret behind it," said Adam.

"Nope. If he knows something, he sure hasn't filled me in," said Mark.

They sat in silence for a few moments, each boy deep in thought.

After a while, Kevin broke the silence. "What should we do now?"

"I'm not sure," said Adam.

"Let's go for a walk. I think better when I'm moving," said Kevin.

"Well, I think better when I'm sitting," Mark replied.

"You must think a lot then," Kevin shot back.

Mark was about to argue with Kevin when Adam stood.

"I agree with Kev. Let's go for a walk," said Adam. "Is it ok if we leave our bikes at your house?"

Mark nodded.

Adam crossed the road and walked toward the hotel. Mark and Kevin caught up and walked beside him, one on each side.

CHAPTER FOUR

The boys walked along the street, not speaking as they passed Mr. Casey's house. Mr. Casey was cutting his lawn again as they waved hello. He nodded back with his usual scowl.

"I think blade number 233,487 is out of place," said Mark once Mr. Casey turned away with his mower.

They laughed at Mark's sarcasm as the noise of the mower drowned out their voices.

Ben Casey cut his lawn every second day, even if it was raining a little. Everyone in town knew it was his obsession. His yard was always beautifully maintained and he stood guard over it, grunting at anyone who came too close. Because the Gupta's lived across the street, Mark had cut Ben's lawn a few times after Ben sprained his ankle the previous summer.

"Every time I cut it, he made me go over it *three times*. He kept saying 'It isn't right, do it over.' " Mark imitated Ben's gruff voice. "He paid me well, but I'm never doing that again!"

The boys chuckled and continued walking. They turned the corner at the hotel and walked toward the store. The smell of food followed them from the hotel, where the bar doubled as a restaurant during the day.

"We could go out to the station and talk to Mark's dad and Mr. Chen," said Kevin, returning them to the subject they had all been thinking about.

Adam shook his head. "You heard George. He's tried to talk to Mr. Gupta without any luck. I don't think we'd get any more answers than he did."

"I don't think Dad knows anything anyway," said Mark. "He couldn't even keep it secret that he was taking Mom to Mexico for their anniversary. Before he could even surprise her, Aggie and Martha asked Mom if she was excited about her trip to Cancun. Dad swears he didn't say anything, but he had to have told a lot of people 'cause he doesn't exactly hang out with those two old quacks."

"Yeah, but this seems like a secret you'd take to your grave," said Adam.

"True, but I've known him my whole life, and I just can't imagine him knowing something *that* secret. It would almost make him cool." Mark laughed at the thought.

"Maybe we should go dig around in the Town Archives. We might find something there," said Kevin.

Mark looked at Kevin like he was speaking another language. "Town Archives? What are you talking about?"

Kevin and Adam looked at each other puzzled.

"The Town Archives? In the basement of Town Hall? We went there on a field trip in Grade Three?" said Kevin.

"That was the Town Archives? I just remember a lot of boring old pictures, and it smelled funny."

Kevin had a grin on his face. "You were more interested in the free doughnuts anyway!"

"Ha ha, funny. Although I do remember the doughnuts." Mark's eyes glazed over.

"Anyway, Kev, that sounds like a good idea," said Adam. "Let's see if anyone's there and if they'd let us look around."

"Let's stop and get a drink on the way," Mark interrupted as they neared the grocery store.

"Umm - how about not. You don't need it," said Kevin. "I'm sure there's a water fountain at the town office if you're thirsty." Kevin knew Adam didn't have any money and wouldn't take a hand-out. Avoiding the store just avoided any awkwardness.

Mark picked up on it, but still had a little tantrum. "Yes Mom." he replied.

They turned the corner onto Main Street and immediately saw Town Hall at the end. It was a stone building that looked more like a church than a town office. It had a tall steeple with a clock on the front, built into a section of the roof that covered the double door entrance. Four large pillars supported the overhanging roof. The building looked strange in the town of 250 people, much more suited for City Hall in a small city rather than in a tiny prairie town.

"Looks pretty deserted. Maybe we should come back tomorrow," said Mark.

"Mrs. Jones only lives a block away. You can't tell if anyone's here until you try the door. You just don't want to go into the basement again," said Kevin.

"N-no, that's not it," Mark stammered.

Adam walked up to the double-doors and tried one handle. It was unlocked, so he opened the door and stuck his head inside.

"Hello," he called, hoping to hear Mrs. Jones reply.

Nothing.

"Hello," he called again. Someone had to be there. The door *was* unlocked.

He stepped inside and motioned for the others to follow.

"Hello," came a voice from far back in the building.

The boys didn't recognize the voice because it came from so far away. They looked at each other and Adam shrugged. He walked toward the reception desk and the source of the reply. Usually, Jimmy's mother Lora was sitting at the desk, but she wasn't there at the time.

Adam raised his voice, "We're hoping to look through the archives, if you'll let us."

"Hang on," came the voice from a distance.

Adam looked at the other two and mouthed, "I think it's Wyndum."

Kevin and Mark hung their heads. The last thing they wanted was to listen to Jeff telling them how to be more like him. They'd heard it all before - multiple times. Everyone avoided Jeff so much that when he did get a captive audience, it was usually a long and painful event.

Mark started to turn toward the door, but Kevin grabbed him giving him a disapproving look. Mark hung his head, disappointed that his friends wouldn't let him get away.

They heard a door open and saw Jeff appear far down

the hallway leading to the reception area. He walked to the front desk with a large grin on his face – he had an audience!

"Sorry about that, I was just working on important Mayor stuff. Too important to go into details with you right now." The look on his face screamed 'I'm important - just ask me.'

"So what can I do for you boys? Need some advice about girls? I'm pretty successful with them you know. Don't know how I get time when I'm in the big city at Mayor meetings and everything."

"Actually, Mr. Wyndham, we were just wondering if we could look through the archives," said Adam.

"That's pretty boring on a summer holiday, isn't it? It's a nice day out. You should be riding bikes on the bike track. You know, I was a pretty great bike racer in my day. They called me 'Windy Windham' because I rode like the wind. That was before the internet and cell phones and stuff like that..."

"We're just going to help Adam look for pictures of his Dad," Mark interrupted. "His mom doesn't have many ... and ... we thought there might be some in the archives." Adam was impressed with Mark's cover story. He realized that they should have thought about it before walking in the door.

The look on Jeff's face changed when Mark mentioned Adam's father. Most of the townspeople had sympathy for Adam, having lost his father so young.

"Oh ... I see ... Yeah ... I guess there *could* be some pictures from baseball tournaments or church picnics in the files," said Jeff. "I'll let you go down and look for a while if you want. If you find any, you can make a copy at the photocopier over there," he pointed to a machine in the corner. "That's one of the best copiers out there. I researched it myself. Just 25 cents per copy and you can leave your money in the jar."

"Thanks," replied Adam.

"Follow me."

Jeff led them to the back corner of the building where the narrow, poorly lit stairway led down. It made you feel that you descended far into the earth.

As they exited the stairway, Jeff turned on the lights and the boys realized that they really were quite far underground. The ceiling was at least 12 feet high. The main floor was just over ground-level, leaving no room for windows in the basement, which added to the feeling of depth. The ratty old wiring that ran the lights was completely exposed and looked like it could start a fire any moment. Everyone who saw the basement had an uneasy feeling, so it was almost always empty.

"You might find some pictures over in those files." Jeff pointed to a row of cabinets. "It's all organized by year then alphabetically - that's what I've been told. Oldest files in the cabinets on the left and they get newer to the right," he pointed as he spoke. "I haven't looked through any of them in years. Thank God for Lora. She keeps them all straight."

"Ok, thanks," said Adam, hoping Jeff would just go back upstairs for a while.

"Yeah, Lora ... I wouldn't be lost without her, but she takes care of all the boring stuff. I *could* do it, but I have more important things to manage. That's what being at the top is all about. You have to have people beneath you to take care of the boring things and free you up to really *manage.* You know what I'm saying?"

The boys nodded, but weren't really listening. They could tell that Jeff was about to give them a long boring speech about how great he was. *If only his phone would ring and get him out of here*, thought Adam.

"Where is Mrs. Jones?" asked Kevin.

"Oh, well, being that I'm a great manager, I gave her the afternoon off. Told her I'd watch the front desk for her."

"Can you tell if someone comes in the door from down here?" asked Kevin, trying to lead Jeff to the obvious answer.

"No, there's no way of hearing it. Too deep, and the floors are too thick..."

There was an odd pause as Jeff was slow to catch the train of thought.

"Now that you mention it, I'd better get back up there. I don't want anyone thinking I'm slacking on the job. I have a reputation to uphold!"

With that, Jeff turned around and headed for the stairway. He paused and turned to face them again.

"I'll come back and get you in about an hour when it's almost closing time. If you have any questions or you're done before that, just come up and find me. My office is across the hall from the top of the stairs."

"Ok, thanks again," said Adam ending the conversation.

Jeff winked, gave them a big smile that clearly meant 'you owe me and I'll make you pay later', then turned and climbed the stairs.

After Jeff was gone, Mark put his face in his palm. "That guy is *so annoying*," he said.

"Nice job getting him out of here Kev," said Adam. Mark nodded in agreement.

"Thanks, but I just couldn't stand listening to him anymore."

Adam grinned.

"So where do we start?" asked Mark.

"Who knows? Just pick a cabinet and see what you can find. I doubt anything is filed under 'S' for secret, or 'P' for pin," said Kevin.

With that, each boy found a filing cabinet and started searching. Adam began at the oldest section and the others spaced themselves over the rest with Mark at the end.

After some time, Mark called out, "Whoa! Guys… come look at this!"

Adam and Kevin ran over. He held a picture and turned it toward them. It was a picture of a two-headed calf.

"Why'd you call us over for this?" said Adam, a little upset.

"It's kinda cool and gross at the same time! It's from the Anderson's farm in the 60's. I heard someone talk about it once, but thought it was just a story."

"Yeah, but you made us lose our spots. Next time it's something cool, let us know before calling us over," said Adam again, a little less upset. The two-headed calf *was* interesting.

They returned to the files and continued from where they had left off. There were pictures of church picnics, school functions and sporting events, but no records of anything they were looking for. The only picture they found of Edward McTaggart was a class picture in grade 8, around the same age as Adam. He was easy to spot because of the resemblance.

"AAAAAAHHHHHHHHHH...."

The loud scream from close behind made the boys jump. Kevin let out a very feminine whimper.

Jeff was laughing hard behind them. "S-s-sorry guys, I just had to. You were so *intense* looking at those files."

The boys forced out a chuckle.

"Yeah, you got us good," said Adam.

Jeff was clearly pleased with himself, although he could tell that Kevin wasn't impressed, probably because of the whimper.

"I was just coming down to tell you it's closing time soon. You've been here well over an hour."

Adam looked at his watch and confirmed the time, surprised it had passed so fast.

"Are you or Mrs. Jones going to be here tomorrow?" Adam asked.

"I'm pretty sure that Lor...Mrs. Jones will be here. Are you intending to come back?"

Adam nodded. "I probably will, but I don't know about these two." He looked at his friends.

"Ok. Just don't start acting like his neighbor," said Jeff pointing at Mark, "We had to throw him out of here a few times when he didn't want to leave."

"Yeah, he's unique, that's for sure," said Mark.

"Are there any other files that George wouldn't have gone through?" asked Adam.

"Well, he went through everything down here, and there's not really anything else on the main floor. I think he's gone through it all."

Adam was disappointed. He should have realized that George would have already gone through everything at Town Hall. George had even told them about going through the original buildings.

Jeff saw the disappointment on their faces. Kevin was still looking unhappy over his un-manly whimpering.

"Did anyone ever tell you about the secret door?" he asked.

The boys looked at each other, shrugging shoulders and indicating no knowledge.

"I didn't think so. Only a few people even know about it. Come with me, I'll show you."

Adam went from disappointment to excitement in a heartbeat.

Jeff headed toward the corner of the basement opposite of the stairs. The boys were curious to see what Jeff was talking about, so they followed close behind.

He opened an old wooden door to a long, narrow storage room that ran along the back of the basement. As they stepped inside, they saw boxes of decorations stacked high throughout the room. Some of them looked as if they would topple over at any minute. Some were neatly stacked on shelves, yet others were stacked hap-hazard on the floor.

They wound their way through the maze of boxes trying not to trip or knock anything over. When they neared the corner that was under the stairs, the forest of boxes opened in a clearing.

In the dim lighting under the stairs Adam saw a dark panel on the wall. It didn't look like a door, but more like a patch over a large hole in the wall, starting a few inches off the floor. It was made of individual boards running up and down with two boards nailed across to hold them all together. A large bolt in each corner seemed to anchor the panel to the wall.

"Here it is," said Jeff, pointing at the panel.

"That's a door?" said Mark

"Well, I don't think the wood panel is a door. I think it's covering an opening for a door that was never finished. Most people don't agree with me and argue that it's just covering some bad foundation work. I'm pretty good at construction though, if I do say so myself, and I think there's a doorway behind this that they boarded up. The Fire Hall is on the other side of the park over there," he pointed in the direction of the Fire Hall. "I think they meant to dig a tunnel to link the two and never finished it. There was another one just like this in the basement over there until they built the new fire-station."

Adam looked carefully at the panel and then at the clearing while Jeff spoke. *Why would someone leave this area free of boxes when the rest of the storage room is packed so tightly?* he wondered.

"Do you have a light on your phone?" he asked Mark.

"Yeah," he said reaching into his pocket, "but don't use it too long or you'll kill the battery."

Mark tapped the screen a couple of times and a beam of light streamed from the back. Adam took the phone and pointed it first at the floor, then the surface of the panel. It looked old and worn. *Maybe they used old boards to build the panel?* he thought.

Adam moved the light up and down the right side of the panel but didn't see anything interesting. He continued with the light on the left side and stopped halfway up. The three boys gasped at the sight.

Perfectly formed in the cement was the bowtie symbol.

CHAPTER FIVE

"You saw that, hey. Pretty cool...It's just the sign of the stonemasons that built this building...I'm pretty sure." Jeff didn't sound completely convinced of his own statement.

Thoughts ran through Adam's head. The area seemed to be cleared so the panel could be opened, but there were no visible hinges or latches. A panel that large and thick would need some big hinges, but there only seemed to be nails holding the boards together, along with the bolts holding it to the wall. Adam moved closer to examine the panel. Some of the nail heads on the boards that held the panel together had small shiny scratches on them. The top edge seemed to be rounded off in the middle and smoother than the side and bottom edges.

"Ok boys, time's up. I've got lots of important things to do yet today, and I'm sure your parents are looking for you to get home. It's after 5 o'clock." He ushered them back out of the storage room with a wave of his hands.

They knew that Jeff's important things to do probably involved an online dating site, since every woman in a hundred-mile radius already knew Jeff, and each likely had the same opinion of him.

Adam didn't hear Jeff talking as they made their way out of the storage room and back upstairs. He tried to figure out if what he just saw could really be a door. If it was, how did it open, and what was it hiding?

"... and that's how I became the youngest Mayor ever, but it was just because of how much everyone likes me." Adam began to understand Jeff's words again as they walked outside through the main doors.

"Thanks for letting us look at the files," said Adam.

Jeff smiled his now-you-owe-me smile. "No problem, anytime. Just keep it between us that I showed you that door, ok?" The boys nodded and wondered how many stories they'd have to hear in order to pay for the knowledge.

Jeff walked to the back of the building where he parked his car as the boys walked up Main Street.

"Do you really think that's a door?" asked Mark. "It just looks like someone tried to cover up a hole or something."

Kevin shrugged and looked at Adam, who seemed deep in thought.

"I wouldn't think anything of it, but the symbol next to it makes me wonder if there's something to Jeff's story. Did you see that storage room? Why would you have the area around that panel clear and the rest of it stuffed to the ceiling, unless you needed it to open." Adam kicked a small stone as he spoke.

"You're saying it's still being used as a door?" Kevin looked at Adam, puzzled.

"Yeah. Something about it makes me think so, but I don't know what."

"We know Jeff would have opened it for us if he knew how, so it can't be him. It would have to be Mrs. Jones. She's the only other person working there." Kevin looked puzzled by his own thoughts.

"There's the Town Councillors too," said Mark. "They meet there once a month, but I don't know if they have door keys."

Adam looked at the others. The more he thought about what he had just seen, the more his suspicion and curiosity grew.

"I better get home; I'm getting hungry. Mom'll be mad if I'm past 5:30," said Mark after looking at his watch.

"What are you guys doing later?" asked Adam. "It *is* a Friday night."

"I have to babysit my sisters. Mom and Dad are going out tonight," said Mark, disappointed.

"You're just going to put them in front of the TV and eat snacks anyway," said Kevin. "Your parents will probably buy you whatever you want just for doing it too."

"It's a lot more work than that! You're just lucky your older sister takes care of *your* little sisters so *you* don't have to," said Mark, trying to make it seem like he was offended.

Kevin ignored Mark. "I can probably get out for a couple of hours tonight. Why don't I come get you when I'm done eating?" he said to Adam.

"Sounds like a plan," said Adam, happy that he wouldn't be stuck at home with his mother.

"See you tomorrow," said Mark as he started walking home.

Adam and Kevin waved a weak see-ya-later.

The two started walking home together, as their homes were in the same direction, not far from each other. Kevin's family farm was on the edge of town, across the train tracks from Adam's house. Kevin was considered a farm boy, even though he was closer to the school than some of the kids in town.

They parted ways at the intersection and Adam headed home. As he walked in the door, he realized that he would be making himself something to eat once again. There were no smells of things frying, baking, or simmering coming from the kitchen; there never was. How he wished that there would be! To come home to a cooked ham with all the trimmings, or even just pork chops and potatoes would be a great treat. He had been at Kevin's house for meals before, and it was how he imagined Christmas in normal houses. And if that was *normal* for Kevin, what would Christmas *really* be like there?

Not for Adam, though. His mother rarely cooked anything, unless you count toast as cooking. Since Adam turned 8, it was his responsibility to fend for himself. Mary made sure there was canned fruit, canned vegetables, bread, butter, milk and eggs on hand most of the time, but not much else. She worked part-time stocking shelves at the local grocery store, so it was strange that she wouldn't bring home better food.

Part-time work at a small-town grocery store didn't pay much, but at least it got her out of the house.

Sandwich meat, God, how Adam hated sandwich meat! He'd had it fried, stewed, baked, and plain, with every combination of the few spices they kept on hand in the small kitchen. He dreamed that one day he would have a steak all to himself. He wouldn't care how it was cooked; he would have it however most people ordered it.

Mary was still at work because the store closed at 6 pm. It usually took her until 6:30 to get home after cash out and clean-up, so Adam had almost an hour before she would be home.

Being Friday night, it was Campbell's Beef Stew night. Adam opened the two tins and emptied them into a glass bowl, then started heating the stew in the microwave before sitting down in the chair to think.

He thought about the storage room in Town Hall. In his mind, he pictured the panel on the wall. Maybe it would have opened to the right, but there would have been wear on the left edge of the door where it would have hit the wall. It couldn't open to the left because there was no mark where it would have hit the stairwell, and the top was unusually smooth and rounded. Even if it did open at all, where was the latch? It wouldn't be far from the door, he reasoned, because whoever built it would want to get in and out as fast as possible.

"Adam!"

Adam woke up startled. He had drifted off to sleep while he was thinking. Mary stood there and looked at him.

"Is the stew done?" she questioned him.

"I..It..should be," he replied. Did he really start it, or was it just a dream? He was still drowsy.

"Did you butter any bread?" she questioned him again.

"N..No. I don't think so," he replied again.

She sighed. "Well, go do it then."

Adam walked to the kitchen and buttered bread. The clock on the stove said it was 6:35 pm. He must have had a good nap.

Kevin would be there any minute. He rushed buttering the bread, dished up two bowls of stew, then sat down and ate as fast as he could.

His mother made her way out of the bathroom and sat down to eat. "Are you going out tonight?" she asked.

"Yeah, Kev should be here soon."

"When will you do the dishes?"

"In the morning after you get up." Adam knew that was what she wanted to hear.

"Just be quiet when you come home tonight."

Adam shook his head in agreement. He knew Mary would fall asleep watching television later that evening and would be angry if anything woke her up before she was ready.

There was a knock at the door.

Perfect timing, thought Adam as he put on his shoes. He stepped outside to see Kevin and his bike.

"I thought we'd ride instead of walking. It's going to be light out until late tonight," said Kevin.

"Sure, let me just get mine from the garage."

Adam walked into the small garage and picked up his bike. A thought struck him, so he stopped and set his bike down again. He ran to the back and moved the envelope full of pictures from where he had found it to his hiding spot behind the right heat shield as a precaution.

"Just because it's going to be light out for a while yet doesn't mean you have to take your sweet time," Kevin joked as Adam came out of the garage.

"Where are we going?" asked Adam.

"Dunno. We could just ride around town for a while."

"Sure. It'll give me time to think. Let's go to the school and see if anyone's there."

They pedaled toward the school, and soon Adam was lost in thought.

"Still trying to figure out that door?" asked Kevin.

"It just doesn't make sense. I wouldn't be suspicious if it wasn't for the stories George told us and symbol in the cement, but I can't think of how it opens," said Adam, clearly frustrated.

Kevin swerved to miss a pothole. "If only we had more time to look at it. Maybe we missed something," he said. "But we won't be able to with Jeff there, and Mrs. Jones would never leave us alone in that basement. She'd be too afraid we'd wreck her files."

"I guess we just have to break in then," said Adam expecting Kevin to laugh.

Kevin was silent.

"I was kidding," said Adam.

"I'm not exactly thinking of *breaking* in," said Kevin, "but maybe we could get a key and go in without supervision. That way, we wouldn't be *breaking* in."

Adam looked at Kevin.

"You're the last person I would have expected to come

up with *that* plan," said Adam. "The only problem is, how do we get a key?"

"That's not hard. Jimmy," said Kevin.

"Jimmy has a key?" said Adam

"No, but his mom does," said Kevin.

Adam realized that Kevin was right.

"Do you think he knows where it is?"

"We can always ask him. If we explain everything, he'd probably help us," said Kevin, "Besides, he'd love the adventure."

"He'd help us by stealing his mom's keys?" asked Adam.

"*Borrowing*. Just *borrowing*," said Kevin. "Besides, I know he's gone there alone to use the copier before."

Adam thought about it for a moment. "It can't hurt to ask, I guess. Where do you think he is tonight? His mom had the day off, so maybe they went out of town."

"We're almost at the school. Let's see who's there and if anyone's seen him. After that we can check his house," said Kevin.

They turned the corner by the dance hall and continued pedalling into the schoolyard. They didn't see anyone on the playground side of the school so they continued to the baseball diamonds on the other side.

As they pedalled around the side of the school, they saw an older boy and girl sitting close together on one of the benches in the baseball dugout. It was the most private spot in the school yard.

The two separated when they noticed the boys. Kevin stopped, so Adam stopped too.

"Well, I'm pretty sure that Jimmy didn't go out of town," said Adam. "Isn't that his brother with your sister?"

Kevin turned red, partially embarrassed and partially angry.

"Yeah, let's just go." He turned and rode back the way they came.

They pedalled a while in silence. Kevin obviously didn't want to speak about what they had just seen, but Adam was curious.

"How long have those two been seeing each other?" Adam asked after seeing Kevin's face soften.

Kevin had calmed down just enough. "Not long. They hit it off on the last day of school and they've been texting each other ever since."

"He's a year older than her, right?" Adam asked, trying not to upset Kevin.

"Yep," Kevin replied. Adam felt the tension building again, so he dropped the subject.

They continued riding in silence toward the Jones family home. At the Fire Hall, they turned onto Young Street and rode halfway up the block to the Jones' driveway.

They leaned their bikes against the house and walked around to the back door. Adam rang the doorbell and heard footsteps approach.

Jimmy opened the door. "Hey, I was just going to try and track you down. Hang on, I'll come right out."

He closed the door. A moment later he opened it again and stepped outside.

"I was just watching TV and lost track of time. Too nice to be stuck inside today," said Jimmy.

"Your brother didn't seem to waste any time getting out of the house." There was a distinct edge to Kevin's voice.

Jimmy looked sheepish. "Look, I can't control what my brother does with your sister."

Kevin was turning red again. "He just better be good to her...or else..."

Adam stepped in, "Kev, Jimmy doesn't have anything to do with them dating, so don't get mad at him, okay?"

Kevin considered it for a moment. "Yeah, you're right. Sorry man. Just...you know...your brother is like...and it's my sister..."

"Hey, I understand. No problem. I'll try and let you know if there's anything funny going on as long as you don't blame me for anything that happens between them, deal?" said Jimmy, always making deals of one type or another.

Kevin nodded his head in agreement.

"So, what did you want to do? Ride bikes to the school?" said Jimmy.

Kevin cringed at the suggestion.

"No, we just came from there...you don't want to go there," said Adam, jerking his head toward Kevin without Kevin noticing.

Jimmy caught on right away.

"Actually, we wanted to talk to you about something, but not right here. Let's walk over to the park by the Fire Hall and sit on the benches," said Adam.

Jimmy agreed, so they started walking.

As they reached the end of the block near the Fire Hall, the boys stopped. Aggie and Martha walked by on another of their many trips around town. As soon as they had passed by, the boys crossed the street.

Aggie turned and looked at Jimmy.

"Keep your shoes tied. You don't want to trip," she said. She turned back around and continued walking with Martha, resuming whatever story they were in the middle of.

Jimmy looked at his shoes. They were perfectly tied. He looked at Kevin and Adam, twirling his finger in the air around his ear. Kevin and Adam laughed.

The boys walked into the park where they found a free bench away from any unwanted ears. There were a few young kids kicking a soccer ball around randomly. All 5 of the Miller kids were flying kites with their parents, laughing and yelling with joy.

The boys sat and began to tell Jimmy everything. He nodded as they told him what George had said and finally about the door in the basement of Town Hall.

"I've seen that a couple of times. It's just some wood on a wall. It can't be a door." He laughed at the thought. "I snuck in there a couple of times when I was supposed to help Mom do some filing."

"Did you notice the symbol beside the door," said Adam.

"Yeah. Are you saying that's the symbol you and George are talking about? I just thought it was like a signature of whoever made the building."

Adam reached into his pocket and showed Jimmy the pin. Jimmy's eyes widened.

"That's exactly the same as the mark in the basement!" said Jimmy, "But what if Jeff is right and it stands for an organization of builders? Sort of like the Masons? That seems the most likely."

"I think George would have found at least something about them in all his research," said Adam.

"Yeah, probably. So what do you guys want to do?" Jimmy asked.

Kevin and Adam looked at each other, trying to decide who was going to ask. Adam motioned to Kevin, as it was Kevin's idea.

"Well...we would really like to get a good look at the door again."

"Good luck with that. Mom won't let me go near the storage room when she's there."

"Yeah...well...we were hoping to go there when she isn't..." said Kevin.

Jimmy registered what was being asked of him.

"No no no... do you know how much I would get yelled at if I stole her keys..."

"*Borrowed*," interrupted Kevin.

"...and then let my friends into her place of work! She'd go ballistic! I'd be grounded for a lifetime!"

"But you've gone there by yourself to use the copier before," said Adam.

"That's different. She knows I won't get into any trouble there by myself. Besides, do you know how hard it will be to get the keys without her knowing? She practically sleeps with them."

"Aren't you just a little bit curious?" said Kevin.

"No fair, you guys are double-teaming me."

"Yeah, that means he's curious," said Adam.

"It would be quite an adventure," said Kevin.

"A great adventure," added Adam.

"Quit it," Jimmy said without much conviction.

"Then go get the keys," said Kevin.

"Go get the keys," echoed Adam.

Jimmy looked at them with a fake scowl, saying nothing for a moment.

"Ok, ok...I'll try and get the keys if you agree to my demands," said Jimmy, back to his normal form. He looked at Kevin. "*You* can't give me a hard time when my brother makes your sister sad...at all...not one mention of it. We both know it's going to happen."

Kevin opened his mouth to reply and was cut off.

"AND...when I say it's time to go... it's time to go. No questions. Drop everything and we leave." Jimmy was adamant.

The two boys shook their heads in agreement.

"And last but not least, Adam has to fix my old bike so I can sell it, and you have to help him." He pointed to Kevin.

"Anything else?" said Adam.

"Nope, that should cover it. When were you thinking of going in?" asked Jimmy.

Adam hesitated for a moment. "Well...tonight sounds good to me," he said.

Jimmy stared at Adam with no expression on his face. Slowly, he began to nod. "I think we can make that work," he said, pausing after the last word. "We should wait until it starts to get dark before we go in, though. That way, there's less chance of someone seeing and telling my parents. Agreed?"

The boys nodded in agreement again.

"So, should we meet you at Town Hall later so you can get the keys away from your mom?" asked Kevin.

"No, you don't need to. Mom and Dad went out with the Gupta's tonight and I know where she keeps her spare key. They won't be back before 11 o'clock." The grin on Jimmy's face annoyed Kevin and Adam, as they realized they had just been fooled. Jimmy knew all along he would have no trouble getting the keys.

"You...You....ooh..." Kevin didn't know whether to laugh or yell at his friend.

"Should've seen that one coming," Adam laughed.

"Alright, we have a little over an hour until it gets dark out. Why don't we start fixing that bike," said Kevin.

CHAPTER SIX

The bike was an easy fix for Adam. The chain was loose and kept slipping off the sprocket. It was also in desperate need of oil. He moved the rear wheel to tighten the chain while making sure it stayed in a straight line with the frame. When he was done, Kevin oiled the chain while Adam adjusted the handbrake. By the time they finished, they were able to take it for a few test rides before it started to get dark. A little after nine o'clock, they rolled the bike into the shed, ready to be sold.

"Shall we," said Kevin, motioning in the direction of Town Hall.

"I just need to get the key. Do we need anything else?" asked Jimmy as he walked toward the house.

"Do you have a flashlight?" asked Adam.

Jimmy opened the back door and stopped. "Yep, I'll grab one. Just wait out here. I don't want you to see where the spare keys are hidden."

Adam and Kevin nodded and stayed put. Jimmy returned a minute later carrying a flashlight.

"Isn't there an alarm system in the building?" Kevin asked.

"I know the code, so it's not a problem."

They walked to the end of the street and turned the corner. Town Hall was straight ahead to the left. The main doors were well lit by a pair of floodlights, while other floodlights illuminated the pillars, making them look bigger than they actually were.

"I forgot how much light is out front," said Jimmy. "I'm never trying to *sneak* in; I've always had permission. We could try the side door, but I don't remember if there's an alarm panel near there. I might not be able to make it to the front door in time to disarm it if we go in that way."

"What happens if you don't shut it off in time?" asked Adam.

Jimmy looked at them. "Do you remember a couple of months ago when we were in class and heard that loud siren go off? Someone tripped the alarm in the Fire Hall. Town Hall has the same alarm."

"Oh yeah! Man, that is one loud siren. The school's nearly a mile away," said Kevin.

"So if we don't get it shut off in time, I'll be in big trouble."

Adam had a thought. "Why don't *you* go in the front door and open the side door for me and Kev? If anyone sees you going in alone they won't think anything of it. We'll stay in the shrubs by the side door."

"That sounds good. Just stay hidden until you see me crack the door a little, ok?"

They split up and the two boys walked into the park

making a wide circle around the building. The door was on the west side of Town Hall near the middle of the building. A row of bushes acted as a border between it and a number of backyards that faced it.

From their hiding spot in the bushes, they could see the dimly-lit side door while they waited for it to open. They waited and waited, but the door wasn't opening, so they started to panic.

Adam whispered, "Did he get lost in there? Maybe he can't find the side door."

"If he had trouble with the alarm, we'd know it by now," whispered Kevin.

Then, to their relief, the door opened a crack. Adam and Kevin sped to the door and stepped inside.

"What took you so long?" asked Adam, closing the door behind him.

"Sorry, had to use the bathroom. I couldn't hold it any longer."

Adam rolled his eyes. Kevin gave Jimmy a light punch on the shoulder.

Jimmy led them down the short hallway, and after a couple of turns they were down the stairs and into the basement. Because there were no windows, the lights weren't visible from the outside. Adam understood how easy it was to lose track of time down there without any natural light.

Jimmy led them back through the storage room door and fiddled with a switch until the dim lighting started. After stepping over and around many boxes, they were back at the clearing.

Jimmy turned on the flashlight and handed it to

Adam. "Go to it, you've got about an hour."

Adam pointed the flashlight at the wooden panel and started a search pattern. He pointed it at the ceiling which was wide open, exposing the floor joists and some really tattered wiring for the lights. He pointed it under the stairwell, deep into the corners and anywhere else he could think of, but still saw nothing unusual. He paused at the symbol, but it looked like a simple impression in the cement.

"If either of you notice anything, you'll tell me, right?" he said.

"You mean other than the handle back here that says 'pull me to open secret door'?" said Jimmy, straight-faced.

Adam hesitated for a second before realizing it was a joke, which made Kevin and Jimmy laugh.

"Thanks," he muttered, pretending to be angry as he returned the light to the panel.

He paused for a moment in thought. "Follow my logic. If the panel opened to the right, there would be wear on the left edge of the door where it hit the wall, but there isn't any." He pointed to the left edge. "It couldn't open to the left, because it would hit the stairwell and make a mark at the top of the boards here." He pointed to the top right edge.

The other two nodded in agreement.

"If you look at the face of these boards, you can see they're worn, and the nail heads are shiny." He pointed to some of the nails. "Normally they would be rusty or dull, unless they came in contact with something - like being opened against a wall, but there isn't enough room on either side to open it fully."

The act of speaking it out loud had an instant effect on Adam. He realized how the door would move, but still didn't know how it was latched.

Jimmy spoke. "If I had a secret society and a secret room with a secret door, I wouldn't just want to have a handle hidden somewhere to open that door. I'd want a key to give to the members, wouldn't you?"

Adam thought about it for a moment. "Do you think this pin is a key?" He pulled the pin from his pocket and held between his fingers.

"Sure, why not. Try and stick it in the one on the wall. What's there to lose?" said Jimmy.

"Stand back," said Adam as he walked to the side of the panel. He placed the pin in the depression and immediately heard a click. The door fell open like a drawbridge, but not fast enough that you would get hurt by being in the wrong place. Adam noticed a pair of large springs in the lower corners of the opening that took the weight off the door. They were fastened to the large lower bolts. The upper door bolts were fastened to cables that ran through pulleys at the top of the door frame and disappeared into the wall.

Jimmy's jaw dropped, and his eyes were wide in amazement. Kevin was smiling and looking at Adam.

"George is looking less crazy by the minute," he said.

Adam laughed. "At least you didn't scream when the door opened!" he said, referring to the incident earlier that day.

Kevin shook his fist at Adam with mock anger.

"Well, now we know why the top of the door is smooth here," said Adam pointing to the top, "You grab it here to close it when you leave, I assume." He demonstrated in the air.

"I know *you* like knowing how it works, but *we* don't really care. *We* see a secret room that's just been opened. Much more interesting, don't you think?" Jimmy elbowed Kevin as he spoke.

"Ok ok...but I'll go in first. We don't want something to scare Kevin." Adam grinned as he spoke.

Kevin shook his fist at Adam again, smiling.

Adam stepped onto the door and stopped just before the opening. He pointed the flashlight at the latch on the ceiling, then followed a cable from it to a hole in the wall. The hole opened up behind the symbol in the cement and inside looked like a ball of steel at the end of a lever.

The pin must be a magnet! thought Adam. He couldn't wait to test it on something.

"...remember...secret room behind secret door..." Kevin tapped Adam on the shoulder to get him to keep moving.

Adam pointed the flashlight into the room. It was long and narrow, just like the storage room that led up to the drawbridge door, but lacking the Christmas decorations. It smelled like damp paper, and was cold. The walls and ceiling seemed to be carved out of rock. Filing cabinets lined the left wall, and a strange door was carved into the rock wall at the far end.

"Do we look through the files or check out the door?" asked Adam

"Let's think. We could read a bunch of boring old paperwork, OR we could check out another secret door that happens to be in a secret room. Hmm, so difficult to choose," said Jimmy, full of sarcasm.

Adam shook his head while Kevin laughed.

Adam walked to the end of the room and shone the light on the door. It was made of metal, had a big handle, and seemed larger than the opening it sat in. He shone the flashlight around the frame and stopped on another bowtie symbol. It was in the wall on the right side of the door. He pulled the pin from his pocket and manoeuvred it into position. The sound of mechanisms moving came from the wall. With his other hand he slid the door into the door frame.

"Cool, retro Star Trek door!" said Kevin.

The door slid easily on its track, even though it was very heavy. Adam shone his light down and saw a row of large ball-bearings. They looked as if they had just been greased. The door itself was thick and heavy, but slid easily on the track. The tunnel on the other side looked as if it had been carved out of rock, the same way the file room was carved, although it was only wide enough for two people.

Adam stepped through the doorway and shone the flashlight back toward the door frame. As he suspected, there was another bowtie symbol next to the door on the other side.

Although he wanted to inspect the mechanism, he knew his friends wouldn't let him stop. He shone his light straight ahead and walked toward what looked like a dead end. When he reached it, he found that it was just a visual trick and the tunnel turned sharply right.

A loud bang from behind startled them all. Adam shone the light back at the sliding door and saw that it had slammed shut behind them.

"I sure hope we aren't locked in here!" said Kevin. "I really should have used the bathroom too."

Adam had a nervous chuckle. "Let's just check ahead a little further and then we'll go back. Maybe there's more storage here, or it'll come out at the Fire Hall."

Adam led the way down the tunnel. It curved slightly so that in the distance you couldn't tell if it continued on or ended. After a short walk, Adam stopped when he came to an intersection. The tunnels now led forward, right and left.

"What do we do?" asked Kevin.

"I say we keep going straight," said Adam.

"Sounds good," said Jimmy. "Lead on."

Adam continued through the intersection. The tunnel switched and now curved the opposite way, but they still couldn't tell if it continued or ended ahead.

A short time later an opening appeared ahead. When they reached the clearing, they stopped and looked around. There were eight tunnels branching off from the clearing including the one they had just exited.

"Jimmy, stay there so we know which tunnel we came from," said Adam. Jimmy nodded and stayed just inside the tunnel.

Adam shone his flashlight into each of the tunnels, noticing something strange. Each seemed to have the same curve to the right, giving the illusion that they ended in a short distance. There didn't seem to be any differences between them, so whoever was using them had better know where they led or have had a map to guide them.

Adam looked at the others. "I think this is where we

stop for now. I don't want to get lost."

"Agreed," said Jimmy. "Besides, we need to start making our way back home."

Jimmy led them back the way they came. When they reached the sliding door leading back to the file room, Adam placed the pin in position. He listened to the mechanism working and tried to slide the door. It wouldn't move. He looked at the other two, concerned, and tried once more. It still didn't move.

"You just hold that pin in there and let *me* open the door," said Kevin, being the strongest of the three.

Adam placed the pin in position and heard the mechanism. Kevin pulled with all his strength. It didn't even budge.

The boys looked at each other and thought the same thing - *We're trapped!*

CHAPTER SEVEN

"That sucks," said Jimmy. "We've gotta get out of here, lock up Town Hall, and get the keys back to *my* place before my parents get home."

"We won't be going through *that* door to get out. I pulled as hard as I can and it didn't even budge," said Kevin

Adam was thinking. He pulled the pin out of the impression and put it back in again. He heard the distinct sound of mechanisms working, but not quite the same as when it was activated on the other side of the door.

"Something isn't the same when I try it from this side. It sounds different. That's strange because the track looks well-maintained. I would think that whoever does the maintenance would have fixed that problem."

"Regardless," replied Jimmy, "we need to get out of here somehow, so we'll have to follow the tunnels. There has to be another exit somewhere."

"Jeff said that they had the same door in the Fire Hall. Maybe we could go that direction?" asked Kevin.

"Good thought, but even if we could get into the Fire Hall we don't know the code for the alarm," said Adam.

"Well, I say we go right," suggested Jimmy, "unless one of you has breadcrumbs or a really long string."

"Why right?" asked Kevin.

"Ok, then left. I don't care, as long as we can make it back here somehow. If we always go one way, we just do the reverse so we don't get lost if we can't find an exit."

Adam nodded. "If we get to any intersections where we can turn or go straight, I say we just go straight. It'll be less confusing."

Kevin and Jimmy agreed.

"Lead on." Jimmy motioned for Adam to go first.

Adam led them to the opening where all the tunnels met. He pointed the flashlight down the first tunnel on the right and continued. The others stayed close behind.

After passing another intersection, Kevin spoke.

"These tunnels are bothering me."

"In what way?" asked Adam.

"Well, some of our farmland is around here. We pick stones that are baseball sized and larger and put them on piles. Once in a while, when the piles get too big, Dad hires Ron Nagy to dig a big hole and bury them with his excavator. He digs a hole that's 10 to 15 feet deep, and I've never seen him hit bedrock."

Adam and Jimmy weren't following Kevin's logic.

"We aren't 10 feet underground, so these caves aren't in natural bedrock. They were built, not chiselled out of rock, is what I think. How do you make *this* rock," he patted the wall, "in dirt and sand mixed with clay? Plus, you have to have it seal enough to keep the water out."

Adam stopped and looked at Kevin. "That's pretty

observant of you! I am honestly surprised by you right now."

Kevin wasn't sure if Adam was mocking him or paying a genuine compliment, so he replied indignantly, "I'm not as dumb as you think I am!"

"I'm not kidding. I think that's a great observation. These tunnels have been bothering me too, and I couldn't figure out why, but you figured it out faster than we did."

Kevin's expression changed to one of pride.

Adam continued, "Just look at this wall," he shone his flashlight to his right. "It's not like concrete, and it's not like solid rock either. I've never seen anything like it, have either of you?"

Jimmy and Kevin both shook their heads, indicating they hadn't.

Jimmy looked at the other two and tapped his watch, reminding them that they needed to get moving.

The tunnel continued on its curve to the right for a while, switching to curving left for about the same distance. It curved back to the right once more before straightening out for a short stretch. In the straight section they reached a tunnel branching to the left, but they kept walking straight.

"How far do you think we've gone?" asked Jimmy.

"I haven't got a clue. It seems like 10 blocks, but might only be one," replied Adam, "this place makes it hard to judge."

Jimmy tripped and hit the ground with a hard slap. As he fell, he let out a loud scream that echoed through he tunnels. Adam whipped around and shone the flashlight at him.

"You ok man," asked Kevin.

"I'm ok, just tripped on my shoelace."

Adam felt strange, suddenly remembering the advice Aggie had given Jimmy near the Fire Hall earlier.

"I guess you should have listened to Aggie after all," said Kevin. He obviously remembered Aggie's advice as well, but it didn't bother him the same way.

After helping Jimmy to his feet once his shoe was tied, Adam started down the tunnel at a faster pace. "Let's make some time. If anyone's down here with us, they know we're here now."

After one more curve in each direction, the tunnel straightened out and they could see another sliding door in the distance. It seemed like it was a mile away, but only took them a minute to get there.

Adam shone the light at the door, then around the sides and bottom. It appeared the same as the other sliding door they had come through. Even the impression of the pin was in the same spot.

"I hope this works," said Adam, feeling in his pocket for the pin.

"*I* hope this door leads out and nowhere else," added Kevin.

They pondered the possibilities as Adam placed the pin. The sound of mechanisms moved in the wall for a second and then stopped.

"Here goes," said Adam, as he pulled sideways on the handle.

The door slid open easily. Cold air rushed past their feet.

Adam shone the flashlight down and saw that the rollers the door travelled on were freshly greased, just like the first door. As he shone the light through the doorway, it revealed a small room on the other side. The room was stacked with boxes, all about the same size and shape. They were beer boxes.

"The hotel!" exclaimed Jimmy. "This has to be the cooler for the bar!"

No sooner had he finished his sentence when they heard a loud bang echo in the tunnel behind them. It sounded the same as the sliding door slamming shut earlier, but much closer.

"Someone's coming! Go!" said Kevin, quiet, but with panic in his voice.

There wasn't a clear path to the main cooler door, but they climbed carefully and stepped quickly. Thankfully, the cooler wasn't locked from the outside, probably because it was Friday night and the hotel bar would be busy.

The three boys ran down a short hallway and sprinted up the stairs. The sight at the top stopped them immediately as they realized they had entered the bar. It was only luck that no one had noticed them.

Jimmy moved slowly toward the exit door. There were no people or tables in the way, so they walked as inconspicuously as possible. They were going to get out without being noticed.

"Hey, you're not allowed in here!" The voice of the hotel owner boomed as he stepped through the door connecting the bar to the hotel. All heads turned to look after hearing the outburst.

Lorne Argue was a large man with a large voice. Some

of his size was from being overweight, but most of it was purely genetic. He rarely had trouble in his bar because his size intimidated even the bravest drunk patron.

Lorne stared at the boys, chasing them out the door with his eyes.

Jimmy spoke in a timid voice, "We...we were hoping to buy a couple of bags of Doritos. This is the only place open in town right now, and we were just walking past."

Jimmy's cover story sounded pretty reasonable, at least to Kevin and Adam. Lorne continued staring at them, making those few moments seem like hours to the three boys.

"You're all underage. You can *not* be in here, understand?" Lorne's voice had dropped in volume, but was still powerful.

They shook their heads in agreement and walked toward the door. The only thing they wanted was to get out before whoever was chasing them in the tunnel caught them.

"So, what kind do you want?" asked Lorne.

They stumbled to a stop, surprised. "Uh, just nacho cheese?" Jimmy managed to say.

"How many bags?"

They fumbled through their pockets and found some money.

"Whatever this buys," said Jimmy, handing over a couple of bills and some coins, "and keep the change."

Every second they stood there felt like a minute. Lorne turned, then paused and turned back again.

"You go wait outside," he pointed to the side door, "I'll

bring them out to you."

The three nodded and made their way out through the side door like speed walkers in a race, each one trying to get out first.

"Wow, that was too close for me," said Kevin once the door closed securely behind them.

"We're not safe yet. Whoever followed us might be in the bar looking for us right now," said Adam, his heart still pounding.

"They won't know it was us. They didn't see us. We were just walking past and went in to buy some Doritos, right?" Jimmy repeated the sentence slowly.

"Yeah, and we're going back to Jimmy's after," Kevin replied. Adam nodded in agreement.

They waited in silence. When the door finally opened, it startled the boys. They had so much adrenaline in their veins that none of them would sleep well that night, if at all.

Lorne stepped out, holding 3 bags of Doritos.

"Next time, just call first and someone will meet you at the side door," he said. "That way, I don't get in trouble if the police are here. I'm sure one of you has a cell phone, right?"

The boys nodded their heads in agreement.

Lorne paused and examined them. "So...did you happen to see anyone leaving here in a hurry? You *did* come in *this* door, right?"

"Nope, no one. Not since we came in and left again," replied Jimmy. Jimmy wasn't really lying, as they hadn't seen anyone leave.

Lorne watched them for another few moments. "Ok...now go." He waved them away, and they moved without hesitation.

They walked south toward the old Lumber Yard and stopped just past Ben Casey's.

"Let's not do that again," said Kevin.

"Yeah, that was too close," said Adam.

Jimmy looked at his watch.

"10:47," he said in a quiet voice, "we need to keep moving. My parents will be home soon."

"I'm more worried that whoever was in the tunnels will be waiting at Town Hall," said Adam, with Kevin nodding in agreement, "but you'll just have to risk it."

Jimmy looked like he was going to reply, but realized they were right. Normally, that comment would have been a jab at Jimmy, but at that moment it was merely a fact - it was better if he went alone. It would be easier to talk his way out of trouble if it was only him and not the group.

"You two are so gonna owe me for this."

"No way. You suckered us into fixing your bike. This makes us square," said Kevin standing firm.

Jimmy muttered a quiet, "Yeah, I guess."

"If we run, we'll draw attention, so let's just walk fast," said Adam.

With that, they started off to Town Hall.

CHAPTER EIGHT

Minutes later they neared Town Hall.

"You guys keep going and meet me by the Fire Hall," said Jimmy. "I'll give you a minute head start."

Adam and Kevin walked as normally as possible past Town Hall. They didn't look at it, even though they wanted to - given the events that evening. Instead, they walked until they were past the Fire Hall, turning back to see Jimmy closing the door behind him.

Adam watched the door, anxious to see Jimmy come out again. As time ticked on, he began to worry. In his mind, Jimmy ran into the faceless thing that followed them through the last part of the tunnel. It was at least 400 pounds of pure muscle and 9 feet tall. It grabbed Jimmy and forced him to recount his evening, including the names, descriptions, and locations of his accomplices. It finished him off by doing horrible things. When it was done, it would sneak up behind Adam in the dark, grabbing him and...

A hand touched Adam's shoulder. He jumped and let out a quiet scream, similar to the one Kevin had done earlier. It was only Kevin.

"Whoa, calm down," he whispered. "Look." He pointed up the street toward Jimmy's house where a car was pulling into the driveway. Jimmy's parents had just arrived home.

Adam watched as the car pulled into the driveway and 2 people stepped out. He heard the doors close and the murmur of quiet conversation as Jimmy's parents walked toward the house.

A hand clamped down on each of their shoulders in the darkness. They both jumped in shock, but managed not to scream. Jimmy was standing behind them, trying to hold in the laughter from shocking his friends.

"Don't do that!" exclaimed Kevin.

"How did you get here? We only took our eyes off the door for a minute," said Adam.

Jimmy was trying to control his laughter. "That was so worth it! You two look like you might need to change your pants!"

Kevin and Adam looked at him unimpressed.

He composed himself and continued. "When I let you in the side door earlier, I noticed an alarm panel. I locked the front doors from the inside, ran to the side door, and was out of there in no time. I went behind Town Hall and walked to the Fire Hall through the trees. "

Kevin and Adam were still looking at him unimpressed.

Jimmy was still smiling. "Ok. You don't owe me anymore. The look on Kevin's face alone was priceless!" Jimmy was enjoying his moment.

"Good to hear...," said Kevin. "Oh, by the way, your parents are home," he continued, grinning because he was able to give Jimmy the bad news.

Jimmy's smile disappeared in an instant. He looked at his watch.

"I have 3 minutes to get home. You two have to come in and distract my parents while I take the key back to their bedroom." Jimmy's tone implied there would be no discussion.

They nodded their heads and ran toward Jimmy's house.

"How are we supposed to distract them?" asked Kevin.

"Why don't you show them your interpretive dance? That'll keep them occupied," said Adam.

"Not until you show them the pink tutu you wear when no one is watching."

Even though they were still wound up from the night's events, they all had a good laugh at the comments.

Arriving at the house, Adam and Kevin followed Jimmy up the steps to the back door. They stepped in and took their shoes off in the small entryway. Jimmy looked at them and mouthed, "I need 2 minutes."

"Trevor or Jimmy?" Mrs. Jones' voice came from around the corner.

"Jimmy - and Adam and Kevin," Jimmy replied as they entered the kitchen single file.

"Oh, hi boys!" said Mrs. Jones, "Isn't it getting late for you to be out?" She was standing behind the counter holding a glass of water. James Jones the Second (his friends called him Jim) entered from the living room as she spoke.

"Wait here, guys. I have to use the bathroom." Jimmy motioned his head slightly toward his parents.

"Uh, well...I don't really have a curfew," Adam answered, "but Kevin needs to be home in about half an hour. We just figured we would walk Jimmy here on our way home."

"Where did you get the Doritos?" Mr. Jones glanced at the bags and then looked at them with a fatherly 'don't-lie-to-me, I-can-read-your-thoughts' expression on his face. It made the boys feel even more uncomfortable than they were already. They had forgotten about the Doritos, even though Adam was still holding his and Jimmy's bags from when they parted at Town Hall.

"Actually, we bought them from Mr. Argue at the bar," replied Adam. "We knocked on the door and no one answered, so we just sort of stepped inside...a little..."

Mr. Jones had a surprised look on his face. "I don't know if that was smart, brave, or incredibly stupid." He laughed, but Mrs. Jones still wore a frown. Upon seeing his wife, he also returned to a frown, staring at them once again.

There were a few awkward moments of silence, and once more those moments felt like minutes to the boys.

Mrs. Jones took a sip of her water and set it on the counter. Mr. Jones started to turn in the direction of the bedrooms. They had to think of something quick.

"Uh...so...I hear Trevor is dating Kevin's sister," blurted out Adam, grasping for any subject.

The awkwardness created by that one simple statement worked. Mr. Jones stopped in his path and turned to listen to the conversation to come. Kevin had a look of I-can't-believe-you-just-said-that on his face mixed with a small amount of anger that he kept contained.

"Oh...We thought they were just friends right now," said Mrs. Jones, looking at her husband to see if he knew any different. "That would be wonderful for Trevor. She's a lovely girl."

Mr. Jones was nodding his head in agreement with his wife.

Adam had a bad feeling deep in his stomach. He knew the discussion made Kevin very uncomfortable, but it was all he could think of at the time. It was necessary, though, and worked long enough that Jimmy appeared in the kitchen again.

"Here's your Doritos." Adam handed the bag to Jimmy.

"Thanks...I'm just going outside for a minute, ok?" Jimmy looked at his mom.

Mrs. Jones nodded. "Don't be too long. Kevin needs to be home soon," she added, glancing at the clock on the stove.

Adam and Kevin said goodnight to Jimmy's parents and made their way outside. The group crossed the street before saying anything.

"I can't believe we made it!" said Jimmy. "Thanks for keeping my parents occupied guys. You did great! What did you talk about?"

Adam looked at Kevin. "I'm sorry. It's the first thing that came to my mind," he said.

Jimmy looked puzzled at first, but caught on quick. His face twisted in fake pain. "Oooooh, you did? Wow."

Kevin looked at Adam. "It's ok, man. I have to learn to deal with it from other people too, not just my friends. If they're dating, they're dating."

"Still, I didn't mean to make you uncomfortable."

"If you don't quit apologizing I really will get uncomfortable. People know I hang out with you." Kevin grinned.

Adam smiled as well. All was fine between him and Kevin again.

"Ok, you can hug on your way home," said Jimmy, "I better get in the house."

They laughed and turned to part company. Kevin stopped and turned back. "Your dad asked where we got the Doritos, so we told him the story about going into the bar. He laughed, but your mom doesn't look impressed."

Jimmy nodded at Kevin. "Thanks. I can talk my way out of that, no problem!"

With that, Kevin and Adam waved a quick goodbye, turned and walked for home.

The moon was nearly full that evening, and the air was cool, but not cold. The boys walked to the end of the block in silent thought.

Adam was going through the evening in his head, although it wasn't in order. His thoughts skipped from scene to scene out of sequence. It skipped from running through the tunnels to opening the first door, then back to Jimmy's house and stopped at the point where Lorne Argue brought them the Doritos.

"He asked us if we saw anyone leaving in a hurry," Adam muttered in a quiet voice.

"What was that?" asked Kevin, bringing Adam out of his thoughts.

"Lorne asked us if we saw anyone leaving. I forgot about it until now, but it seemed a little strange at the time. He said 'in a hurry'."

"He was probably looking for someone who skipped out on his bar tab," said Kevin.

"But this is Grayson. Lorne knows everyone in this town, and would know exactly who ran out without paying. I don't think he was asking for *himself*."

"Wait, are you saying that whoever was behind us in the tunnels asked Lorne if he saw anyone?"

"Yep."

"That would mean we would have *just* stepped outside when the person came up from the cold room into the bar."

"Yep."

They both stopped.

"They *have* to suspect us," said Kevin.

"I don't think so. I bet Lorne didn't even say anything about us being in his bar. He's got a keen sense for drunks lying to him, but Jimmy even convinced *me* that we just went in for something to eat."

"Still, I think we need to be on our guard. News that we were in the bar will spread through this town fast."

"When we go back into the tunnels, we'll have to make sure we're quieter. Hopefully tomorrow." Adam looked serious.

Kevin nodded, "I just want to look through the files. There's got to be something in there to explain all of this."

"You *must* be curious if you're willing to *read*. Not to mention breaking into Town Hall again." Adam laughed, soft punched Kevin in the shoulder and started walking again.

"It's not really breaking in when you have a key and know the alarm code. We're not looking to steal anything...I just hope you can convince Jimmy to 'borrow' the keys again."

"He won't be a problem. He wants to know what's going on as much as we do."

They stopped at the corner where they would have to part.

"Come and get me as soon as you can get out of the house tomorrow," said Adam, hoping it would be early.

Kevin nodded. "See ya tomorrow."

"See ya."

Adam turned toward his home and remembered he had dishes to wash in the morning.

CHAPTER NINE

Adam couldn't remember when he finally fell asleep. The previous night's excitement made his mind work hard when it should have been calming down. His alarm woke him at 7 am so he could wash the dishes before his mother woke, but he still felt tired, as though he hadn't slept at all.

He dragged himself out of bed and threw on some clothes, making sure to put the pin in his pocket. He tiptoed downstairs to eat some breakfast and wash the dishes. Mary didn't have to work that day, and she hadn't fallen asleep in her chair the night before. He knew she would be sleeping late that morning, or just lying on her bed as long as she could.

Adam ate fast and then washed the dishes. By 7:45 am he was outside sitting on the step, waiting for Kevin to arrive. It was another beautiful summer day, and the birds sang in appreciation. The lack of a good rest, combined with the birdsong, kept Adam in a delightful daze until Kevin arrived nearly an hour later.

"You look like I feel," said Kevin with a weak chuckle.

"I slept so bad that I can't even come up with a smart reply, and you always make it so easy." Adam gave him a smile. His mind was starting to work again, now that he had someone to talk to.

Kevin sat and handed Adam a plastic travel mug. "Here, have some coffee. I thought you would have slept as bad as I did and might need something to get you started."

Adam looked at him. "Since when do you drink coffee?"

"I don't. I just tried to think of something that would help me get going today. I don't really like the taste much...Anyway, bottoms up!" Kevin tipped his cup to his lip and took a big swig.

The first sip shocked Adam. The coffee was strong and bitter. Kevin had tried to kill the overpowering burnt taste with a lot of sugar.

Adam coughed and took a couple more swigs. He put the mug down and looked at Kevin. "That's a lot of sugar."

Kevin smiled, "Yeah, I made the coffee strong too. I figure that if the coffee doesn't wake us up, the sugar will."

Adam laughed at Kevin's logic, followed by another swig on the mug. He wiped his mouth after a small cringe from the aftertaste. He didn't want to insult Kevin, as it was thoughtful of Kevin to make the effort. The more he drank the concoction though, the easier it was to drink.

He and Kevin sat silently sipping away for a few minutes, hoping the mixture would soon give them some energy.

Adam broke the silence. "So, one of the thoughts I had last night is that we need to get the keys to Town Hall again. It's going to be difficult to keep getting the keys from Jimmy's mom, so we should make a copy at the hardware store."

Kevin nodded in agreement. "Good idea."

"When we go in, we should spend a bunch of time looking through the files," added Adam.

"I want to go in right now, but I know that would be crazy," added Kevin while Adam gulped the last of his coffee down.

Adam tried hard not to make a face while finishing the coffee, although he *was* feeling the haze leave his mind more each minute. Maybe Kevin's mixture was working, he thought.

"I think we should bring Mark with us this time," said Kevin, "He might remember something he heard from George that could help us."

Adam agreed. "We should get him and Jimmy over here and have a meeting as soon as possible. That way we can tell Mark what happened last night." Besides being Adam's workshop, the old garage doubled as a meeting place for him and his friends. He had salvaged some old lawn chairs and a coffee table from the dump so they had places to sit. Sometimes, if there was nothing else happening, they would hang out in the garage all day. They never stayed too late, as Mary would send them home if she saw lights on in the garage. Adam was sure she just didn't want to pay for the extra power.

They put the travel mugs in the garage and walked toward Jimmy's house, since it was closest. Adam could feel the full effect of Kevin's concoction soon after they left. His mind flew through images and ideas at a rapid pace. It made him feel like running the rest of the way.

When they arrived at Jimmy's house, Jimmy was attaching a 'For Sale' sign on the bike Adam and Kevin had fixed. It already seemed like a week since they did the work, even though it was the previous day.

"Mom, I'm going with the guys," yelled Jimmy toward the house.

"Ok, be good," came the muted reply.

The three walked toward Mark's house, and made generic small talk along the way. Adam told Jimmy they were going to have a meeting at the garage to tell Mark about the previous evening, but they shouldn't speak about it while they walked. The rest of the short walk to Mark's was filled with typical teenage teasing and sarcasm, light-hearted without real intent to harm.

Adam walked to the side door and rang the doorbell. The ring stirred the sound of excitement inside the house. Siri and Miri could be heard exclaiming, "Someone's here!"

After a short time, the door opened a crack and little eyes appeared. "Mark, it's just your friends," yelled the mouth belonging to the eyes, as they disappeared from the crack in the door. Immediately, the first set of eyes was replaced by another nearly identical set.

"Yep, just your friends again," yelled the other sister.

A hand reached through and opened the crack while another pushed the face out of the way. "Go away, Siri..."

Siri struggled against her brother's hand, but gave up soon and ran away. Mark smiled at his small triumph. He looked at Adam and held up his index finger telling Adam to wait. Adam stepped away from the door and joined Jimmy and Kevin on the driveway. Shortly, the door opened again and Mark stepped out, still chewing his breakfast. He was washing down the food with a canned soft drink he had just opened.

"You're having a Coke for breakfast?" Kevin's face showed how poor of a dietary decision he thought that was.

"shhhh......" Mark ushered the group off the driveway and back the way they came. "Mom and Dad don't know, and I don't want them to find out."

Kevin shook his head while the other two smiled. *Too easy of a target, too early in the day,* thought Adam.

"So, what happened last night?" asked Mark.

Adam made the motion of a zipper over his lips. "We're going to my garage." Mark caught on quick and was silent for the rest of the trip.

They all took seats around the small rectangular coffee table, with Adam across from Mark. Adam started telling the story, with Jimmy and Kevin filling in the holes and providing small skits of live-action replay. Mark was so intent on the story that he forgot he had a soft drink in his hand.

When they finished telling the story, they sat in silence for a while. Recounting the events brought out their curiosity as they thought about the previous night.

"Wow! That's all I can say." Mark looked at each of them in turn, breaking the silence. "I'm not sure if I'm happy or mad that I missed being there!" He sipped his drink for the first time since the story started.

"Adam and I were thinking, Jimmy, that we can't keep having you *borrow* the keys from your mom. You might get caught," Jimmy was nodding in agreement as Kevin continued, "so, we want to make a copy of the key."

Jimmy's nodding in agreement turned to head shaking in disagreement halfway through the sentence. "No way. That was way too close last night." He folded his arms in weak defiance.

Adam and Kevin looked at each other. They knew Jimmy was just as curious as they were, but Jimmy sensed an opportunity to get something out of his friends.

"Don't try and tell us you aren't bursting with curiosity after last night?" asked Adam.

"Of course I'm curious, but I'll be grounded for the rest of my life if I get caught. I actually *do* want a girlfriend someday! You have to be able to leave the house for that." The politician side of Jimmy came out, trying to minimize the bad press if he got caught doing wrong.

"Ok, we understand," said Adam. "How about this; if you get caught, we'll *swear* to everyone that *we* forced you to come along with us. Kevin threatened to crush you, and I said you might have an 'accident' riding your bike. Will that do?" Kevin looked hurt that he was being positioned as mean.

Jimmy was thinking it over. "Just *one* more time?"

"Yep," said Adam.

"Deal." Jimmy looked pleased.

"Do you think you can get it today?" asked Adam.

Jimmy cringed a little. "I'll try. Town Hall is open every second Saturday, but not today, so Mom's at home."

Adam looked confused. "Yesterday Jeff said your mom was working today."

Jimmy laughed. "If it wasn't for my mom, Jeff wouldn't know what day of the week it is. She wasn't there yesterday, and Jeff never comes in on a Saturday during work hours, so he has no clue."

Adam seemed satisfied with the answer. "If she's at home, won't that make it tough to get the keys?" he asked.

"She always goes out for groceries on her Saturday off. Usually around 10 or 11 am. That'll give us about half an hour."

"That would work. The hardware store is only a block from your house, so we can do it quick. Does anyone have any money to pay for it?" Adam asked, slightly embarrassed.

The others emptied their pockets and came up with a few dollars.

"Are we planning on going back in tonight?" asked Mark. The others nodded yes. "Ok. I'll get a couple of good flashlights."

"I want to get in at least an hour earlier tonight. I know it's still light out, but we want to get everyone home in time for their curfews," said Adam.

There was general consensus in the group.

"We're going to check the files tonight. Wandering through the tunnels will likely get us lost, or caught. We need to find some information about the symbol and why the town and tunnels were built. Hopefully something will tell us what is going on around here," added Adam.

"Can I take a look at the pin?" asked Jimmy, "I

haven't had a good look at it yet."

Adam placed the pin on the table and Jimmy picked it up.

Adam continued, "I think that we should have a lookout at the top of the stairs just-in-case someone comes in Town Hall. Just a precaution. The other 3 can go through the files without worrying that someone is sneaking up on them." Adam was remembering Jeff's surprise earlier.

"I'll be the lookout," said Kevin before anyone else. "I'd rather do that than look through paperwork."

"Buuuuuurrrrrrrrrrrrp.........," Mark let out a deafening belch, then slammed down the empty Coke can.

"Gross," said Jimmy, "I think I saw chunks of your breakfast fly out!"

Mark grinned, happy with himself.

"Here's your pin back," said Jimmy as he placed it on the table.

As soon as he set it down, the Coke can flew across the table and stuck to the pin.

CHAPTER TEN

"Cool, it's a magnet!" exclaimed Mark.

Adam, more than the others, understood the significance. His face showed he was confused and surprised.

"That shouldn't happen," he said, almost to himself.

Jimmy looked at Adam. "Aren't Coke cans made of aluminum?" he asked.

"I haven't heard any different," Adam replied.

Mark looked confused. "So?"

Adam answered, "Aluminum isn't attracted by *any* magnet. At least, none that anyone knows about."

Adam stood up and walked toward his tools. He began digging through a pail full of parts, setting aside a few items.

"Maybe they changed the material in the cans," stated Kevin.

"We're gonna test your theory right now," said Adam, returning to the table holding a few items. "Mark, pull the pin off that can and keep them apart until I ask for them."

Mark did as was asked while Adam set 2 items on the table and another on the floor. The first item on the table was a large bolt. The second looked like a lowercase 'h', but missing the lower left leg. The third item on the floor looked like a metal hockey puck.

"Mark, hang on to the pin and put the can on the table here." Adam pointed to an open spot near the end, making a line out of the three items on the table.

"So, I have a strong magnet on the floor that I found. The bolt is made out of typical steel that is very magnetic. The second thing is the crankshaft of a bicycle; the part that the pedals are mounted on. It's made of pure aluminum. Last, the Coke can. We'll test all three with the magnet, then the pin, sound good to you?" Everyone agreed.

Adam sat next to the table and picked up the magnet. He brought it near the bolt. Ding! The bolt stuck to the magnet as soon as it was close. Adam pried the bolt off the magnet and set it back in its original position. He looked at his friends and nodded.

Next, he brought the magnet near the crankshaft. Nothing happened, even when he touched the magnet directly on the part. Adam tapped the magnet against it a few times to make sure and then moved on to the can.

He brought the magnet closer and closer to the can. Again, he was able to touch the can with the magnet, and it was clearly not attracted.

"That's exactly what I expected would happen. Now let's try the pin." Adam held his hand out to Mark, who handed him the pin.

There was nervous anticipation in the garage as Adam started the second half of his experiment. They had all learned in school that what they were doing was called the "scientific method", although it seemed natural to Adam.

He brought the pin to the bolt slowly, not sure if there would be any attraction. Closer and closer he moved, until the two were touching. There was no obvious attraction.

"Nothing. Not even a weak pull," Jimmy stated.

"Yeah, zero," replied Adam. "Now, the part I've been waiting for!"

He brought the pin slowly toward the crankshaft. At nearly 4 inches away, the pin pulled from his grip and stuck itself to the crankshaft. The nearby can was sucked into the group as well.

Four faces registered amazement. "Well, Doctor McTaggart, your experiment is a success!" said Jimmy, half-kidding and half-serious.

Adam now understood how the pin worked as a key. "What an easy way to keep a door locked. Just use science people don't realize exists. All this pin does is magnetically attract some aluminum to unlock a latch."

"How can you know so much about this stuff and suck at school," said Mark. "Even Kevin has better marks than you."

Adam shrugged off the comment. "It takes a lot of effort to barely listen in class and still pass."

"Not that I don't enjoy teasing Adam, but doesn't this just bring up more questions?" Kevin asked, looking at each of them as he spoke. "I mean, it makes me wonder what we're discovering."

"Yeah, I know. If George saw any of this, he'd be

freaking out," added Mark.

Adam's mind was in high gear again. After that discovery, the possibilities streamed through his thoughts as he narrowed them down to a few realistic scenarios.

"Seeing this, I'm sure there has to be some sort of scientific discovery hidden in Grayson. I'd put money on that, and you know I don't have much to bet," said Adam.

The others didn't know if they should laugh.

"Do you think that's why someone is destroying towns? They're trying to find this discovery?" asked Kevin.

"That makes sense," said Jimmy.

"Yeah, but how are *we* supposed find it?" asked Mark.

"It's gotta be in those tunnels somewhere," said Jimmy.

"I agree, but where? Those tunnels are confusing. Without a map, I don't want to go wandering through there again," said Kevin.

"Maybe there's a map in the file room," said Mark.

Jimmy thought about it and agreed. "Yeah, you're right. If we don't have a map, we could get stuck in the tunnels until someone rescued us. We'd be in huge trouble if that happened. Let's look for a map before we go in there again."

"First, *you* need to get the key," Adam looked at Jimmy who reluctantly nodded, "and *we* need to help Jimmy any way we can."

"What are we standing around here for!" said Mark, heading for the door.

"Someone's excited about something other than a video game," said Kevin, jerking his thumb in Mark's direction.

"Hey, you had all the fun yesterday. My turn," Mark turned and stepped out the door.

The remaining boys filed out of the garage, smiling at Mark's excitement.

After a short walk, they arrived at Jimmy's house. Jimmy led the way through the back door and into the kitchen.

"Hello," called Jimmy, "Mom, are you here?"

"I'm in the bedroom. Be out in a minute," came the reply from down the side hallway.

Soon, Mrs. Jones stepped into the room and found the boys seated around the table. "Oh, hello. I didn't realize you were all here. What are you boys up to today?" she asked.

"Not sure, we're just discussing options," replied Jimmy. "Are you headed out for groceries this morning?"

"No, I did that yesterday on my day off. I'm just going to work around the house today."

The boys snuck disappointed glances at each other, followed by awkward silence.

"Is it ok if we hang out in the basement for a while?" Jimmy asked.

She nodded approval and they sauntered into the basement, dragging their feet in a lazy fashion.

"That just sucks. I forgot that she did her shopping yesterday," said Jimmy, disappointed at himself for the lapse. He plopped down on the old sofa against the wall. The others found an old rocking chair, a beanbag chair, and another part of the sofa to sit down. They sat for a while, each lost in their own thoughts.

"Mark, go tell Jimmy's mom about one of your video games. That'll put her to sleep for a couple of hours," Kevin joked.

"Why don't you go weed her garden, farmboy," Mark snapped back.

"Actually," said Jimmy, "Mark has a good idea. Mom's been complaining that she needs her garden weeded for the last week. What if we offer to do it for her...for pay, of course. Just a couple of bucks each?"

"How does that keep her outside?" asked Mark, skeptical about any manual labor.

"We just keep asking her 'Is this a weed?' and make her look at the plants. I need less than a minute to get the key and I'll slip it to one of you. That person goes and makes the copy."

"Let's give it a try. How do we decide who works and who goes for the key?" asked Kevin, never afraid to work.

"I'll go," offered Mark.

"No, you should stay. You'll be the most important person for this task. Mom will believe you don't know the difference between a carrot and a dandelion." Jimmy's natural smooth talk nearly slipped the outright insult past Mark. Being told he was the most important person for this job made Mark let the comment pass.

"Let Adam go," said Kevin, "I don't mind doing the work."

Adam opened his mouth to protest, but stopped when he saw Kevin's stern face.

"Ok. We'll only have to keep her occupied for a couple of minutes until I give Adam the key, and then again when he gets back. Everyone give him your money so he can pay," said Jimmy. They dug in their pockets and handed him some change and bills.

"Now, what do we tell her about Adam leaving and coming back?" Jimmy wondered out loud.

"Tell her there's still something wrong with the bike you're selling and Adam is going to fix it for you, but he needs to test drive it first," said Mark.

Jimmy face broke in a wide smile. "I like the way you think. Some of my charm is wearing off on you."

Mark's face broke into a wide smile as well. "I wouldn't call it 'charm'. It rhymes more with bull spit."

Adam and Kevin laughed at the insult. Jimmy's smile changed from mischievous to embarrassed, which made the others laugh even more.

"Ok, everyone remembers what they're doing?" asked Jimmy, changing the subject. The others assured him yes and followed him up the stairs.

Mrs. Jones was walking into the kitchen at the same time as the boys.

"Mom, I have a deal for you," said Jimmy, sounding like a cross between a game show host and a salesman at a used car lot. Mrs. Jones barely batted an eye, having heard that opening countless times.

Jimmy continued, "For a small fee, my friends and I will pull all the weeds in your garden."

She eyed him closely. Jimmy had made her an offer that caught her interest. "How much is the 'small fee'?" she asked.

"Whatever you are willing to pay," Jimmy replied, poker-faced.

Mrs. Jones picked up her purse from the kitchen table. After rifling through it she pulled out some money. "Here. This is what you'll get when I'm satisfied the job is done." She pulled the money away as Jimmy reached for the bills and shook her finger at him. "You guys must really be bored," she added.

"Just one little thing, though," said Jimmy, "while we're pulling weeds, Adam is going to take another look at my old bike. It's making a noise that'll make it hard to sell. I'm paying him to fix it for me."

Mrs. Jones turned to Adam, "You make sure he pays you well for your work, ok?"

Adam nodded.

Jimmy jumped in, "I'll pay him fair...why don't you take them out to the garden so they can get started? I'm just going to change into work clothes." He pointed at Mark and Kevin.

"Are you sure you want to do this?" Mrs. Jones looked at the three boys who weren't doing the talking. They all nodded yes.

"Alright then, follow me," she said, leading them out the back door.

Jimmy took the opportunity to run down the hallway while Adam stayed in the kitchen waiting. Jimmy returned, walking while pulling on a new shirt, and slipped a ring of keys into Adam's hand. It had more keys on it than Adam expected.

"It's the gold key in the middle. It's worn more than the others," Jimmy whispered to Adam. "Get back here as quick as you can."

Adam agreed as the two stepped outside. Jimmy opened the shed and Adam pulled out the bike he was supposedly fixing.

Jimmy turned toward the garden when he heard his mother say, "Not that one Mark, it's a carrot...." He grinned and waved 'go' at Adam. Adam hopped on the bike and pedaled out of the driveway.

The Hardware Store was half a block up and a block west of Jimmy's house. It was one of the newest buildings in town. It was also a place Adam loved and hated. He loved seeing all the tools and parts on the shelves, and often imagined what he could build with them. He hated it because he couldn't afford anything in the store, even the cheapest tools.

He parked the bike between the Hardware Store and post office, so that it was hidden from passer-by's, and ran into the store. He needed in and out fast because Kevin didn't know how to work slowly and there weren't many weeds in the garden.

Adam sped to the main counter. He could see the key-cutting machine behind it but no one was manning the counter.

"Can I help you," came a young girl's voice from behind, startling him. He turned around.

Lacey Lang stood with her hands on her hips, looking at Adam. She was a plain girl who was more comfortable wearing jeans than a skirt. People in town said she knew her way around the store and was pretty handy with the tools as well. Being a year younger than Adam, he didn't know her much, except for seeing her at school.

Hoping Lacey didn't notice she startled him, Adam said, "Uh...is your dad around?"

Lacey looked at Adam, "No, I'm the only one here at the moment."

Adam looked disappointed.

"Well, what do you need? Maybe *I* can help you?" Lacey asked. The tone of her voice showed she was tired of people underestimating her abilities.

Adam sensed that, which was odd as he never usually sensed people's feelings, but being underestimated was something he knew. "Cut me a copy of this key," he said, holding it out to her.

Lacey took a second to process what Adam had said. Whenever someone wanted something at the store, they always asked for her dad and then her mom. Rarely would customers give her the chance to prove her abilities, so Adam's request took her off guard.

She took the key and smiled. "Ok, it'll just take a minute."

She checked the key against the blanks hanging on the wall and found a matching one in a short amount of time. She took both keys and bolted the original into the left side of the key cutter, and the blank into the right.

After checking the alignment of both keys and the travel of the cut, she turned on the machine and it started working.

"What do I owe you?" asked Adam over the hum of the machine. She told him, and Adam realized he had more than enough money to cut a second key. He handed her all he had and asked for another key, insisting she keep the change. Lacey beamed, happy to be taken seriously and given a tip as well.

When the keys were finished, Lacey handed them to Adam. "The original key is pretty worn. The copies may be a little bit small, so you might have to jiggle them in the lock," she pointed out.

Adam thanked her and left the store. He felt proud of himself, as his actions made Lacey happy. She had copied the keys with more skill and speed than Adam expected, which was a pleasant surprise.

He pedaled into the driveway at Jimmy's and parked the bike outside the shed. As he stepped to the edge of the garden, Mark spotted him. Mrs. Jones was facing Mark with her back to Adam.

"Ooooh...now I see the difference. *These* are peas, and *these* are weeds...," said Mark.

Jimmy was smirking as he walked over to Adam. "Did you get it fixed?" he asked, giving a wink.

"All fixed," he replied. "Can I wash my hands in your house?" He winked back at Jimmy.

Jimmy caught on. "Follow me. Mom, I'm just taking Adam in to wash his hands," he called. She nodded her approval.

In the house, Adam handed Jimmy the keys and Jimmy ran down the hallway toward the bedrooms. Adam followed and decided to wash his hands in the bathroom anyway.

He washed them quickly and was starting to dry them when Mrs. Jones walked past the bathroom door. She was supposed to be outside! She was going to catch Jimmy!

Adam stepped into the hallway behind Mrs. Jones as Jimmy stepped out of the bedroom, nearly bumping into his mom. Adam's stomach tightened.

"What are you doing in my room?" asked Mrs. Jones, startled.

Jimmy was taken by surprise as well, and was lost for words.

"He was trying to find something to get the grease off my hands," said Adam, hoping there was a bathroom in the master bedroom.

Jimmy followed along, "Doesn't Dad have that hand cleaner for mechanics in your bathroom?"

Mrs. Jones looked from Adam to Jimmy, "No, It's in the garage. Now stay out of my room." She moved Jimmy out of the way and walked past. "I have a headache from Mark's questions. You show him which ones are weeds and let me know when you're done."

Jimmy agreed, and the boys sped outside. Mark and Kevin stood in the garden looking toward the house.

"Why didn't you stop her?" Jimmy looked at the two, anger in his voice.

"Hey, there's only so many ways I can pretend I don't know the difference between a weed and a radish. Farm-boy here was no help." Mark jerked his thumb at Kevin.

"*I* helped! Who do you think pulled most of the weeds?" Kevin replied. "We *did* promise to weed the garden. Besides, she would never believe *I* wouldn't know what a weed looked like."

Mark looked insulted. "I asked her a question, bent down to pull the weed, and when I looked back she was halfway through the door. I couldn't just drag her back out again."

Adam diffused the situation. "You guys did great, really. We got the task done and in the end no one's in trouble, alright?" Everyone seemed to calm down as he spoke, agreeing in turn. "So let's get this garden finished and we can all go home for lunch. We can re-group later."

They did as Adam suggested, and finished weeding the garden. Mrs. Jones inspected their work, and thanked them all for their help. She handed equal amounts of money to Mark and Kevin. Adam received more, and Jimmy was given nothing. When he began to protest, she reminded him that he owed Adam for fixing the bike, so she paid Adam on his behalf. Besides that, she was going to make him weed it for free anyway. Surprisingly, Jimmy didn't complain at the explanation.

Before they could say anymore, Mrs. Jones invited them to stay for lunch. It was just sandwiches, but they were more than welcome. That would be quicker than going to their homes and meeting again later, so they all agreed to stay and thanked her for her offer.

Even though they were simple sandwiches, Adam loved them. Real beef, slathered with the good mayo and mustard, not the cheap stuff he had at home. They even had something labelled 'sub sauce' that added a wonderful tang to the flavor. He ate his sandwich quickly, and Mrs. Jones insisted he have another. It didn't take much to convince him, and soon he felt over-stuffed, but didn't care.

After eating, the boys helped Mrs. Jones clean. Adam loaded the dirty dishes in the dishwasher while Mark wiped the table and Kevin swept crumbs off the floor. When they were done, they left the house and headed back to Adam's garage, where they could come up with a plan in private.

CHAPTER ELEVEN

The boys sat around the old coffee table in Adam's garage once again. "I made 2 keys at the hardware store," said Adam, "so we have to decide who keeps them."

"Since Jimmy knows the security code, I think he should keep one," said Kevin, "and I don't want one, so it'll be either you or Mark." He pointed at Adam.

Adam handed a key to Jimmy.

Mark spoke up, "If I take it home, my sisters will find it and lose it, so Adam should keep the other key."

Adam silently accepted. "The only thing we need now is the security code. You can just tell it to *me*, if that makes you more comfortable." The three looked at Jimmy.

"If I didn't trust you guys, I would never have *'borrowed'* the keys in the first place. Besides, it's not like its rocket science to figure out."

The others looked at Jimmy puzzled.

"Who had the system installed?" Jimmy added.

They thought for a few seconds before it dawned on Adam. "It's Jeff's birthday, right?"

Jimmy laughed, "Yep, 1027 - October 27th. Of course, he wouldn't use the year. He's still 29 you know."

They all laughed. Typical Jeff.

"Since Town Hall is closed today, when do we want to try going in?" Mark was almost vibrating with anticipation.

"Calm down. We'll get there soon enough." Kevin grinned at Mark's excitement.

"The sooner the better, but I think we should try after 5 o'clock. That's when the stores are closed and most people are at home eating. There isn't a car driving in this town until 5:30, so there's less chance of being seen," said Adam.

"That makes sense. In the meantime, we can each get a flashlight and grab a bite to eat. Maybe meet back here at around 4:30? If they ask, tell your parents that we're playing some baseball at the school," said Jimmy.

They all agreed and left one by one. When they had all gone, Adam cleaned up the coffee table and hid the money from Mrs. Jones in his hiding spot. He placed it in the small tin can and closed the plastic lid, slipping it back to its original location.

With quiet steps he walked into the house. His mother was in her usual spot watching an old British soap opera on the TV. "Did you have some lunch yet?" she asked without turning her head.

"Yeah, at Jimmy's. We helped his mom weed her garden and she fed us a sandwich," he replied, stepping toward the stairs.

"I'm going to the store for a couple of hours this afternoon. They need help unloading a truck that was supposed to be here yesterday." Still, she didn't turn to look at Adam.

Adam stopped at the foot of the stairs. "I'm going to eat something early so I can meet the guys at school and play some baseball. I'll be quiet when I get home tonight." His mother grunted, barely acknowledging that he had spoken.

Adam continued up the stairs to his room. He opened the top drawer of his beat-up dresser. The drawer was filled with wires, nuts, bolts, screws, and miscellaneous parts that Adam had saved from pulling apart things he found. He knew he had an old flashlight that needed a new bulb buried somewhere in the parts. He also had some various energy efficient bulbs he had pulled out of other broken lights. He intended to convert the flashlight from a conventional bulb to an energy efficient bulb eventually, and that moment seemed like as good a time as any.

He pulled out the parts he needed and set them on top of the dresser, then dug around until he found the soldering iron he would use to connect the pieces together. He had bought the iron at a garage sale for a dollar. It came with solder and soldering paste, enough to last him a long time. Soon, it was heated up and ready to work.

He removed a bulb assembly he ripped from a newer flashlight that had been crushed. Next, he inspected the old flashlight and pulled it apart. After some soldering, modifying, fitting and re-fitting, he assembled the flashlight, including two almost new batteries he had found. He turned on the flashlight to inspect, and it worked. It wasn't the brightest light he had ever seen, but it was good enough.

Adam heard the door close as his mom left. He worked for a little while longer getting the flashlight just right and cleaned up the left over parts and tools, except for the soldering iron as it needed some time to cool. He tiptoed down the stairs, careful not to make much noise, even though his mom was gone. It was a habit too hard to ignore.

He sat down in his mom's chair again, intending to rest for a while, but his mind kept going over questions from the previous night's events. Why were there tunnels beneath the town, and how were they made? What was so important that someone took the time to build them? Who built the security locks, and how did they manufacture the pin that attracted aluminum?

His brain wouldn't stop pelting him with questions, so he sat in the chair, eyes open and staring straight ahead. Slowly, his eyes fell to the picture of Edward. He remembered the day he first noticed the lapel pin and later found the envelope containing it. He saw the envelope in his mind and realized that he hadn't looked through the rest of the pictures and papers.

He sprang out of the chair and ran outside, jogging to the garage. If anyone had seen him, they would have thought he was up to something just by seeing him move.

In the garage, Adam grabbed the envelope, spread the papers on the coffee table and looked at them one by one. The first one was the only one he had taken time to look at before he found the pin. It was the Town Hall Grand Opening picture. He examined the faces of the people standing together in the picture. So many looked familiar, probably because many of their grandchildren through great great grandchildren still lived in Grayson.

The next paper was old and tattered. Hand drawn on it was a picture that looked like a crude spider. Legs curved out in all directions from a circle at the center. A ring tied the legs together. At the bottom of the picture "E.M." was written; his father's initials. *He* must have drawn the picture. It was the first thing Adam had ever seen written by his father. Surprisingly, his own handwriting was similar, even though he had only seen the two letters.

He turned the paper over. On the back he saw a list with simple symbols.

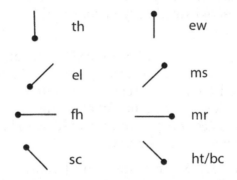

Feel five from floor, was written at the bottom of the page in his father's handwriting.

Adam thought it was strange. What did it mean?

The next pictures were just buildings in town. The Grain Elevators (only one was still standing, but he had seen pictures of the other three), the Church, the hotel, and one that was labelled "school." It was an old one-room schoolhouse in the picture. Adam was pretty sure the school he attended, while being old itself, was built on the site of the one in the picture.

He sat back and wondered for a while. What if some of the tunnels led to these buildings? They had to come out somewhere?

After thinking for a few more minutes, Adam hid the envelope again, hoping he would find something in the file cabinets later that would make sense of everything.

He ambled back into the house and opened the fridge. What to eat today? There was bread, luncheon meat, mustard, ketchup, and some pickles in the fridge. He closed the door. After the sandwiches he ate for lunch, he couldn't bear the thought of more luncheon meat. In futility, he opened and closed each of the cupboard doors. Stale crackers, old spices, dry pasta - nothing that he was interested in eating.

Glancing at the clock, he noticed it was almost 4 pm and the guys would start arriving soon. He grabbed a piece of bread (stale rye bread; discounted at the store) and forced it down one mouthful at a time with a glass of tap water. It tasted terrible, but it would keep his stomach from grumbling later in the day.

Back outside, Adam waited until Mark and Jimmy arrived, then Kevin a few minutes later. Each boy had a small flashlight in his hands. Adam's homemade light was by far the largest. All the others fit into each owner's pocket, but Adam's was the size of a police flashlight.

"Do you want to leave that here for now?" asked Kevin. "People will suspect something if they see you walking around with *that* light. I've got an extra one you can use."

Adam agreed. Kevin was right.

"Come to the garage for a minute. I want to show you something," said Adam.

They followed him into the garage and he grabbed the pictures from their hiding spot, spreading them out on the coffee table for all to see.

Mark immediately identified his great-great-grandfather in the first picture, as did Jimmy and Kevin. They looked at Adam, then back to the picture. No one could identify anyone resembling Adam.

"I thought the McTaggart's were one of the founding families? Why don't I see someone that looks like you or your dad?" asked Mark, even though they all thought the same thing.

"I don't know, maybe they took the picture," Adam replied.

"What about your grandparents?" asked Mark again.

Adam felt uncomfortable under the gaze of his friends.

"My dad's parents moved overseas when he died," said Adam. "At least, that's what I've been told. I've never heard from them, although I *have* seen their picture. My mom's family disowned her - that much I know - but not much else." He paused for a second and continued. "You all know my mom. She barely acknowledges me. She never answers any of my questions about our family. Most of what I've learned is from other people in town."

The others realized they were making Adam uncomfortable, so they looked back to the picture.

"Does anyone recognize the lady in the picture?" asked Kevin. They had all noticed her, but none had wanted to point it out for fear of being teased.

"She must be from my family tree, 'cause she's not ugly like you three," Jimmy teased, thinking he would beat them to a punch-line.

"That's gross! You just admitted you're attracted to your great-great grandma!" Mark shot back at Jimmy.

They all had a chuckle while Jimmy stammered in protest.

"Sounds to me like no one knows who she is," said Kevin, and the others agreed.

They saw the rest of the pictures, but nothing seemed interesting to them. The hand-drawn picture and list weren't as interesting to the others as they were to Adam.

"It's 4:37. Should we go hang out in the park until we try going in?" asked Adam. "I'm assuming that my mom will get home soon after 5 and I don't want to be here when she gets home."

Jimmy agreed. "We can hang out in the park behind Town Hall and slip in the side door one at a time. I'll go first and shut off the alarm."

The others nodded and soon they left for the park. As they passed the Fire Hall, they noticed a lot more traffic as it was just after 5 pm. They hung around the trees in the park until all seemed calm and headed for the back of Town Hall.

Jimmy looked down the side of the building. "Follow me one at a time, every couple of minutes," said Jimmy, and he stepped around the side of the building.

The others waited against the wall. After two minutes, Kevin started around the corner to the side door.

Slam! He and Jimmy collided hard.

They both staggered for a second, regaining their composure while offering 'are you ok's' to each other.

"Why'd you come back?" asked Adam.

"The key won't work! I tried it a bunch of times and it wouldn't unlock the door."

Adam nodded his head. "Lacey said that the keys might be tricky because the original was so worn. Try jiggling it up and down while you turn." Adam made a jiggling and turning motion with his hand as he spoke.

Jimmy looked uncomfortable about trying again, but nodded, checked around the corner, and left. That time Kevin kept looking around the corner to make sure Jimmy got in before following. He gave the others a thumbs-up, waited thirty seconds and rounded the corner the same way Jimmy had done.

Their stealth worked, and soon they were all inside Town Hall, hearts pounding from being somewhere they weren't allowed and excited at the thought of finding answers to their questions.

CHAPTER TWELVE

The hallway was dimly lit by a safety light on the wall above the alarm panel, making it eerie and dark in the spot where the boys stood. There were no windows in the hallway, but some natural light flowed from the hallway exit ahead.

"Let's leave the lights off just in case we get stuck in the tunnels again," said Jimmy. "There are windows and safety lights all over the main floor, so we don't need light until we get to the basement." The others nodded.

"Shouldn't there be safety lights in the basement too?" asked Mark.

"You would think," replied Jimmy, "but I don't know why there aren't any. Mom always told me not to get stuck down there if the power went out because there's absolutely no light." He shrugged, and motioned for the others to follow.

Trying to be quiet, they made their way through the building and down the basement stairs. Kevin waited at the top of the stairs, as hidden as possible. The others continued on toward the storage room.

After winding through the maze of boxes, Mark

examined the drawbridge door.

"Hard to believe this is a door," he said.

Jimmy pulled Mark toward the boxes, moving him out of the way. Adam placed the pin against the wall and they watched the drawbridge door slowly fall.

"That is just *cool*," said Mark with a wide grin on his face.

"That's what *I* thought," said Adam, "but the other two just rushed me into the room."

"You would still be here tinkering if we didn't," said Jimmy.

Adam shrugged, switched on his flashlight and stepped inside. Mark was right on his heels, his flashlight searching everywhere. He seemed in awe of the secret file room.

"I'll bet these files are sorted the same way as the files in the main part of the basement, so let's just do what we did before," said Adam. They each walked to one of the well-worn wooden file cabinets that lined the left wall.

Adam flipped through the first cabinet, but nothing caught his eye. He found financial records from the Town, as well as financial records from the monitoring station. Not knowing the cost of everyday expenses like power and water, all of the bills looked like a lot of money spent.

A quiet noise in the direction the storage room caused them all to look. The drawbridge door was closing by itself.

"You guys keep reading; I'll try and open the door," said Adam, walking while pointing his flashlight around the opening.

He found the impression right away and re-opened the door soon after. When he turned back to the files, he saw the worried look on Mark's face lighten as the door fell open. Mark must have been putting up a brave front with all of his excitement for adventure earlier, but the thought of being locked in the file room made him quickly give up his cover.

"It must be on some type of timer. I'd love to figure it out, but I'll do that later," said Adam. "At least we know we can get out next time it closes." The statement didn't seem to relax Mark much.

Adam kept searching his files. He found more and more financial records, but nothing else. After a half hour, he decided to move to the next cabinet and immediately had better luck. The first drawer he opened had a file labelled 'Ed McTaggart'. He pulled the file and started to look through it.

'Director of Special Site Operations,' was Edward's official title, according to the file. Adam had never heard that before. Although he knew his father was in charge of the monitoring station outside of town, he didn't know what else Edward was responsible for. What was a "special" site?

Adam leafed through the papers in the folder trying to see if anything stood out. Mostly he saw the minutes of meetings discussing the monitoring station, pretty boring stuff. He stopped at a picture. It was a headshot of Ed, who must have been in his early 20's. Adam pulled the page out to look at it more closely.

"Listen to this," said Jimmy.

The other two turned toward him.

"Following the destruction from the battle of

Tunguska, Larix fled after we recovered the object. Special teams lead by Gupta and McTaggart attempted to track him for the following month, but once again he has disappeared. Meetings to discuss the future of the object will take place August 18 at headquarters." read Jimmy. "Signed, Clay Campbell, Director, Sentinel League, August 4, 1908"

"Did you say Tunguska 1908?" asked Mark.

"That's what it says. Why, is it near here?" replied Jimmy. Adam looked as curious as Jimmy to hear what Mark knew.

"You guys never really read or watch anything educational do you?" said Mark looking slightly frustrated.

Jimmy was going to reply, but Adam stopped him and motioned for Mark to continue.

"Anyway, I just watched a documentary on Tunguska. It's an area in the middle of nowhere in Russia. In 1908 something exploded and wiped out everything for miles, and no one knows what caused the explosion. There have been a lot of theories over the years though. People have said it was aliens, swamp gas, a meteor, and even an invention by Nikola Tesla."

"Nikola who?" asked Jimmy

Mark palmed his forehead and was about to start in on Jimmy, when a hurried knock interrupted. It came from the drawbridge door.

Adam looked at the others with a worried face as the adrenaline started pumping. He bolted to the drawbridge door and fumbled with the pin. It felt like it took an hour to lower the door. Kevin stepped into the room in a hurry.

"Someone's here!" Kevin panted as he spoke, visibly excited. "I heard the door open and someone said that Jeff must have forgotten to arm the alarm again, so I assume there are at least 2 people."

"Who was it?" asked Mark.

"The voices are so hollow in this building that I couldn't tell, and I didn't exactly hang around to find out."

Adam grabbed a light and ran out the door. He danced through the box maze, shut off the lights, and retraced his steps. Once back in the file room, he pulled the pin from his pocket.

"I hope this works," muttered Adam as he looked at the others.

He placed the pin, and the drawbridge started to retract. Adam looked slightly relieved. He turned to the others, "If they come in here, we're in trouble."

The others nodded.

Even though everyone was nervous, Mark was by far the most visibly stressed. His eyes darted between the other three and he couldn't stop playing with his hands. "W..w..what are we going to do? Not go into the tunnels?" He looked at the others in the silence. "Guys? ... Guys?"

They said nothing but each boy understood what had to happen, so they walked to the tunnel entrance.

Adam spoke as he opened the door. "You guys wait further inside the tunnel and I'll keep this door open a little to watch the drawbridge. It goes down slow, so if it starts to move, I'll just close the door the rest of the way. We'll have to wing it from there."

The others filed past and Mark looked terrible. Adam

positioned himself where he planned, then slid the door into position and waited. He heard Mark fidgeting with his hands, and after a few long moments he gave a "shhh" in Mark's direction.

Thoughts ran through Adam's mind. What if the people came into the file room? The boys couldn't stay in the tunnel on the other side of the door in case the people continued into the tunnels. Should they try the same tunnel they had already been down? Someone was already suspicious in that direction and it was probably being watched. Should they try the tunnel to the immediate left instead of right this time? That probably led to the Fire Station where they would be trapped. Maybe one of the tunnels straight ahead, but where could they possibly lead?

Adam's thoughts were interrupted by the sound of a simple click. He recognized it immediately as the start of the mechanism to open the drawbridge door. He slid his door shut and hoped that the sound of the drawbridge lowering hid the sound of it closing. He turned to the others and whispered, "Go!"

Mark's eyes couldn't have gotten any wider after hearing that single little word. The others grabbed him and forced him to move down the tunnel. At any other time he would have been teased about the look on his face, but that was far from anyone's mind at the time.

They stopped at the junction to all the other tunnels and all looked at Adam. Adam paused for a moment and pointed at the second tunnel to the right, next to the one they had previously taken.

They ran down the tunnel, again curving gently right. In their haste, they didn't notice they ran through an intersection. Immediately afterward they nearly hit a wall, as it blindly turned to the right. It continued left after a couple of steps, and left again after a few more, opening into a room.

They swept their flashlights around trying to take in the size of the room they had just entered. It was only 8 feet high, but was a wide open expanse, with a few support columns scattered throughout.

"Whoa," Kevin commented quietly.

Before they could say anything else, an all-encompassing light blinded them from above.

Adam's heart raced, and all he could think was,

We're dead!

CHAPTER THIRTEEN

Adam was sure they had been caught in a trap.

How's Jimmy going to talk us out of this one, he thought as his eyes adjusted to the light streaming from the ceiling. It seemed to get less intense with every passing second, and soon his friends began coming into focus.

The rest of the group squinted in the light. Mark seemed to struggle the most, but soon they were all looking around the room. What seemed like minutes was only a few seconds, and they were all jerked back to reality by the sound of the file room sliding door slamming shut.

Mark was breathing really fast and deep, filled with fear. "W..w..what d...d..do we d..do?" he whispered.

Adam thought quickly. "Pick a column and hide behind it. Stay there for a couple of minutes. I'm going back down the hallway to listen. Go." He waved them to their hiding spots.

They walked as quietly as they could while Adam tiptoed up the hallway a short distance. He heard his own heartbeat sounding in his ears and it almost drowned out all other sounds. As he listened, he heard footsteps getting louder as they got closer. Two people were walking together, sometimes in step with each other and sometimes not. Louder and louder the footsteps grew, until Adam was sure they would come face-to-face at the next footfall.

The walkers broke their silence, further away than Adam had imagined, but close enough to hear. "Ellie knows more about this than she's telling us, you know," said one of the walkers. It was Don Chen. His voice was unmistakable.

"Yeah, I know. You know how stubborn she can get. Probably because of her age." Gurpreet Gupta's voice echoed through the tunnel as well. He chuckled at his own comment.

Their pace was casual and didn't seem to be getting closer, much to Adam's relief. They stayed silent, and slowly the sound of their footsteps dwindled, but Adam couldn't tell what direction they took.

During that time, Adam had a chance to look up at the ceiling. The light coming from it was strange, like nothing he had ever seen before. It was as though the entire thing was glowing and there were no individual points of light. Light came from every square inch, with a roughly defined edge at the walls. He was amazed, staring at it until he was interrupted by the sound of another door closing far down the tunnels. The light from the ceiling slowly dimmed and soon went out.

"Are they gone?" whispered Jimmy, clicking on his flashlight and stepping out from behind a column far back in the room. The others popped their heads out from columns even further back.

"I think so, but I don't know where they went or for

how long." replied Adam. "Could you guys hear them from back there?"

The others looked at each other and shook their heads in the light Adam had pointed at them. "Not really," said Mark, "but please tell me one wasn't my dad." He frowned, as he already suspected the answer.

"Sorry, but it was your dad and Don Chen."

"Could you hear what they said?" asked Jimmy

"Mr. Chen said 'Ellie knows more about this than she says', and Mark's dad said she's stubborn because she's so old."

"Who's Ellie?" asked Mark.

They all shrugged their shoulders and looked at each other.

"So, what now?" asked Jimmy.

Adam thought for a moment. "Let's try and find another exit in this room. You and Mark walk up this wall," said Adam as he pointed to the wall on the right, "and Kevin and I'll walk up this wall. Look for a way out of here. Be quiet, sound carries a long way in these tunnels."

They agreed and each group started walking. After a minute they realized just how massive the room was. Through the columns the teams saw each other's lights, but the low ceiling and large room played tricks on their eyes in the darkness. Eventually, the teams ended up at the far wall walking toward each other, meeting somewhere in the middle.

"Nothing?" asked Adam.

"Nope," replied Jimmy.

"Why would you have this huge empty room and only one small entrance and exit? There should be another way out," Adam thought out loud.

"I don't think you have to worry about the latest building codes when you're building in secret," replied Jimmy.

"Yeah, but even a hundred years ago they must have had a little thought about being trapped in a big underground room." Adam said, half in reply to Jimmy and half in thought.

"Well," said Kevin, "Why don't we just continue looking at the walls until we get back to where we came in. You go the way you were going and we'll keep going the way we were going."

The others nodded and continued down the walls. Adam was looking more intensely at them, hoping that the others had missed something. Soon, they met at the entrance having found nothing.

Adam continued to scan the walls near the entrance when he noticed a strange impression on the inside corner of the wall. The impression was simple. It was a tall rectangle made up of 4 squares. It wasn't deep in the rock wall, and was easy to miss. The angle of the flashlight made it stand out a little from the surrounding wall.

"What's that?" asked Mark, butting in between Adam and the wall.

"If I knew, I would tell you," replied Adam, slightly annoyed by Mark's curiosity.

Adam touched the top square. Nothing happened. He felt the impression, starting at the top square and sliding his finger to the bottom square. He understood how it could be missed easily, as he almost didn't feel it carved into the wall.

As soon as he had finished touching the impression, Mark stuck his fingers on it, like a child imitating everything they see. Adam was slightly annoyed by that, even though he knew Mark was just nervous.

In an instant they were blinded by the lights again. Mark yelped a little, but their eyes seemed to adjust a little quicker than the previous time.

"Did *you* do that?" Jimmy questioned Mark.

"I don't know," he replied.

"What did you do?" Jimmy asked again.

"I DON'T KNOW!" Mark shot back.

The lights faded back to darkness again.

"Cover your eyes," said Adam, so they did.

The lights came back on and faded to darkness again.

"That's just cool," said Adam as everyone opened their eyes.

"What did you do?" asked Mark.

"I noticed that you slid your fingers up when the lights turned on, so I slid my finger down and it turned them off. Slide up for on, down for off. I bet there's one of these by every door."

"This place seriously freaks me out," said Mark. "Secret tunnels, light coming from nowhere, magnets that shouldn't be magnetic..."

"Yeah, it's pretty cool," replied Adam, still trying to examine the light from the ceiling.

"Maybe we should we keep the lights off," said Kevin. "They'll know someone's here if the lights are on. We'll also know if they come into the tunnels if the lights turn back on again."

Adam nodded, "Good thinking." He slid his finger down and the lights slowly fizzled out. "Lets go back to the junction and take the next tunnel to the right. Agreed?"

They nodded in silence and turned to the doorway.

"What do we do if we hear a door open again?" asked Mark, clearly still nervous.

"Just follow Adam and be quiet," said Kevin. "We need to stay together."

Adam led the way back to the main junction. He stopped at the entrance to the first tunnel on the right, shining his flashlight against the walls just inside the opening. After trying different angles he felt the walls.

Light blinded them again.

"QUIT DOING THAT!" exclaimed Mark, as the lights turned off again

"Sorry," replied Adam, as he continued feeling the wall.

He worked his way down in a back-and-forth pattern. Near the bottom of the wall, he felt something. It was small, but not an imperfection in the wall. It was a raised bump, like a circle, and a line attached to it, almost like the hand of a clock pointing to 7 or 8 o'clock. He shone his flashlight on it, and could barely get a shadow, let alone see it. Whoever made this tunnel and these impressions knew how to hide them in plain sight.

"Feel five from the floor," Adam muttered to himself.

"Come feel this," he said to the others, "close to the floor."

They all took turns.

"What do you think that is?" asked Kevin.

"I'm hoping it's a marker for the tunnels. If you know the tunnels and know where to find the mark, you can figure out where you are pretty easily. You guys stay here for a second. I'm going to check the tunnel to Town Hall."

Adam walked over to the tunnel and felt the wall near the floor again. In a couple of seconds he nodded his head, stood up and checked the next two tunnels the same way.

"12 o'clock is the way to Town Hall. 10:30 is the way to the bar. 9 is the big room. Should be easy enough to remember," he said, shuffling past them. "Let's see what happens at 7:30."

Adam started down the 7:30 tunnel when Mark stopped him.

"What if this is the tunnel Dad went down? We should go back to Town Hall," he said, still nervous.

"The door to Town Hall doesn't open from this side, remember? And the cooler to the bar is probably still locked this early, not to mention that it's probably being watched. This is our only option," said Jimmy.

"As for meeting your dad and Mr. Chen, that's a chance we have to take. I don't want to be stuck down here any more than you do. Besides, we've only got a one in six chance of taking the same tunnel as them anyway," said Adam.

"Same odds as Russian roulette," muttered Mark.

The others laughed at the remark, even under the

circumstances.

Adam led them through the tunnel and they followed single file. Mark stayed close to Adam, followed by Jimmy and Kevin. After a short distance, they reached another 4 way intersection. Adam motioned for the others to stop and felt the wall near the floor of their current tunnel and the tunnel that intersected. Next, he went to the tunnel on the other side of the intersection and felt it as well.

"The intersection we keep walking straight past in each tunnel has a marker that feels like a circle. I'm guessing it makes a ring connecting all the tunnels - like a shortcut," said Adam.

"Shortcut to getting lost," muttered Mark.

They continued in silence, trying to minimize the sound of their own feet in the tunnels. No matter how hard they tried, every footstep echoed both ahead and behind.

The tunnel itself was laid out strangely, curving right to begin with, switching left then right again. Because of the curves, it was difficult to judge exactly what direction they were headed. Shining their lights forward or backward looked like a dead end due to a trick of the light, the color of the tunnel and how it was constructed. It seemed to be built so you could easily get lost.

Curves left, curves right, on and on they walked. How many curves was that so far? Adam didn't know.

As the tunnel continued, they walked louder and louder. Mark dragged his feet more each step, walking with his shoulders hunched and hands dangling. The monotony of the tunnel had seemed to calm him down, but because he was so excited earlier, Adam guessed that Mark's energy was pretty low.

Adam stopped the group and motioned for them all to sit down. Kevin and Jimmy looked confused, but did as Adam indicated. Mark looked happy to have a break.

"If I was down here alone in this tunnel, I think I'd go nuts," whispered Kevin. Everyone nodded in agreement.

Jimmy added, "Yeah. It feels like I've been walking on a treadmill. I'm tired of walking but don't feel like I've gone anywhere. It's depressing."

Adam agreed. "We'll take a short break. We don't know how much further to the end of this tunnel, and with our luck we'll have to turn around and go back."

As Adam finished speaking, blinding light came upon them once more.

Not again! he thought.

CHAPTER FOURTEEN

After a moment, the light faded from blinding to bearable. As soon as they were able to see, Adam signalled for the others to stay quiet. He knew it would be difficult with nerves on high and hearts pounding.

They waited in the strange light, listening for the smallest noise. Being far down the 7:30 tunnel, the sound of footsteps and soft voices weren't able to make the distance. Once in a while, one of the group would move as though they heard something, only to re-adjust and dismiss the thought.

Time ticked slower as they waited, and soon the ceiling faded back to black.

Even though the flashlights were still on, it took a few moments for everyone's eyes to adjust to the darkness once again. In that time, they took deep breaths to calm their nerves.

"Better get moving," said Adam as he stood up. The others followed his lead.

Adam continued down the tunnel. It curved left then right a few more times before it started going down slightly. After a while it flattened out, and soon Adam thought he saw the tunnel straighten. A few paces further, a door began to appear, bottom first. After a few more steps, the full door was in view at the top of a ramp. Just twenty steps back the tunnels looked as if they continued forever.

Because they wanted out of the tunnels already, each boy had the urge to rush up to the door, but Adam stopped as they reached the bottom of the ramp. "We don't know where this leads. I'll open it and take a look while you wait here," he whispered.

The others agreed.

Adam shone his light around the door as he approached, searching for the impression. Before he reached the door he found it exactly where the other ones had been.

The door looked like another slider, so he placed the pin and pulled the handle. The mechanism was quieter than the one in the file room, and so was the movement of the door. He opened it a little and peered through but saw nothing in the darkness. He shone his light into the crack and realized there was something in the way. As he pulled the sliding door open he found another door on the other side.

The door was normal and plain, like an interior door in a house. It was painted a strange green color and had an old style knob. The lock assembly looked like it took a skeleton key like to the ones Adam had seen in old cartoons. He turned the knob and pushed on the door, but the lock held it in place. Unless they had a skeleton key, they weren't getting through that way.

Adam called the group to the door and they each took turns looking at it. When Mark saw it, he smiled.

"I know where that door leads," he said, happy that he knew something the others didn't.

He paused, and the others stared at him. Jimmy rolled his hands in a 'get on with it' motion.

"The weather monitoring station," he finished.

"Are you sure?" asked Kevin.

"Oh yeah. That door leads into the basement."

They looked at him and said nothing.

"I used to play down there when Dad needed to do things at work. Once the twins were born, he had to take me along on weekends, and I would end up in the basement. Unless there's another door around town that is painted the same green as this one, it leads into the basement of the weather station."

"Did you ever ask him about it?" asked Jimmy.

"Yep. He just said it was a storage room where they kept old equipment."

"So how are we going to get through?" asked Kevin.

They all looked at Adam, who felt strange in their gaze.

"So?" asked Mark, looking at Adam.

"So what?" Adam shot the question back.

"You're the mechanical guy, can't you figure something out?"

Adam looked at Mark, paused, and then decided to put his mind to the task.

He thought out loud, "Ok, so far we've gotten in and out of the tunnels just by using the pin as a key. We've made it here, and now it looks like they added another door and another lock. Why would they do that?"

The others shrugged while following Adam's logic.

Adam thought for another moment and then spoke. "Nobody has this type of magnet lying around," he said showing the pin, "so the sliding door had to be safe enough. Did they put the second door up just to hide the sliding one? It *is* just a common old door."

"It worked for me," said Mark. "I've seen this door fifty times and didn't think anything was strange. If I saw that sliding door, I would have wanted to see what was on the other side."

"There's got to be a way to get through this door with the pin. *I* wouldn't go through the trouble of building all of this," Adam motioned to the tunnels and the doors, "only to have a standard lock on this last door."

He moved in to take a closer look at the lock. He shone his light around the rectangular lock plate. The paint beside the lock plate was scratched in one area. Adam placed the pin on the scratches and immediately heard the bolt sliding. He tried the handle and opened the door just a crack.

After looking back at the guys and giving them a thumbs-up, he opened the door as slow as he could. It opened easily but made a small creak. Adam worried that it was loud enough to alert anyone that might be in the building, so he paused and listened. Once he was satisfied that no-one was coming to investigate, he finished opening the door. He waved for the others to follow and slipped through.

The basement of the monitoring station was empty, except for an oil furnace and some shelving units with old computer equipment on them. The dirt floor smelled musty, causing a slight gagging feeling in Adam's throat.

Mark slipped past Adam and walked to the stairwell. He made a motion telling everyone to stay put as he disappeared up the stairs. A minute later he called back down.

"Nobody's here, you can come up."

Jimmy and Kevin climbed the stairs while Adam closed both tunnel doors, since he had been keeping them open as an escape route.

"There's no alarm in here, so nothing to worry about - except being here without permission," said Mark.

"Better to be caught here than in the tunnels," replied Kevin, "...at least for us three." He pointed at himself, Jimmy and Adam.

Even Mark agreed. "At least I might be able to talk my way out of being found here with you guys. Not so much in there," he pointed downstairs toward the tunnel.

"If the tunnel leads here, it has to be more than just a monitoring station," said Adam. "I always wondered why they built it at the bottom of a valley instead of up on the flat prairie. At least up there you could see the weather coming."

"If I have to hear that joke about it being 'so flat you can watch your dog run away for three days', I'm gonna punch someone in the throat," Kevin said, half joking.

"Whoa big guy," said Jimmy, "no one was going to say that. Calm down. We're all sick of hearing that joke too."

Mark brought them back to the original subject. "I asked Dad why they built this place in a valley once. He said that they don't have to see the weather; they use the data from the instruments in that big golf ball looking thing about a mile south of here."

"Oh yeah, I remember seeing that ball. It's in the middle of nowhere," said Kevin

"Mark, are there any files here?" asked Adam.

"Nope. Everything's always been electronic, as far as I know."

"Do you know any of the passwords?" asked Jimmy.

"Nope."

"Are you sure?"

"Yep."

"A while ago you were pretty sure your dad didn't know anything about all of this either," said Jimmy.

"Yeah yeah, so I was wrong about that - but I've spent loads of time here being completely bored, so I know there are no files here. If there were, I'd have probably looked through them for something to do," said Mark.

"So, nothing to do here I guess. We might as well head back to town while there's still some light outside," said Kevin.

Reluctantly, Adam agreed.

They stepped outside onto the balcony that surrounded three sides of the monitoring station's upper floor. The station was built into a hill, with the back side of the basement buried and the front side exposed. One steel fire exit was the only access to the basement from the outside as there weren't any windows. The balcony covered the basement, and in turn was covered by an overhanging roof on all four sides.

After closing the door, Mark told the other three to look away while he punched in the code to lock the door.

It was a keyless entry keypad. "I'm not supposed to know the code, but I've seen Dad do it enough times to remember," he said.

They climbed down the stairs and started the trek back into town. Walking quietly, each was lost in their thoughts. The monotony of their footsteps didn't help, having been mentally tired from the excitement in the tunnels.

Step after step, they trudged along, and after they had made it halfway home, Adam's brain started firing again. He pictured the tunnels from outside, like a map viewed from above. Lines and curves were drawn on the mental map, and a picture came into view.

He remembered something that got him excited.

"We need to get back to my place. I think I have a map there."

The others looked at him wondering how he could suddenly realize he had a map, but then seemed to get excited as well.

They picked up their pace and Mark started complaining soon afterward.

"Slow down! I'm not built for this," he said, gasping for air.

Jimmy laughed. "Just what *do* you think you're built for then?"

"I'm fast in short sprints, but not long distances!"

"I'll bet you are Gimli," Jimmy mocked. The others laughed at the 'Lord of the Rings' reference.

"Funny guy," Mark replied.

"No, really, I believe you," said Jimmy. "You've had

years of training with all those short sprints between the couch and fridge."

"Not funny," replied Mark between great puffing breaths. "At least I'm not skin and bones like you and Adam. You guys are built for jogging long distances."

"Kevin's not having any problem, and he's not built like a stick," replied Jimmy, faking insult. He loved teasing Mark, and often said it was one of the few ways Mark ever got his heart rate up, so he was only looking out for Mark's health. "Besides, we're not even jogging. You could barely call this speed walking," his eyes gleamed with fun.

Mark grumbled and was quiet from then on, trying to conserve his energy. Soon they were at the edge of town and walked more casually toward Adam's house. They waved at a few passing cars, trying to look as if they were only out for a walk. They didn't want to raise any suspicion.

After a few minutes they arrived at the garage, ready for a rest and curious to see Adam's map.

CHAPTER FIFTEEN

Adam grabbed the papers from their hiding spot. He thumbed through them as he sat down; stopping when he found the page with the spider-looking diagram and his dad's initials at the bottom.

"I think this is a map of the tunnels," he said, "or at least a guide."

They passed it around, each examining it for a short time.

"I don't follow," said Kevin.

Adam placed it on the table, with the spider picture face up.

"Look. The dot at the center is the junction, and the eight tunnels branch off from it, each curving slightly to the right," he said. "There's the ring tunnel that runs through them all." He pointed to the ring in the picture. "It's not the best drawing I've ever seen, but look at the symbols on the other side." He flipped the picture over. "They're the same as the symbols I felt on the wall in the tunnels.

See how they look like the hand of a clock?"

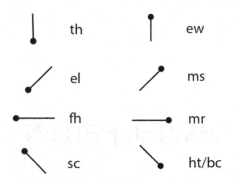

"Look here," he pointed at the first one. "See the letters next to it – 'th'. Remember when I felt the marker and said Town Hall was at 12:00? That looks like it's pointing at 12:00 to me."

Understanding lit upon their faces as Adam spoke.

"Look, the one that points to 10:30 is labelled' ht/bc'. hotel and Ben Casey makes sense to me," said Jimmy.

"I always knew there was something fishy about Mr. Casey," said Mark.

Kevin looked at him, "And you never even had a sniff about your dad."

Mark was about to argue back when Adam continued speaking. "9 o'clock doesn't make sense to me, but 7:30 is probably 'ms' for Monitoring Station, and 3:00 'fh' has to be Fire Hall. Any others jump out at anyone?"

No one offered any more suggestions.

Adam thought out loud again. "We know these 5, so now we only have 3 more to figure out. They could go anywhere, but most likely in the direction they started out. I would bet 'sc' goes to the school, but the other two I haven't got a clue – 'ew' and 'el'."

"Would the 'el' stand for Ellie? Isn't that what you heard them say in the tunnels?" asked Jimmy.

"Good thinking," said Adam. He sat quiet for a moment. "That brings up a whole other issue. Who would Ellie be? I don't know anyone named Ellie or Ellen that lives here of any age. I know enough stubborn old people that live here, though."

"If you follow the 'ew' line you could get near Ms. White's place, but I'm pretty sure her name is Nora. That would have to be a really long tunnel, because she lives a few miles out of town." said Kevin. "Dad and I delivered a side of beef she bought from us once. I've never seen her myself, but Dad said she's old."

Adam added, "Mom told me that Mr. Garagan delivers groceries to her every week. I guess she doesn't have a car and never comes to town. From what I've heard of her I doubt she's involved."

"Do we confront Mark's dad with what we know and see if he'll tell us anything?" asked Kevin. "Obviously he's the leader of this Sentinel League."

"I don't think he'll tell us anything. We might waste too much time before *we* end up disappearing," said Adam.

"If we can find out who Ellie is, maybe we can get some answers from her, directly or indirectly," said Jimmy.

"That's not a bad idea. Personally, I would like to look through those files again, but it seems like we can't get enough time to just sit and read without getting caught," said Adam.

"I don't think there's much more in the files. I think the papers you have here," Jimmy pointed to the pile on

137

the table, "are more information than you're going to find there, other than bill payments. Plus, look how long it took to find the one note about the Sentinel League. We wasted a lot of time there."

Adam thought for a moment. "You're probably right. I hate to admit it, but finding Ellie seems like the next logical choice. If we're going to get into trouble asking questions, we might as well ask the person in charge."

"Just what I was thinking," said Jimmy.

"But how do we find her?" asked Mark.

"We go back into the tunnels, one more time," said Adam.

Mark groaned. "I think I've had just about enough excitement today. It wasn't *your* dad that almost caught you earlier, it was mine. I'm not worried about him, but he'll tell my mom and then I'll be in it deep."

"We have to go back in and find out who Ellie is," said Adam.

"Even if we do find her, she's not going to tell four teenage boys what she won't tell the head of the 'Sentinel League'," Mark responded full of sarcasm.

"I don't know, Jimmy can be pretty persuasive," said Adam. "We have to try, at least."

"Should we take the obvious tunnel? The one labelled EL?" asked Kevin.

Everyone agreed, even Mark, although his response was weak.

"I'm in," said Jimmy, "but, can we go out to the monitoring station to get back in the tunnels?"

They looked at him as though he were speaking a

language they didn't understand.

"Why would we go all the way out there when Town Hall is so close?" Mark asked, not because Town Hall was closer but because the other option involved more exercise.

"Let's see; if we get caught in the tunnels together, we're all in trouble. If we get caught in Town Hall together, I'm in trouble."

"Oh, suck it up princess! You want to go back in as much as the rest of us, or at least me and Adam," said Kevin.

Jimmy tried to appear insulted, but the others ignored him.

"Some of us need to be home by 11 tonight, so if we're going to do this we better get moving," said Mark.

They left the garage after Adam hid the papers again and walked south to Assiniboia Avenue because it ran in front of Town Hall. Walking that way would offer them a view of most of the building. Only the west side wouldn't be seen; the one with the side door they entered earlier. If all was clear, they could turn at the Fire Hall and slip through the trees near the back of the park, approaching Town Hall from the south and lessening the chance of being seen.

As they approached the Fire Hall, a car behind them honked quickly. The driver stopped next to them and rolled down the window.

"Did you guys find out how to open that secret door?" asked Jeff with a smile. "I didn't think so," he continued without letting them reply. "A lot smarter people, like me, have never been able to figure that one out. Anyway, off to work I go. A mayor's job is never done. I have lots to do - busy busy busy. See ya!"

And with that, Jeff drove ahead to Town Hall and parked at the back. The boys stayed where Jeff had stopped them.

"Lots of work, more like free internet," laughed Jimmy.

"That throws a wrench in that plan," said Kevin. "What now?"

Adam paused for a second. "Off to the monitoring station, I guess."

Mark groaned, as the others knew he would.

"Let's get our bikes and meet behind the gas station," Adam continued. "It'll be a lot quicker that way, ok?" He looked at Mark.

Mark's groaning faded somewhat. "We'll have to hide them in the trees near the station," he added.

They all nodded.

"See you in 15 minutes," said Adam.

CHAPTER SIXTEEN

Fifteen minutes later the four boys met behind the gas station and began their trip. The bikes were much faster than walking, and soon they were coasting down the hill into the small valley where they would find their destination.

Mark stopped at the bottom of the hill and the others stopped beside him.

"Let's hide the bikes in the trees over there," said Mark as he pointed to a clump of Poplar trees on the south side of the road, lower down in the valley.

"Good thinking," said Adam. "The bikes will be lower that the road, and that means car lights won't see the reflectors."

Mark didn't realize that the comment was a compliment. "Oh, I didn't think of that, it's just the closest bush so I won't have to walk so far."

The others laughed as Mark realized what he had said.

They hid the bikes, climbed back out of the deep ditch and made their way to the station. Mark unlocked the door and they were soon inside making their way downstairs. Standing in front of the ugly green door they said nothing as Kevin waved Adam past. Adam opened both doors and they were back inside the 7:30 tunnel.

They walked along at a steady pace through curve after curve, not speaking while trying to step as light as they could, keeping their noise to a minimum. They walked by flashlight because the glowing ceiling was better used as a warning system. It didn't seem as far to the junction from the monitoring station as it did when they travelled the opposite way earlier.

Adam bent down and felt for the marker indicating the 1:30 tunnel. It was five inches from the floor, just as he expected. The marker wasn't visible at all, no matter how he angled the flashlight. After confirming he was at the right tunnel, he nodded to the others and continued walking.

After a short distance they stopped at the familiar 4 way intersection. Adam felt for the symbols then nodded his head and said, "This is the ring that crosses all of the tunnels. The marker feels like a circle, just like on the map."

They continued down the 1:30 tunnel. In the same way as the others, the tunnel was built to look like it ended after a short distance, but as they walked it just kept going.

"This place drives me crazy," said Mark after a while. "Have we walked more or less distance than we did in the tunnel to the monitoring station?"

As he finished speaking, the tunnel straightened out and another sliding door appeared.

"I'd say less," Jimmy answered Mark, straight-faced. Mark shook his head.

"Any guesses where this door leads?" asked Kevin.

"As long as it isn't under an outhouse, I am happy," said Jimmy.

"The way these tunnels are, it could be anywhere. I tried to think of the houses in the general direction it seemed to start, but I'm lost," said Adam.

"As my dad likes to say, 'There's no time like the present'," said Kevin, motioning Adam to the door.

Adam placed the pin and listened to the almost familiar sound of the mechanism again. That one sounded slower than the others he had opened so far. He pulled the handle expecting the door to slide easily, and it didn't budge. It surprised him a little, so he pulled harder. The door moved a little, but not easily. A puff of air rushed through the crack of the door and quickly made its way to all their noses. It smelled like a beer bottle that had been in a ditch on a hot summer day, mixed with a hint of old cheese.

"McTaggart, if you're going to do that at least wait until I'm not around!" Jimmy teased.

"That smells more like a Jimmy Jones special," replied Adam with a smile. "Kev, give me a hand."

Kevin stepped up, and the two pushed the door open even though it moaned in protest. The sound made the hair on Adam's neck stand up. He hoped it didn't carry far down the tunnels.

Adam pointed the flashlight back at the base of the door. The track was unmaintained; rusty and needing oil. It seemed strange, since all the other ones were so well cared for.

"Nobody's used this door in a while," said Adam. "I

don't think we'll find Ellie here unless she died and your dad talks to ghosts." Adam looked at Mark smiling.

"If he catches me in here, you'll be the ones talking to a ghost," replied Mark looking nervous again.

Adam chuckled and turned to see where the door had led them. He shone the light on a narrow stairway with rickety old slats. It climbed at an angle that made it nearly a ladder instead of stairs.

"Glad you're going first." Jimmy's voice startled Adam it was so close.

"How do I get stuck going first every time?"

"You're the key master, so you've inherited the lead position," Jimmy said, "like a king...or dictator."

Adam shook his head and turned to the stairs. *I hope they hold,* he thought, looking at their poor condition.

The stairs creaked under each footstep. After the silence of the tunnel, each creak was like the crack of a nearby lightning strike. Thankfully the stairs held until he made it to a small landing. Shining his light around, he saw the small room he had climbed up to had no windows and only an old wooden door that looked to be made of worn barn wood. The handle had a bolt mechanism that was manually opened from the inside and probably keyed from the outside. It would allow someone to get out from the inside but not in from the outside without a key.

Adam pulled the bolt and opened the door, then understood what EL stood for. Not Ellie. Elevator. The old grain elevator. That explained the smell, even though it had been closed since before he was born.

Mark followed next, then Jimmy, and finally Kevin.

"Elevator. I should have guessed that one!" said

Kevin, "But I was more worried about opening a door into my basement family room while my parents were watching TV."

"We *are* pretty close to your house," said Adam.

"Well, back we go," said Jimmy, turning back to the stairs.

"Are we really going back down there?" asked Mark as he looked at Adam.

Adam nodded. "We have to get back to the monitoring station for our bikes before it gets too late. It'll be quicker through the tunnels than on the road, right?"

Mark thought for a moment. "Yeah, I guess you're right, but I'm going down first. I don't know if those stairs will hold farm boy again." He walked to the door leading to the stairs.

"If they hold you, they'll hold me!" Kevin retorted.

Mark was already through the door and starting down the stairs. The others followed close behind. Once down and through the sliding door, Adam tried sliding it shut, but it only moved a few inches making a loud squeal as it slid. He pushed it open and closed a little, trying to free the movement.

Mark cringed at the sound. "You're gonna draw too much attention with that noise!"

"You already did," said a low, gruff voice. A bright light from the tunnel blinded them.

CHAPTER SEVENTEEN

Being from a small town, most of them recognized the sound of a shotgun loading a shell into the chamber.

"Don't move 'cause I don't wanna clean your brains off the walls," said the gruff voice.

Having never been held at gunpoint before, the four boys were completely stunned and silent. Adam almost lost control of his bladder, and somewhere in the back of his mind he was intrigued by that fact, as he thought it was only a myth. At that moment it was no myth, and he wondered if anyone else in his group wasn't as lucky as he.

Adam snapped back to reality.

"I said what the hell are you doing here and how the hell did you get in? Hurry up!"

"M..m..mister Casey?" Mark mumbled. "Is that you?" Mark stepped to the front.

"Answer the questions!" The voice yelled back, lower and gruffer.

Adam's brain was racing. He had to come up with something quick, before they got shot. Jimmy spoke before him, though.

"We were just going to Kevin's house and decided to check out the old elevator."

He paused for a second, and the voice was all over him. "That does NOT explain how you got in here!"

"Hang on... just a second. We're nervous... and... you have a gun..." Adam spit out the words, giving Jimmy a chance to think. If there was any time he needed Jimmy's talent for creativity it was right then.

Jimmy continued, "We were bored so we came here to look around. I jiggled the handle on the door at the top of the stairs and it opened. We came down the stairs and that sliding door opened a little when we pulled on the handle."

The story sounded logical to Adam. Most days he didn't like Jimmy's ability to come up with a story in an instant and have it sound completely natural. That moment wasn't like most days, and Adam just hoped the story worked.

"...told them to seal that bloody door..." grumbled the voice. "Nice story kid, but I'm taking you to the boss."

Adam's heart missed a beat. *He's taking us to Mr. Gupta. Mark's in big trouble!* he thought.

"Follow me and be quiet...Now!"

The light moved down the tunnel.

Slowly, they followed the light back toward the junction. Adam was first, followed by Mark, then Jimmy and Kevin. When they reached the intersection to the ring tunnel, the light moved right.

Adam followed, the others tight behind him. Mark's breathing was intense and sounded like it was right in Adam's ear. Mark was obviously afraid of what was going to happen.

After they passed the first intersection, the light turned right at the second. "Not much further," said the voice.

Adam thought the tunnel they were in had to be the one that ended up at the hotel. When they reached the intersection where they had gone straight the first time, the light went left.

"Come on...quick now!"

Mark let out an odd noise that was pure fear. It sent a shudder up everyone else's backs, but they continued following. The intensity of the light made it impossible to see anything beyond.

"Stop," the voice commanded. "Wait."

Adam heard a familiar mechanism working, followed by the sound of a sliding door.

"Come here and hold this door," another command came from the captor.

Adam held the door with his foot while squinting in the light that was pointed straight in his face.

"Put these on." A hand shot into view and handed something to Adam. "Take one, hand the rest back. Put them over your head and pull the string tight around your neck, but not too tight."

Mark whimpered as he slipped the bag over his head and tightened the string. The others did the same - without the whimper.

"Grab the hand behind you and follow."

The rough hand of the captor grabbed Adam's hand, and Adam grabbed Mark's. They walked forward a few steps and stopped. The sound of creaking metal moving, like a heavy door opening, echoed in the room. The hand holding Adam's pulled him forward some more and then let go. Adam felt the captor walk past, back in the direction they had come from.

"Take a few steps forward and stop when you find the wall."

Adam did as he was told and soon bumped into the wall. Mark wasn't paying attention and bumped into Adam, causing Jimmy to stumble as well. They heard the metal on metal creaking again, sounding like a door closing.

"You just hold tight here until I get back. You're locked in a jail cell. If you try and pull the hoods off, the cords will just keep getting tighter until you go unconscious. I won't tell you what happens after that."

With that, they heard him walk away. A door opened and then closed. Muffled footsteps sounded on the stairs, getting quieter and quieter until they couldn't be heard anymore.

"I'm dead I'm dead I'm dead I'm dead," Mark kept repeating, making himself a nervous wreck.

"Quit that," snapped Kevin.

"It's not *your* dad coming back here to find you in a jail cell with a bag on your head!"

"Who knows, maybe it *is* my dad," answered Kevin.

Adam interrupted. "Mark, are you sure it's Mr. Casey?"

Based on where the tunnel branched, Adam thought it could have led to Ben Casey's house, or any other house on that block.

"Pretty sure. He never did talk to me much. Did you hear him change his voice after I said his name?"

"I always thought he was the type of guy who would have a jail cell in his basement," added Jimmy. "Probably collects torture devices too, like these hoods."

Mark whimpered again. "You don't think – he wouldn't – you know –"

"He'll probably start with you first," said Jimmy, picking up on Mark's fear. "I'll bet he's still angry at the way you cut his lawn."

"Y---y—you're k-k-kidding, right? Just trying to scare me?"

"If I were like him, I would definitely start with you. Easiest nut to crack. He's probably got old dental equipment he'll use on you with no freezing." Jimmy was starting to enjoy teasing Mark.

"Ok Jimmy," said Adam, stopping Jimmy from continuing. "He's just teasing you Mark."

"Not funny - at all," stated Mark.

"Sorry man, just trying to lighten the mood. Didn't think you would take me *that* seriously," said Jimmy sounding sheepish.

Silence surrounded them again, each boy listening for their captor's return.

"Can anyone see anything out of these hoods?" asked Kevin, breaking the silence.

"Not me," replied Adam.

"Nope," replied Mark.

"I think I can make out something," said Jimmy.

"What can you see?" Adam asked, excited.

"Umm, well, it looks like a cat."

"Really?"

"Yeah."

"What color? What's it doing?" asked Adam.

"I think it's a black cat. It's in a coal mine at night," said Jimmy, laughing at his own joke.

"We're stuck in a jail cell, our heads are in hoods that will choke us if we struggle, and you have to come up with that *lame* joke? I hope it's your *mom* that comes here and finds us," said Mark.

Jimmy chuckled, "Sorry, but I get a little giddy when I'm in trouble."

"Ok, no more joking around," said Adam. "We need to be ready for the *Boss*."

"You mean my dad," said Mark.

"Whoever. We need to stick to Jimmy's story," Adam responded. "We've never been in the tunnels before, right?"

The others agreed.

Soon, they heard faint footsteps on stairs. Their captor wasn't alone. By the sound of the footsteps there were 2 sets of feet, the captor and the Boss.

The door opened and closed again. Footsteps approached and stopped, followed by silence for a few seconds.

"How did you get into the tunnel?" the captor's gruff voice asked, startling them.

"We already told you," replied Kevin.

"I don't care! Tell me again!" demanded the captor.

Jimmy spoke up, "We were bored. We were going to Kevin's house and decided to check out the old elevator. We were just gonna look around. I saw the door at the top of the stairs and tried the handle. It opened. We came down the stairs and tried the handle on the sliding door. It opened a little when we pulled on it, but it was stuck, so we worked it back and forth for a while."

He paused and took a breath. "After we got it open wide enough, we stepped inside to check it out. You pointed a gun at us after that."

The captor and the boss whispered to each other.

"How long did it take you to get the door open?"

Adam listened as Jimmy paused, trying to understand the reason for the question.

"Oh, I don't know. I guess it was a while. That door was good and stuck."

Good answer, thought Adam

"Did you see anyone else by that door?" questioned the captor.

"No," answered Jimmy. It was the truth, but Adam had a feeling in his stomach as if Jimmy were still lying, even though he knew different.

"No strange noises, no strange sounds?"

"Nope. Nothing other than the squeal of the door," Jimmy answered in a definite tone.

Silence. Adam had heard the term 'deafening silence' but only then understood what it meant.

"Get them out of there," the voice of the other man said. It wasn't Gurpreet Gupta, but they all recognized it right away.

"Mr. Chen?" Mark asked, surprised. Without thinking, he tried to pull his hood off and it began to choke him. He made an awful gagging sound and bumped hard into Adam.

The captor moved quickly. The door to the cell opened and a moment later Mark was taking in deep breaths, coughing as he exhaled.

"Thanks – cough – Mr. Casey – cough cough," Mark managed to say.

Soon Adam felt a hand circle his neck with a strange shaking motion. The hood loosened immediately, and Mr. Casey pulled it from his head.

The light in the room hurt his eyes. He hadn't realized just how well the hoods blocked the light. He had thought they were in a dark or dimly lit room, but the one he was looking at was bright and sterile. His mind had pictured an old steel cage, twisted and battered. In reality, it looked futuristic, with an odd design of round steel bars wrapped tightly together diagonally, painted bright white. The floor was so white and shiny that it was hard to look at for long. He looked up and realized that the ceiling was glowing in the same way as the ones inside the tunnels.

Don Chen stood in front of them, smiling kindly. It seemed odd but genuine to Adam. Ben Casey stood next to Don, distrust showing from every line on his face.

"Why don't we all grab a seat," said Don, motioning the boys to sit on a bench attached to the wall near the cell. He grabbed a wooden chair that had been sitting near the desk in the corner of the room, but Ben remained standing, arms crossed.

"...too young...troublemakers...shouldn't tell them nothin'..." Ben grumbled.

"Thanks for your concern, Ben. Ben here is the head of security. You'd be surprised to hear some of the things he's done in his lifetime," said Don.

Probably not too surprised, thought Adam as he sat down.

"Ben shouldn't have brought you through the tunnels, but it would have been worse to have him march you through town with a shotgun at your backs," said Don, giving Ben a disapproving look.

Ben shrugged like he didn't care and Don turned back to the boys.

"I'll bet you have some questions," he said.

Some questions? thought Adam, *that's an understatement.*

"I can answer some of them, but not all," Don continued. "We usually don't tell anyone what *exactly* goes on here until they are at least 16, sometimes up to 18."

"Who is 'we'? And why not before 16, Mr. Chen?" asked Adam

Don paused. "Don. Call me Don. Well, as far as the age is concerned, we feel that we need to wait until people are responsible enough to make informed decisions *before* they hear the full story, that's all. The age of 16 seems to be where that has already happened for the majority. That's why I'm not telling you everything right now. We've always had plans in place for this exact situation - where someone underage finds out about us, either accidentally or on purpose, but we'll get to that part later."

Ben grunted again, as though he didn't approve of the plan.

Don continued, "I *can* tell you that we are members of an organization called the Sentinel League, and, as the name implies, we keep watch on things. In fact, the entire town was built by members of the League."

"And you're the head of the Sentinel League?" asked Mark.

"No, not me. I'm Third in command here."

"Who's the leader?" asked Mark, curious about his dad.

"I'm not going to tell you that. I will tell you that your dad is second in command, though, because that's what you're really asking. I wish he could have been here so he could have told you himself."

"What about *my* dad?" asked Adam.

Don frowned at the question. "He *was* Number 2. Gurpreet took over when he..." Don didn't finish his sentence.

"So George was right! I just thought he was completely crazy," said Mark.

"Actually," said Don, "George was a high ranking member of the League in his day."

The boys were surprised by the news.

"How can that be? He obviously doesn't remember anything," said Mark.

"Well, he had an accident and lost some of his memory. Because of that, he became suspicious of everyone. We keep him here to watch him; make sure he doesn't get himself into trouble. That's why he's your neighbor, Mark. He was put there so your dad could watch him back when your dad was Number 3."

"But George left because he thinks we're all going to disappear next," said Mark.

Don smiled and nodded, "He's been 'directed' to another site of the Sentinel League. He's fine."

Thoughts raced through Adam's head. It was difficult to decide what to ask next, especially with all the information he was hearing.

"It seems pretty strange to have these tunnels under the town," said Adam.

"Well, they aren't here to bootleg alcohol like the ones in Moose Jaw, if that's what you're thinking," Don answered.

Actually, Adam hadn't been thinking that at all, but it would have been a great cover story.

"So, why *are* they here?" Adam pushed for some answers.

"The tunnels were built in order to help hide a secret and let us do things without being seen. They are constructed to confuse and are easy to get lost in. They are also difficult to get into in the first place, which is why Ben was so rough with you. The door you came through hasn't been used since the rail line was taken out. We were sure it was locked, but we never check it from the other side." Don looked at Ben, as if to say Ben needed to add that to his list of duties.

"What are you hiding down there?" asked Mark.

Don laughed, "Sorry, but I'm not going to tell you that."

"Does everyone in town that's over 16 know about the Sentinel League?" asked Adam.

"No. Over the years, due to births and marriages, we have a number of people who live here that have no idea. Usually, you inherit the honor from your parents, but the Senior League members ultimately decide who gets invited to join. We've had a few people who never quite measured up."

"Jeff Wyndum. There's no way he knows about this," stated Jimmy. "He'd have told everyone he ever met about it."

Don's smile weakened. "Yes, sadly, Jeff has been left out. It's a shame, because his father was part of us and was a really great man. We don't know what happened with Jeff. He had lots of potential."

Adam tried to ask the next question, but was too slow.

"How is the ceiling glowing? I've never seen anything like that before," said Kevin, pointing up. Adam was glad Kevin referenced the ceiling above them, not the one in the tunnel.

"Ahh, yes. I'm so used to them that I forget that they are unique. Well, they are basically living organisms that give off light."

"Bio-luminescence?" asked Adam.

"Why, yes. Exactly."

"But that's only in the beginning phases of scientific research," Adam stated.

Don looked impressed. "You're right, Adam. In the rest of the world, yes - but not here. Here, we've been using it since the tunnels were constructed at the beginning of the 1900's."

Adam was shocked by the news. One of his favorite things was to sit in the school library and read different magazines featuring cutting edge science. He knew that, as far as was being reported, that kind of bio-technology was years away.

Don continued, "I see you're surprised, but don't think into it too much. It works great in the tunnels. The organisms live off the carbon dioxide and water in the air, and release oxygen into the tunnels. Part of what we protect here is information, such as this bio-luminescence."

"Why wouldn't you release that kind of technology to the world? It could do a lot of good," said Adam.

Don thought for a moment before he responded. "I know that's what you think. It seems perfectly logical that releasing technology like that would do no harm. The problem is you can't think about how the general population would benefit; you have to think about those who would try to harness it as a weapon. What if, instead of releasing oxygen, you modified it to do the opposite – consume oxygen and release carbon dioxide? Or something worse? You could harm a lot of people."

Adam and the boys nodded in understanding.

Don continued. "It's been proven in history, time and again, that most technological leaps are first used to gain power over others before becoming part of society. Some things are better off not being in the hands of the general public until they are ready."

Adam thought about that for a moment. "Do you mean that the Sentinel League releases knowledge when they think people can use it properly?" he asked.

"No. I've probably said too much already. It is a continuous philosophical debate in the League, and I'm not the best qualified to answer that question. Let's just say that there are people strongly on both sides. Being able to see both sides of the debate comes with time and it's a good example of why we wait to induct new members."

Adam nodded his head and another question popped up.

"Are Langenburg and Waldron connected to Grayson somehow?" asked Adam

Adam's question caught Don off guard. He paused to compose himself and responded, "Langenburg and Waldron are both sites of the Sentinel League. When we came to this country at the beginning of the last century, we found sites that we could use for various activities. Those two sites were set up for different reasons."

"So, that means we're in danger as well," said Adam

Don looked Adam straight in the eyes. "Yes." He paused for a couple of seconds, "The good news is that Grayson is a special site, and we have a few strategic advantages that the others did not. Of course, I can't tell you about any of those right now."

"What happened to all the people?" asked Adam.

"We aren't sure. We haven't been able to get any of our people into the sites yet to investigate."

"You must have an idea what's happening there," stated Jimmy.

"We do."

"But you're not going to tell us," stated Jimmy again.

"Right."

"You think the people are safe?"

"We don't know."

"Who is doing this?"

"Well, I can give you a partial answer for that. You see, there is a group of people out there who are searching for something that the Sentinel League is protecting. They've been looking for a long time."

"What is it?" asked Mark

"I can't tell you," said Don. "Only Number 1 knows that."

"Why only Number 1?" asked Mark.

"The fewer people who know about something, the easier it is to keep secret."

"What if something happens to Number 1? The secret will be lost forever," said Adam.

Don smiled. "Don't worry about it. Everything has been thought of."

Don's words didn't comfort Adam.

"Are you going to tell us any more about it?" asked Mark.

"No. You know almost as much as I do now," said Don.

Adam was curious about the secret. Did his dad know what it was?

"You've heard enough from me for now. Let's move

on to our current problem - what to do with you?" Don pointed at each of the boys, one at a time. "As I said earlier, we've had a plan in place for a long time to deal with this exact situation."

Adam was nervous, as were the others. They weren't 16 yet, so they wondered what the Sentinel League would do to them.

"You know what *I* would do with them," said Ben with an eerie look on his face.

Don looked at Ben as though he were considering whatever Ben was thinking. After a pause he continued, "Well, here is what we've decided. You aren't old enough to be full members of the League, so we're going to make you all 'Junior Initiates'. That means you will be watched carefully for the next few years until you can become full initiates. How does that sound?"

Adam went from nervous to excited in a flash. Becoming a member of a secret organization was better than anything he could think of. He was sure his friends felt the same way. Besides, anything would be better than being handed over to Ben.

"Can we talk to our parents about the League?" asked Kevin.

Don paused to think. "Yes, but absolutely no one else. If you do, Ben will be allowed to implement *his* plan."

Ben grunted what Adam thought was a happy grunt, although his face didn't change. Adam didn't want to know what Ben's plan was, but thought Jimmy wasn't far off about Ben and torture devices.

"...and maybe Adam shouldn't say too much to *his* mother yet," Don continued.

Adam was surprised. He assumed that she knew about the League, being married to the former Number 2.

"Why not?" Adam asked.

"Well, your mom has been out-of-sorts with the League ever since your dad died. She blames the League for...things that happened. We've offered her help - but you know her, she's pretty stubborn sometimes."

Suddenly, Adam recalled what he overheard in the tunnels, although his mother wasn't any older than Don. "She's not Number 1, is she?"

Don laughed, "No. Why would you think that? She wants absolutely nothing to do with the League."

Adam shrugged, happy with the answer. He was a little angry with his mother, though. The League could have helped her, maybe gotten her a better job, but instead she made Adam go without a lot of things.

"She knows you will find out in a few years anyway, but she may not be too thrilled that you are part of the first ever 'Junior' members here in Grayson."

"I won't say anything to her," Adam said shaking his head. *Even if I did, she never listens anyway*, he thought.

"Good. So I take it that you're all interested in becoming members?"

All four heads nodded in agreement.

"Well then, I guess we have to make an oath," said Don.

"You're really going to do this?" Ben asked, sounding upset at the thought.

Don nodded.

"We'll make it simple. Just repeat after me, 'I

solemnly swear that I will give my life in service to the Sentinel League'."

Life? thought Adam.

They repeated the oath. Ben grunted.

"Ok then. When you turn 16 there's a more lengthy and involved oath."

"So when do we get keys to the tunnels?" asked Jimmy.

Don laughed, "In about ten years if you work hard! Not everyone in the League has keys, and very few have access to everything."

Jimmy looked disappointed.

"For now, you'll be part of the *surface* division of the League. You'll do odd jobs and we'll see how it goes from there."

"Will we learn more about the League?" asked Kevin.

"Definitely. You'll get to understand the ranks, responsibilities and history. Some of it is pretty exciting. A lot of it is pretty boring, except when the old timers get together and talk about how they passed the time on watch," he laughed again, "like the time Ben and Gurpreet were on patrol and thought they heard..."

"Ahem," Ben interrupted, "*not* an appropriate story for these young boys." Ben shook his head back and forth slowly.

Don thought for a second. "Yeah, you're probably right Ben. Anyway, there are lots of stories you'll hear. Some are almost true," Don grinned at Ben, who returned nothing but a cold stare.

"What sort of things will we have to do?" asked Mark.

"Well, considering that you are technically lower than the newest initiates, it's not going to be anything glamorous."

Mark groaned at the idea of more manual labor.

"I have some ideas, but I'll have to discuss them with other Senior members. We'll start you off tomorrow morning, just after lunch. How does that sound?"

"Where should we meet?" asked Kevin.

"Let's meet at Town Hall. I'll make sure it's open before you get there."

All agreed in one way or another, Mark with a nod of his head, Kevin with an enthusiastic 'yes sir', Adam and Jimmy with a simple 'ok'."

"If Ben will be kind enough to lead us out, we can continue this tomorrow." Don motioned for Ben to lead.

Adam wanted to ask more questions, like who was Ellie and how were the door locks made, but he knew those questions would reveal that they had been in the tunnels already. He hoped they would learn some of those answers in the near future.

Ben led them through the door and up the stairs. At the top, there was a small landing before another door. Ben hid the fact that he used a familiar pin to unlock it, and they all stepped into a room on the other side.

When they were all through the doorway, Ben closed the door behind them and they saw it wasn't a door at all. It was a workbench, and the room they were in was the tool shed behind Ben's house. It contained an assortment of hand tools, power tools, and gardening equipment.

Mark was shocked. "No way! I was in here when I did all that work for you," he directed his words at Ben, "and

I never would have believed if you told me there was a secret staircase off the back of this shed."

Adam had a thought pop into his head. "Why would you get Mark to cut your grass and not some initiate to the League?"

Ben looked at Adam and answered in the way only *he* would. "Because there *were* no initiates last year."

That surprised Adam, as there were a few 16 to 18 year olds in Grayson he could think of.

"What about this year?" he asked.

"There's a couple."

"Who?" Adam continued

Ben looked at Don, who gave him an agreeing nod.

"His brother and his sister." Ben pointed at Kevin and Jimmy.

They all realized why Trevor and Kassie had become so close so quickly.

"But Trevor is closer to 19 and Kassie is barely 16. Why wasn't he an initiate before?" asked Jimmy.

"Because he was a dip...," started Ben until Don cut him off.

"He wasn't ready yet. That's all. It seems that boys usually do take a little longer to get to that point than girls. All of you have been watched as well, waiting for the right time to induct you."

"What about Dave?" asked Kevin, referring to their classmate and friend who was also Don's son.

"He will be inducted in time, hopefully, but not for a couple of years."

"I'm sure I don't need to escort you home, right?" said Ben, ending the conversation.

They all nodded.

"Then go." He pointed to the shed door.

They didn't waste any time leaving the shed, walking down Ben's driveway. They walked across the street to the front of Mark's house and stopped.

"I am dreading this," said Mark, looking at his house.

"I'm sure it'll be fine," said Adam. "Just don't slip up so they find out we have the key to the tunnels."

"When do we get the bikes?" asked Jimmy.

Adam had forgotten about the bikes at the monitoring station.

"We better get them in the morning. This whole evening tired me out," said Kevin.

"You think you're tired! Try getting choked out by one of those freaky hoods," said Mark.

"That was your own fault. He told you it would choke if you struggled," Kevin shot back at him.

"I'm too tired to argue now. See you tomorrow," said Mark.

"Meet us at 11 behind the gas station," Adam called out as he walked away. Mark gave him a thumbs-up and disappeared into the house.

"Sure is a happy little guy," said Kevin.

Jimmy and Adam chuckled as the three walked home.

CHAPTER EIGHTEEN

Sunday morning came way too soon for Adam. He rolled out of bed at 8:43 am, which was unusually late for him. 7 am was his usual wake-up time, regardless of when he fell asleep. Last night he had fallen into bed around 10 pm, so he had slept almost 11 hours. Lucky for him, being Sunday, his mom wouldn't be up for a while.

He made his way downstairs with the usual amount of stealth and proceeded to make breakfast. He fried an egg and put it on a piece of toast, ate and chased it down with a big glass of water. That would hold him until lunch when he would try to eat a larger meal, as he assumed there would be a lot of labor later.

He left the dirty dishes in the sink so the noise wouldn't wake his mother. She would make sure he cleaned them up later anyway, frowning over how he had left them. He was used to the guilt trip so it didn't bother him much.

Adam left the house by 9:30 and headed for the peacefulness of his garage. He hadn't stashed the pin there the previous night only because he was tired. He slept in his clothes with the pin secure in his pocket. In the silence of the garage, Adam's mind drifted through images of the previous night and some of the conversation with Don. He had mentioned that not all members had keys to the tunnels, and not all of the keys opened all of the doors. That seemed strange. Then again, it also felt strange to think of him as Don and not Mr. Chen.

He shook his head to clear the sleep. *Even Kevin's coffee might be good right now,* he thought, until he remembered the aftertaste. It gave him a shudder that cleared his mind a little. It had only been the previous morning, but it felt like a week ago. The sugar and caffeine rush, followed by the adrenaline and excitement, must have been what made him sleep so long.

He wasn't tired enough to go back to sleep; just in a haze. His brain didn't seem like it was working much at all. It was lazily going through scenes from the past couple of days, almost in disbelief that some of them even happened, when the whole information session with Don came back into focus again. There was so much that Don either didn't know or was holding back, and Adam wanted more answers. It wasn't a general curiosity, though. He felt like he *needed* answers to understand a part of himself.

Who was Number 1? What were they hiding? Was it hidden in Grayson right now?

He needed to find answers so he could at least prepare for whatever was coming. He needed to be able to protect his friends. But how?

It seemed the best course of action was to learn about the Sentinel League and find Number 1. Adam could ask them what was happening. Maybe Number 1 would think Adam was just a kid, so it wouldn't hurt to tell him about the secret. If not, Adam was prepared to use his father's death as a crowbar and pry at some heartstrings, since Number 1 *had* to have been close with Adam's father. Edward *had* been Number 2 after all.

Adam twiddled his thumbs as he slouched in the old chair, feet on the coffee table. Time ticked, and slowly Sunday morning moved on. He couldn't wait until he would meet the others and get the day started. He took a small amount of comfort in the fact that the events in Langenburg and Waldron happened a week apart, so if Grayson *was* next, he should have a few more days to figure things out.

He looked at his watch. 10:13 am. He had wasted some time sitting and thinking, but not a whole lot. Kevin was meeting him at the intersection between their houses around 10:45, so Adam decided to wait for him there. At least he'd waste a couple of minutes walking to the intersection. If he had his bike, he would have gone for a ride around town, as the exercise would calm his mind and waste time simultaneously.

At the intersection, Adam sat with his back against a tree. The tree grew just inside the corner of the sidewalk intersection. It was a shady spot, a little cool on that summer morning. Squirrels ran up and down trees nearby, shaking the odd leaf loose. Summer birds sang songs, sometimes quiet and slow, other times shrill and speedy. Being Sunday morning, there wasn't any traffic noise to interrupt the sounds of nature quite yet.

"Hey, Sleeping Beauty."

Kevin's voice made Adam open his eyes.

"I wasn't sleeping, just relaxing."

"Yeah yeah, and Mark is just big-boned. C'mon, let's go."

Adam smiled and stood up. "You know, a better reference would be Rip Van Winkle, not Sleeping Beauty, although I haven't been here for 20 years."

Kevin looked at him with a slightly raised eyebrow, clearly not understanding the reference.

"When you get home later, look it up," said Adam. He chuckled to himself.

They began walking toward the gas station.

"If I'd've known you were gonna be this tired, I'd've made you another coffee," said Kevin.

"I hope to never be tired enough that I'd need *your* coffee ever again. That stuff would bring on the zombie apocalypse." Adam laughed at his own joke.

"I could've made it taste good, but that's *not* why I made it. It was *meant* to wake you up. It *did* wake you up, right?"

"Yes, but –"

"I rest my case."

"- but –"

"I rest my case!" Kevin said, faking a gavel strike.

Adam laughed. Kevin was right; it did what Kevin had intended, even if it tasted terrible.

A few minutes later they arrived at their destination. Mark was already there, so they only needed to wait for Jimmy.

"How did things go with your dad?" asked Adam.

"I dunno. Good and bad." Mark shrugged his shoulders, but didn't intend to continue on with the subject. Knowing Mark, that wasn't due to him not wanting to continue, but rather his poor communication skills.

Adam and Kevin looked at each other, back to Mark, and back to each other again. Kevin rolled his hand in a circular motion to get Mark to continue.

"Yeah, sorry. Spaced out for a sec. Anyway, when I got home last night I wanted to talk to him, but Mom wasn't feeling good and Miri wouldn't go to sleep. Dad had sent Mom to bed and was trying to get Miri down. I said to him, 'Did you talk to Mr. Chen?', and he just nodded and gave me the 'shh' finger to the lips. I went up to bed and fell asleep pretty quick. By the time I got up this morning, the girls were up again, and Mom was up too, feeling much better...She wouldn't be pregnant, would she? I mean, she was sick last night, right? Man, I hope not."

Adam and Kevin laughed at Mark.

"First, it's *morning* sickness, not evening," Kevin grinned.

Mark looked relieved at the news.

"Second, you took a left turn at the end of your story."

"Oh, sorry. So, where was I? Oh yeah – hi Jimmy!" Mark waved at Jimmy over the other boys.

"Sorry I'm a bit late. Don called my parents last night and told them what happened," said Jimmy.

"No problem. Just hang on and we'll get the rest of Mark's story out of him and come back to yours," said Adam. "But first, let's get going for the bikes."

As they walked, Adam said, "Go on," and waved to Mark. Mark started thinking, trying to remember where he stopped.

"When you woke up, everyone else was up already..." Adam helped Mark get started.

"Oh yeah, that's it. So, everyone else was up already. I couldn't exactly say 'good morning Number 2, what's the Sentinel League all about?'. I can't say anything in front of my sisters, and I don't even know if my mom knows about it, so I just sat quietly and ate my breakfast. Dad stared at me the whole time. When I was done, I told Mom that we had offered to help Mr. Chen – Don – with some odd jobs. She thought it was great that we were getting involved with the community. I left right after that and was standing behind the gas station since 10:30."

"You said that it was good and bad. What do you mean?" asked Adam.

"I've been worried that Dad's going to be mad that I was caught in the tunnels and got inducted into the League out of necessity rather that having earned it, so it's good that he hasn't been able to get me alone. It's bad because if I *could* get him alone, maybe he would answer some of our questions. I still can't believe that he's the Number 2 in a secret organization."

Adam was happy with the answer. "Your turn," he said to Jimmy.

Jimmy prepared his story like a shady salesman prepares his pitch to a customer. "When I got home last night, all was normal. I watched some TV and went to bed. When I woke up this morning, my whole family was sitting at the kitchen table waiting. We usually sit at the table to eat, but this felt like an intervention from the second I walked in the room. Don had called early this morning and told them everything. It turns out that Mom and Dad have been members since they were 16, although Mom grew up at another Sentinel League town.

My parents weren't happy about us poking around at the elevator, but the biggest problem was my brother. He's not too pleased with the fact that he wasn't asked to join the League until recently - after they deemed him worthy - and we just had to do a 'break and enter' as he put it, to get asked to join the League."

Jimmy paused for a second and looked at the others to make sure they were listening. After finding their attention trained on him, he continued. "I only found out a few things from them, and I think some of the things they told me were just to make Trevor feel better about the whole situation. Trevor is a full initiate, and he'll be going away for training, while we are only Junior Initiates. We won't be going anywhere for a long time. We're basically going to be slaves to the local members while they tell us a few details about the League. I don't know for sure if they said that just to keep Trevor happy, or if they were telling the truth, but after hearing them talk this morning, I know where I get my smooth style from."

"I like how you refer to it as 'style'," Mark said, straight faced.

Jimmy gave him an angry look that broke into a smile.

"Use what you've got I say, and I've got a lot," said Jimmy.

"A little or a lot, it still sucks when I step in what *you've* got," Mark shot back. The other two boys roared with laughter.

They teased each other back and forth until they reached the spot where they had stashed the bikes. It was difficult work to get the bikes out of the trees, and even worse to get them back up the steep ditch onto the road again. Adam ended up helping Mark by pulling on the front wheel of his bike. Adam felt like he wasn't just helping pull the bike up the hill, he was pulling the bike *and* Mark up the hill.

After sitting for a minute to catch their breath, the group pedaled back toward town. It was a quiet ride, as they wondered what duties were in front of them, imagining the worst. Kevin imagined cleaning out George's trailer and shuddered. Mark imagined having to shovel manure, which combined his dislike of manual labor with his horror of manure. Jimmy didn't have a fear of doing any particular job, but having to do a job in silence was particularly scary for him.

Adam, out of all three, couldn't wait to see what work was ahead, because whatever it was, it was connected to the League. That connection made him feel closer to his dad than he had ever felt before.

"Meet you after lunch," said Mark as he turned down the street toward home. The others continued on in the same direction, and soon Jimmy turned off as well.

When they reached the intersection where Adam and Kevin would usually part company, Kevin signalled for Adam to stop.

"Come to my house for lunch. I know you don't want to go home."

"I *should* go home. I don't want to just show up at your place and say 'feed me'," said Adam.

"Why not? My family likes you."

"Yeah, but I'd be an inconvenience."

"Inconvenience? How? There's 6 of us at the table already. That little extra you're gonna eat isn't gonna make us go broke! Besides, I eat more in one sitting than you do all day."

Adam laughed at his friend. Kevin always knew how to cheer Adam up, which was why Kevin was such a good friend. Why Kevin hung out with Adam, Adam didn't know. He guessed it was probably because Kevin was just a nice guy.

"Lead on," said Adam, pointing toward the Baranov homestead.

"Before we go, I want to talk to you a little," said Kevin.

Adam felt strange that Kevin had just convinced him to come over for lunch and now was stopping him for a 'talk'.

"Maybe you didn't notice, but I didn't say anything about my family after the other guys were done telling about their evenings with their families."

He was right, Adam didn't think about it, but the Baranov's were probably Sentinel League members. He knew that Kassie Baranov was an inductee, so one or both of their parents probably were as well.

"Sorry, I feel bad that I didn't even think about it," Adam replied.

"That's ok. Last night, after my little sisters went to bed, the rest of us sat up and talked. My parents weren't upset about me getting into the League, although they didn't like how it happened. Kassie was really excited for me, though."

Adam nodded and smiled.

"I found out that the Sentinel League is really old, like centuries. They were around at almost all major turning points in history. If they weren't observing the turning points, they were involved in them. Their mandate is to protect Mankind and let it grow naturally, whatever that means. The name Sentinel League comes from that. They are to watch over Mankind – Sentinel - and it doesn't matter what country you are from or what nationality you are, as long as you share the same ideals – League."

That made sense to Adam. It also made him more curious about the League. He wondered what sort of things they had hidden in tunnels across the globe.

"Did they say anything about how many members there are, or anything about the knowledge they seem to have?"

"Not really. I did ask about the biolumi..lami..loomo..."

"Bioluminescence," Adam finished the word for Kevin.

"Yeah, that. They asked how I knew about that, so I told them about Ben's dungeon, and they laughed. They said that the knowledge of the ceiling light has been around for a long time, but because of the source of the knowledge it couldn't be given to the general public."

"That seems strange," stated Adam.

"That's what I said. They said I will understand it later, once I've learned more. They also said they didn't want to tell me too much because the League will train us in their own way when we're ready....so I asked them if it had something to do with space aliens."

Adam's eyes widened. He didn't know if Kevin was being serious or joking. "Really?...and..."

"They laughed at me a little and said no, it didn't have

anything to do with aliens. Then they said I watch too much TV."

Adam relaxed a little, but was getting even more confused. The Sentinel League was a confusing organization.

"I asked them about Langenburg and Waldron and they told me not to worry about it. If they felt we needed to leave, we'd be going on a long vacation in a hurry, and besides, they weren't called the Sentinel League for nothing. They have knowledge of who did it and we shouldn't worry. Langenburg and Waldron aren't destroyed, just broken doors and windows everywhere. The media are the ones that have made it sound worse than it is, although the people *are* still gone."

"Coming from your parents, that makes me feel better," said Adam. "Did they tell you any more about the disappearances?"

"No, they didn't. It was pretty late when we started talking, so they sent me to bed. When I got up this morning my little sisters were up, so we couldn't talk about it again," said Kevin.

Adam shook his head that he understood. "Thanks for telling me. I appreciate you letting me know."

Kevin smiled and looked back at him. "The reason I didn't tell the other two is because they would have just kept making me feel stupid because I forgot to ask this question or that question. I knew *you* wouldn't, so thank you."

Adam then understood what Kevin got out of their friendship.

"Let's go eat," he said to Kevin as he pedaled past.

"Beat you there." Kevin raced past Adam, and Adam followed.

Down the gravel road they rode until they turned up the long driveway that led to the Baranov farm house. Adam loved the Baranov's yard as it was quiet, peaceful, and well cared for. The Baranov's didn't have brand new vehicles and equipment, as they were considered small farmers compared to everyone else, but whatever they had was well-maintained.

Kevin propped his bike against the house, near the garage door, and Adam did the same. Always neat and tidy, just like the yard.

When they stepped into the house, Kassie saw Adam first. "Hello stranger," she teased.

"Hi," said Adam, feeling a little shy and awkward.

"Hi Adam, you're staying for lunch, right?" asked Mrs. Baranov as she stood at the kitchen counter. The look on her face showed that it wasn't really a question as much as a statement, no matter how it was said.

"If it's ok with you, I would like to."

"She'd be insulted if you didn't," said Mr. Baranov as he stood up from his chair at the table. He had been sitting with his back to the boys. He looked like an older version of his son but more stocky and powerful.

Two girls ran into the kitchen, having heard Adam's voice. One was smaller and obviously younger than the other. "Hi Adam," said the older girl, while the younger one acted shy.

"Hi Karlea. Hi Kelsea," Adam replied.

The older sister, Karlea, had a mischievous smile. "Kelsea has a crush on you!"

"Karlea!!" yelled Kelsea.

Adam blushed a little.

"Don't tease your sister Karlea," said Mrs. Baranov, "and don't embarrass Adam. He's our guest."

Karlea hung her head as Kelsea punched her in the arm. Mrs. Baranov scolded Kelsea with a look, and Kelsea hung her head as well.

"If you two have so much energy, you can set the table," their mother said as Adam and Kevin sat down near Mr. Baranov.

Kassie sat across from Adam and Kevin. "So," she started, "I hear you had an exciting day yesterday." She smiled, staring directly at Adam.

"Ben can be quite a scary guy at times," said Mr. Baranov, "but he's really a decent man."

Kevin coughed. "Could've fooled me. No normal person has a jail cell for home use. That, and those hoods aren't exactly child-proof.

"His job is security and he's good at it. Unconventional, sometimes, but that's why he's here. Once you get to know him more he'll grow on you," said Mr. Baranov.

Adam felt strange hearing so much while the two girls set plates on the table around them. Mr. Baranov picked up on his discomfort.

"Ben works for the *town*, just like you, Kevin and Kassie, but you're *volunteering* this summer," said Mr. Baranov, making the story perfectly clear.

Adam nodded.

"Egg salad sandwiches ok with you, Adam?"

"Perfect, Mrs. Baranov," replied Adam.

"You can call me Charity, Adam. I've told you that before," she said in a gentle voice, "and you call him Mike, especially now that you work for the *town.*"

"Yes ma'am, I'll try," Adam replied.

Charity began setting food on the table, followed by her youngest two children.

"Can I help?" asked Adam, starting to get up from his chair.

"Sit," Charity commanded.

Adam sunk back down.

"What are we going to be doing?" Kevin asked his dad. "Do you know?"

"I don't," Mike replied. "They're talking about it this morning. Most likely it won't be anything exciting. Be prepared for manual labor. Don't worry; they won't work you too hard."

That didn't comfort Adam much. Mike's opinion of not working too hard was a lot harder than most people. He was well-known for his work ethic and ability to accomplish large jobs.

The rest of the family sat at the table and they ate. The room was filled with happy family banter combined with great food. In Adam's opinion, Kevin had a perfect life.

CHAPTER NINETEEN

After lunch, Kevin, Adam and Jimmy walked to Town Hall. Kevin and Adam had stopped to pick up Jimmy since they walked past his house anyway. As they stepped inside, Mark and Gurpreet were already there. Thankfully, Ben was nowhere in sight. They had been afraid he would be their task master, making them clean his torture devices and testing them on the boys.

"Come come," said Gurpreet. "We're just waiting for two more people before we can leave." He motioned for them to take a seat in the lobby area.

Who else are we waiting for? Hopefully not Ben, thought Adam.

"You should consider yourselves privileged. The Sentinel League has rarely had Junior Initiates since it was formed over 1000 years ago," said Gurpreet.

"Did you say *1000 years?*" asked Jimmy.

"Yes," replied Gurpreet, straight faced. "It's been an extremely private organization in its time. You wouldn't have heard about it because you weren't asked to join. That's when all of the members discover it exists. It's a well-kept secret"

Adam thought for a second. So many questions ran through his mind and it was the time to ask. "Why is there a Sentinel League?" It was a simple but loaded question. He hoped Gurpreet would have a good answer.

Gurpreet paused and took in a deep breath. "That is a great question. I'll tell you the basics, because there are a lot of details and we don't have all day. So let's start this off appropriately...In the beginning, we go way back to early Man. They were living in caves and doing all those primal things we learn in school about hunters and gatherers. They lived in small communities, had children, and did what they needed in order to continue living.

At the same time, a group of people lived on an island. How they got there, they didn't know, but they were special. They were human, but they just understood more about everything and were naturally curious.

The island they were on was perfect for living and learning. They never had far to go for food or water, and the weather was always the same. Not having to worry about the essentials of life allowed them to concentrate on learning and building a civilization. And learn they did. They learned about the sciences, mathematics, chemistry, art and other things. They were passionate about knowledge, and lived in peace for generations of time. It was the only true Utopia the world has ever known."

"Sounds like Atlantis to me," said Mark.

"Actually, that *is* where the stories of Atlantis started. The original stories were somewhat accurate, but current stories are more imagination than truth," replied Gurpreet. "The island *was* somewhere in the Atlantic Ocean but they had never named it - at least not Atlantis. They came up with a name for themselves though -

Teneo, meaning 'to learn'."

"You're serious? This is a true story?" asked Jimmy.

Gurpreet nodded. "Because they loved knowledge, they eventually travelled beyond their island. They didn't travel far when they met our ancestors, and this is when things changed. After seeing how difficult the lives of the regular humans were compared to their own, one of the Teneo showed a man how to fashion a bow and arrow, so hunting would be easier. The first thing that man did with the bow and arrow was to kill his enemy, as he now had an advantage. The Teneo had been peaceful for so long that this didn't even register as a possibility when they passed on the knowledge. From that point on, they banned the sharing of knowledge with our ancestors, believing them incapable of dealing with it responsibly."

"Is that why the Sentinel League won't release information?" asked Adam

"Yes and no," said Gurpreet, "but we'll talk about that later. The way the regular humans handled the knowledge wasn't the only problem. The incident affected the Teneo as well. Having only known peace for so long, the act of one human killing another stirred up deep primal urges. They began arguing about how to deal with our ancestors and, over time, two groups emerged. One believed that the regular humans, who they now called Mankind, would evolve to learn everything the Teneo knew, just at a slower rate. Mankind would learn naturally, and in that way would be able to use knowledge responsibly. The other group believed that Mankind would never learn and should be ruled over as slaves, used like lab rats to further their own knowledge. That group felt *they* should decide the fate of Mankind, thinking of themselves as far superior. The rift between the two groups became so deep that the second group stopped referring to themselves as Teneo. They were Decreta, meaning 'to decide'. Some of the Decreta started calling Mankind 'Commons' as an insult, and it's been that way ever since. You've heard of the House of 'Commons' in our own government? That isn't a coincidence."

Adam was shocked by that little bit of information and it showed on his face.

"I see you have," said Gurpreet, nodding toward Adam.

"There are generations of stories since then that bring us to the present time, and you'll learn more of those later. For now, I'll give you the condensed version of the rest. Through time, the Teneo and Decreta fought with each other. There came a point where the Teneo realized they needed our help, so they reached out to our ancestors. That's when the Sentinel League was formed.

We as Mankind were nowhere near strong enough to fight the Decreta ourselves, but we were everywhere. We could keep watch for trouble developing, thereby protecting the Teneo and ourselves. That's where the word 'Sentinel' comes from. 'League' is there because we've always had members from multiple countries. Ever since, we have helped protect the Teneo and their knowledge."

Adam's mind was still on the technology. "If all members of the Sentinel League know about things like the bioluminescence, hasn't anyone leaked some of that information?" he asked.

"Another great question," said Gurpreet. "Yes, there have been leaks over the years, but we try to minimize how much *can* be leaked. An example is the bioluminescence. All of our members know it exists so we've had leaks of the idea before, but they don't know the process to actually create the bioluminescence. Only a few hand-picked members ever get to learn the process of how it is created, and those members would never leak that secret. This is why we hand select initiates to begin. We only invite the most trustworthy people. Usually, we find trustworthiness runs in families, but not always. We invite the initiates, put them through exercises to make sure they are who we think they are, and make them full members."

"What happens if someone doesn't make it?" asked Kevin

"They have their memories *adjusted* and are sent to a new location. I can't tell you more than that."

The boys looked at each other. It had never occurred to them that one of them could be sent away in the future, never to be seen again.

"But that rarely happens. We haven't had it happen in a long time, so don't worry about it. There's nothing you can do to 'study' for it either. We have to have missed something pretty glaring in order for that to happen," said Gurpreet.

His words didn't do much to release the knot in Adam's gut.

"So that's the rough history of the Sentinel League. You'll learn more of the story and details over time. Because the League is so old, there are a lot of them. Right now, though, we are starting you off with some jobs that need to be done. It's just a little manual labor."

Mark groaned.

"Markandeya Gupta – you quit complaining! You most of all could use the exercise, as well as some work ethic," said Gurpreet.

"Markandeya?" asked Jimmy, smirking. Adam and Kevin tried not to laugh.

"Daaaad!" complained Mark.

Gurpreet shrugged.

Mark looked at the others whose faces were wide in smiles.

"What? Did you honestly think my name was Mark? Like out of the Bible? My family is East Indian you know," he stated.

The main door opened and in stepped two men. First was Karl Klein, the local insurance broker. Second was Marius Miller. The boys were surprised that Marius was part of the League. His 5 young children were so close in age that it was hard to believe he had time for anything other than childcare. It was often thought that he had so many children so people would stop calling him by his long time nickname 'Mary'.

"We're ready when you are," said Marius.

Gurpreet nodded to Marius and Karl then looked at the boys. "Well, I hope you're ready." They nodded that they were, although Mark's nod was weak. "You can follow Marius," Gurpreet added and pointed to the door.

Marius led them outside and directed them to his van. Adam realized why Marius was included; he was the only one with a vehicle large enough to fit them all. Adam couldn't figure out why Karl was included.

They climbed into the second and third rows of the van and buckled their seat belts. Karl squeezed into the second row next to Kevin and Mark while Jimmy and Adam, being slimmer built, had an easier time getting into the rearmost seat. Because Karl was so overweight, Kevin and Mark were cramped.

"Gonna be a tight fit here boys," laughed Karl in his slight German accent. "Us 'well-built' men have to stick together." He slapped Mark on the knee and looked at Kevin.

Adam could tell that Kevin didn't like being lumped in with the 'well-built' crew, being that he was mainly muscular.

Gurpreet and Marius hopped in the van, and soon they were moving. Marius drove out of town toward the monitoring station, so Adam thought they would be painting walls or cutting lawns. At the bottom of the hill near the station, Marius turned away from it, going further west down the valley. Soon the valley widened out to an open plain, and Marius pulled off the road into a field. The field was rocky with stone piles everywhere except for one large clearing.

Marius stopped the van and they all stepped out. The adults stretched as if they had been driving for a long time. Mark was pouting, dreading the work to come, while Kevin and Jimmy looked around.

Adam looked at the rocks and thought about Mike Baranov saying the labor wouldn't be too hard. Seeing the stones surrounding him, he wondered just what Mike thought *was* hard labor.

"So, Junior Initiates, do you have any idea why we're here?" asked Gurpreet with a big smile on his face.

Kevin answered with a bit too much excitement. "Picking stones?"

"Well, that's part of it," said Gurpreet, looking at his smiling counterparts, "but, we are guilty of fooling you a little. As it is your first day as Initiates, we thought we'd have some fun."

"I thought only Kevin could think picking heavy stones would be fun," said Mark, still pouting.

Gurpreet gave Mark a stern look, and then his face softened. "We are here to teach you an old Sentinel League game that's played here among the rocks. For centuries it's been known as 'Kurling'."

The boys all exchanged looks, not sure if Gurpreet was kidding.

"Curling?" Jimmy laughed as he asked. "You mean that boring game you old guys play in the winter at the 'curling' rink?"

"It's not just for old people, and it's got a lot of strategy!" Kevin replied, insulted by Jimmy's comment.

"Yes and no, Jimmy," answered Karl. "The ice game of curling has its roots in *our* game, but other than some terminology and the fact that they both have a lot of strategy, they are quite different. How do we know the ice game has its roots in our sport? .... A group of teams is called a Curling *League* of course!" Karl made a huff at the end of the last word.

Marius spoke for the first time since they left Town Hall. "Karl is *obsessed* with League Kurling. And he's quite good at it," Karl's chest started to puff out, "until he plays against me." Marius smiled a mischievous smile.

Karl's chest deflated and he turned red. He spoke a few words in German that Adam guessed weren't compliments to Marius, and then he turned to the field.

"So, a little history first, then the game," said Karl, leading them to the middle of the field. "It all began a long time ago when two of the Sentinel League members, who happened to be brothers, were on watch in a rocky field. They were bored, so they began throwing stones. One of them had an idea to mark out a one foot circle, literally using the size of his foot, and see who could throw a stone into the circle or closest to it." He walked a few paces away from them and marked out a circle using a stick he picked up. "They called the circle the 'button'. That's where the term 'on the button' came from."

He picked up some stones and walked away from the circle, turned and started tossing.

"They played for hours, knocking each other's stones out of the circle. After a while, they decided that each of them would only get 6 stones, of whatever size and shape they liked, and that they should stand at a certain distance – 10 paces to start." Karl walked back to the button, turned and stepped out 10 paces.

"At 10 paces from the button they marked out a two foot square and called it the hack, which was the spot from which they would throw," he said as he picked up the stick again and marked a square using both feet. After picking up a couple of stones, he threw them at the button, landing them close to the center.

"The brothers played like that all day, and realized that they would each only get a point or two because it was too easy to get stones on the button. They decided to move back to 15 paces. At that distance, it was more difficult to hit the button and just as hard to knock the other player out." Karl moved 5 paces further away from the button and re-drew the hack with the stick. After picking up more stones he began throwing them at the button again. Not one of the six he threw ended up on the button.

"I haven't seen any of your stones 'curling', so why call it curling?" asked Jimmy.

Karl smiled at him, "I usually save that detail for last, but I'll tell you now, since you've asked. You remember the brothers that invented the game? Their names were Kurt and Karl, K U R T and K A R L. They combined the first two letters of Kurt – K U - with the last two of Karl – R L - K U R L. My father was such a huge fan of the game that he insisted *I* be named after one of the brothers, actually." Karl seemed especially proud of that fact.

"Are you sure you're not just making this up as part of the initiation?" asked Jimmy.

Karl looked at him, smiling again, "You'd be surprised how many initiates have said the same thing. I should really start introducing the game differently, but for now I'll stick with the tried and true...now where was I?" Karl paused and thought for a moment, scratching his head. "Oh yes, the history. So, the brothers were playing this game they invented and were getting bored. You're probably thinking the same thing." He looked at Jimmy who nodded in agreement.

"Well, one of the Teneo was watching them play. When they started to get bored, he came down to the brothers and asked them to try something different with the game. He hunted around and found 6 stones, all of various sizes and shapes." Karl did the same, picking up 6 very different stones.

"The Teneo explained to the brothers that everything is connected in some way, you just have to figure out how. He said that once you've found out how to connect to an object, you can control it to some degree. How much control depended on many different factors, from the skill of the controller to the size and shape of the object.

Observe."

The boys watched as Karl picked a round stone that fit in the palm of his hand, placed his other hand on top and raised it to the bridge of his nose between his eyes. He closed his eyes for a moment, then opened them and tossed the stone toward the button, leaving his hand in the air. The height and angle that he threw the stone would have put the stone well past the button. Time seemed to slow as Karl watched the stone without breathing or blinking, and a moment before it was over the button Karl dropped his hand. The airborne stone dropped at the same time as Karl's hand, coming to rest in the center of the button.

The boys looked to each other with wide eyes. They couldn't process what they had just seen.

"Did you just do what I think I saw you do?" asked Mark.

Karl winked at Mark and picked up another stone. It was twice the size of the first one. He did the same procedure, raising it to his forehead, closing and opening his eyes, then tossing toward the button. That time he threw it with less power, and it looked like it should land only halfway to the button. Karl made a push in the air and the stone gained speed, flying further and faster in the direction of Karl's push. It landed with a thud at the edge of the button, hiding the first stone from view.

"Nice guard," said Marius.

Karl nodded to Marius then spoke to the boys. "*That* is a guard. It's a basic move in the game, to try protecting the counters. We'll teach you the strategy later. Now, when you're as practiced as me, watch what else you can do."

Karl picked up another stone, a little larger than the first one but flatter. He tossed it high and long and made small correcting motions to straighten its flight. It arced down past the button, and Karl made a quick dropping/pulling motion. The stone moved like it had bounced off an invisible backboard and slammed hard into the stone at the center of the button, popping it out of the circle and remaining at the center.

Adam couldn't believe what he was seeing.

"Nice takeout," said Marius. Karl nodded at him again.

"Because different sizes and shapes of stones behave differently, it's hard to shoot well every time. Add in the selection of only 6 stones per end and it makes for a lot of fun. Today we thought we would just teach you how to get a connection and some basic moves."

Adam had been thinking outside of the game. "If you can control the stones like that, can you control other things too?"

"No, sadly it is limited to certain types of rocks and minerals. We'll teach you how to find stones that you can connect with, and show you *how* to make a connection. This particular field is full of good selections, that's why we play here. Not everyone can get a connection, though, but because you are all descendants of people who I know can do it, you should be able to," said Karl.

Mark gave Gurpreet a look that asked if Gurpreet had the ability. Gurpreet nodded back.

"Is that why those old guys can make so many great shots at the curling rink?" asked Kevin, "I mean, ice curling?"

"No, they're making those shots with pure skill. Those

curling rocks are 40 lbs each, and I've never heard of anyone establishing control of an object even 10 lbs before. Too small and too big don't work, and they have to be the right density. We can't control ice or wood - too light. Iron ore is great to control, but once it's processed we lose control. On top of that, the regular curling rocks are made of granite, and we can't seem to establish a connection with granite at all," said Karl.

Marius added to the conversation, "At one point they made the ice curling rocks with handles made of controllable stone. The thrower could make small corrections to the trajectory without it being noticed. It didn't take long until the handles returned to wood, and then plastic."

Karl nodded. "We've chosen this sport for your first day because so many members love the game, and it gives you a chance to try something you never thought possible. Go find 6 stones each and come back here with them. Try to pick ones with lighter colors and less grainy texture."

The boys walked into the field and picked up stones. Adam found 6 that he suspected would be good, all within a 4 foot circle. He was the first one back to Karl, and showed his haul.

"Good, good. Those will fly nicely...very controllable," said Karl, picking each one up and examining them in turn. "You can wait here until I check the others." He turned toward Jimmy who was returning next, with Kevin and Mark close behind.

Adam examined his own stones while listening to Karl examine the others. "Too small," was said many times, as well as "too hard to control." Adam laughed when Karl examined the stones Mark selected and said, "That's not a stone, Mark, its horse poop."

Each of the others was sent back to find replacements for the ones Karl discarded, but soon each boy had their stones.

Karl lined them up facing away from the van, nearly halfway down the field. It was one of the few spots that were clear of rocks, so each of them piled their stones at their feet.

"Pick up any one of your stones." said Karl, and they followed his direction.

"In order to get a connection with your stone, place it in your hands like this," he demonstrated and they copied.

"When you bring the stone to your forehead, the stone needs to be as close as possible to the point between your eyes. Close your eyes and look into the stone using your mind. Concentrate hard and you will get a positive feeling or none at all. If you get a positive feeling, you have established the connection. If you get no feeling - no connection. Keep trying until you do, and let me know when you have it. I will let you throw as soon as I think you are ready."

Adam thought it seemed strange, but decided to go along with the instructions. He held the stone between his hands, brought it to his forehead and closed his eyes. His mind was blank for a moment, and then it began to see. It looked as if he was falling into the stone and the stone was deep. In a heartbeat he stopped at what he assumed was the middle of the stone, and felt an almost happy feeling. That must have been the feeling Karl was talking about.

He opened his eyes and called for Karl.

"That was quick," said Karl as he walked over. "You got a positive feeling?"

Adam nodded, "Is it normal to see yourself falling toward the center of the stone?" he asked.

Karl looked surprised. "Yes and no. Only the strongest connections have visions associated with them. You must have a strong connection with this stone."

Karl raised his voice to the group, "once you've established a connection, do not lose contact with the stone. If the stone hits the ground, it starts to lose the connection with you, and you have to re-establish. Also, once you throw it and it hits the ground, you have a few moments where there is still enough of a connection that you can manipulate the stone slightly."

He turned to Adam. "Throw it high in the air and keep your hand wherever it is when you release. Concentrate, and once the stone starts to arc downward, wave your hand side to side."

Adam was skeptical, but he threw the stone as hard as he could, leaving his hand in the air where it released. He concentrated on the stone and felt positive energy coming back. As the stone started descending, Adam waved his hand side to side. The stone followed his motion exactly. Adam was stunned.

"Try another one," said Karl, "but this time, pull your hand back halfway and when it reaches the apex, give it a push." He walked away to help Mark, who thought he had a connection too.

Adam brought the stone up to his forehead and again fell to the heart of the stone. He opened his eyes and threw the stone on the same arc as the first one, pulling his hand back with a quick motion as Karl had told him to do. The stone instantly changed direction, racing back at Adam faster than he had thrown it. Without thinking, he waved his hand down. The stone slammed into the ground with a loud thud. The noise drew everyone's attention.

"What happened?" asked Gurpreet from his spot leaning on the van.

Adam shrugged as Karl walked over to talk to him. Adam explained what happened and Karl stood in thought for a moment.

"I never expected you to have that strong of a connection on your first day. When you've practiced a lot and played for years, you can get really strong connections with some of the stones. Just after releasing the stone there is usually a slight delay and the thrower can adjust themselves to a better control position. Obviously that didn't happen with you, and the stone responded to your movement immediately. Try it again, but this time when you release the stone, concentrate on the stone continuing its flight. Re-adjust and then focus on your hand giving it a push."

Everyone had stopped and stared at Adam as Karl was delivering instruction. Adam felt awkward, but picked up another stone and began the process of connection. That stone was a little more difficult to start a connection, or so it seemed, but once he saw himself falling to the heart of the stone, he knew it was done. Eyes opened again, he took his time and prepared to throw, trying to remember everything Karl said. He threw the stone hard and concentrated on it continuing on its path. Meanwhile, he brought his hand back halfway, re-focused and pushed hard. The stone straightened out and shot like a bullet in the same direction that Adam had pushed. It hit a large boulder in the distance and shot off to the side with a big bounce.

"Wow," said Gurpreet.

"I think you owe me ten bucks, Karl," said Marius.

Karl smiled and shook his head. "Gladly," he replied.

"Why does he owe you ten bucks?" asked Kevin.

Marius smiled, "I bet him that Adam would be a powerful thrower like his dad. I didn't think he would prove it on the first day though."

"My dad played this game?" asked Adam.

The three men looked at each other, unsure how to answer.

"He was a great player. Very strong connections with the stones," said Karl.

A while later, each of the others was able to establish connections with their stones too. Jimmy seemed to have the hardest time as it required quiet and concentration, but eventually it worked for him.

Karl and Marius showed them different throws, sometimes privately so the other wouldn't see. Both men were highly skilled and could hit small targets at long distances from multiple angles. The next hour was spent throwing and throwing until their arms were sore.

"That's enough for today," said Gurpreet, seeming quite happy. "Karl would keep you here all day if we let him."

"He's the only guy I've ever met who doesn't get insulted if you tell him he has rocks in his head," said Marius, teasing Karl. The two obviously had a friendly rivalry.

Karl grinned. "With how well you throw, I worry that I really will get a rock in the head," Karl teased back.

They all had a good laugh.

"Do you know what the best part of the game is?" asked Karl.

They all said no.

"There's nothing to clean up at the end! Drop and walk!" With that, Karl dropped the two stones he was holding and turned to the van.

Gurpreet ruffled Mark's hair in a proud fatherly gesture as Mark walked past him toward the van.

They all got in and breathed a sigh of relief to be sitting.

"When do we get to learn how to play the full game?" asked Jimmy.

"Do you still think it's *boring*, like ice curling?" Karl replied.

Jimmy didn't want to admit that he was excited by the game, even though he showed a lot of promise with his throws. "It's alright," he replied back, trying to play it cool.

Karl grinned wide. "How does next Sunday sound? We can practice a little, then try and learn the game by playing a few ends."

"Ends?" asked Jimmy.

Kevin groaned. "How can you say you don't like ice curling if you don't even know what an End is? It's like an inning in baseball, or a quarter in football."

Jimmy shrugged. "It just *looks* boring."

Kevin shook his head, but said no more.

They drove back to town listening to Karl talk about his favorite throws and Marius teasing Karl about every one.

Altogether, Adam had a great day. He was feeling closer to his dad than he ever had before.

CHAPTER TWENTY

The van pulled up at Town Hall during Karl's story of how he once bounced a stone off two others, knocking the shot stone off the button and sticking it for the win. Marius laughed and teased Karl that his shot was mostly luck and not skill. Karl commented that Marius didn't know the difference between the two.

They all piled out of the van, laughing at the comments from both men. As they stepped out, the door to Town Hall opened and out stepped Don Chen.

"Hi guys, did you have a good time?" he asked.

They nodded and he smiled back at them. He looked to Gurpreet, "Can I talk to you?"

Gurpreet's smile faded somewhat. "Nothing bad," said Don.

The two men stepped off to the side and spoke in barely audible voices. Soon, they turned back to the group and Gurpreet spoke.

"Well, I'm glad the first thing you will remember about the League is learning Kurling, and I think you all had fun," he began.

They all nodded their heads in agreement.

"Sadly, it seems that today won't be all fun and games. We have some work that needs to be done, and you four are perfect for the job." He gave them a smile. "Let's just step inside to talk," he continued.

Adam looked at the others and followed Gurpreet into the building.

"Do you still need us?" asked Karl, referring to himself and Marius.

Don turned. "You can go home now, Karl, and thanks for your help. Marius, can you come in for a minute?"

Karl nodded, turned to Marius and shook his hand. "Thanks for the ride. I leave tomorrow for a month of holidays, but we'll have to play another game when I return. I still have much more to teach you," he said with a big smile.

Marius chuckled and shook his head. "No problem, Karl. I'm always ready."

Marius followed the group into Town Hall.

Once inside, they formed a semicircle facing Don and Gurpreet.

"So, like I said, we have some work for you today... sorry! We usually want the first day of initiation to be filled with fun, but that's how it goes. Anyway, the League likes to help out wherever possible, volunteering in the community for people who are in need, like the elderly or people who get hurt."

"Then why didn't someone else cut Ben's lawn last summer? I wasn't part of the League," said Mark.

"No, *you* weren't, but *I* was," said Gurpreet, scolding Mark with a look, "and *you* needed to do something other than play video games."

Mark was a little upset at being scolded in front of his friends.

"Anyway, we have a request for some help, and we've decided to send you four. An elder in the community needs some weeds pulled from their garden, and we've heard that you are experienced at that job," said Gurpreet. "Hopefully Mark has figured out which ones are weeds."

Adam looked to the others again and they tried not to laugh. Obviously, Gurpreet had heard about the job they did for Jimmy's mom.

"It's almost 3:30 right now. Why don't you all go home and have a snack. Come back here around 4:30 in your work clothes," he continued.

"Marius, would we be able to book your van for that time? We just need to drop them off for an hour or so and pick them up again."

Marius nodded. "No problem. I'll be here at 4:30."

"Thanks," said Gurpreet. "Now, go home. See you all in an hour." He waved them all toward the door.

Marius held the door for everyone and Gurpreet locked it once all were out. Adam, Kevin and Jimmy walked toward Jimmy's house, and Marius drove past with a wave.

"Well, so much for the fun," said Jimmy.

"You have to admit, that was pretty addicting," Kevin said to Jimmy.

"Yeah, it actually was. I can't wait to do it again," said Jimmy.

Adam was silent as they talked. He was lost in wonder, picturing his dad Kurling, throwing fantastic shots.

"See ya later," Jimmy called as he turned at his house.

"How come you're so quiet? Didn't you have fun?" asked Kevin as they continued walking.

"Sorry, just thinking. I had fun, for sure...I was just thinking about my dad. You heard Marius say that I shoot like him."

Kevin smiled. "Yeah...I guess it's nice to hear stories about him."

Adam nodded. "It's the only way I'll ever get to know him."

They walked in silence until they were at the corner where they would have to split up once more.

"Meet you back here in half an hour?" asked Kevin.

Adam nodded and turned toward his house.

His thoughts drifted to his mother. She knew about the League, but how would she react when she found out that Adam was now a member? It wasn't like he could sit down with her and have a reasonable conversation about being an initiate - or anything else for that matter.

He was mulling these thoughts over as he arrived home, worried about going in the house for fear of her anger. He had to eat something and get back soon, although he was still full from the meal at Kevin's. After standing and thinking for a moment, he took a deep breath and stepped in the side door.

There she was, sitting at the table waiting for him. The look on her face told Adam that she already knew.

"Sit," she commanded. He did as she said.

"So...where were you today?" she asked.

Adam could feel the anger in her voice. "Learning how to Kurl," he said.

She paused for a long moment. "So, it's true. You're part of the League."

"Just a *Junior* Initiate," he replied, trying to minimize the meaning of his membership.

"There hasn't been a *Junior* Initiate in nearly a century," she replied with a snap.

Adam realized then that she knew a lot more about the League than he thought.

"Are *you* a member of the League?" asked Adam, already knowing the answer.

"This isn't about me," she snapped back again. "I can't stop you from being a member because this whole town is filled with *them. I* stopped acting as a member when your dad died. The one thing I can tell you is that the League is the reason your dad is *dead.*"

She had never spoken so directly to Adam about his father's death, and Adam found it disturbing.

"*They* are the ones that caused him to drink, always talking about the 'danger' coming. 'Be prepared, always on guard'. The only way he could cope with the stress was by getting drunk for the last year of his life." She sobbed into her hands. "And for what? Nothing! Nothing has happened in the last 11 years. They drove him to his grave for nothing!"

Adam was stunned into silence while Mary paused, holding back her tears.

"Don Chen told me everything while you were gone, if you're wondering," she said, gaining control over her emotions. "I told him that if anything happened to you I would never forgive him, and he promised to look out for you."

She almost seemed to care, which seemed foreign to Adam.

"You are to do *nothing* dangerous for them, and I don't want you *ever* to be more than a general member. Once you're done initiation, you won't have to do anything other than go to the odd meeting. That is what I want, understand?"

So many questions ran through his mind. When did she become a member? Were her parents members and that's why she didn't talk about them? Did she meet his dad because of the League? He knew he couldn't ask though, because in her current state of mind she would just break down again. Instead he answered, "Ok, Mom. I'll do what you want."

She smiled at him, which didn't happen often. Adam didn't know how to respond, so he turned to the kitchen. "I'm going out with the guys again, so I came to eat something quick."

She returned to her normal self in a hurry. "There's a new canned soup in the cupboard, if you want to try it," she said in her normal tone, but there was a slight change. Normally she would have told him to make two cans so there was enough for her as well. This time she let him do it for himself.

Adam opened the can and heated the contents as fast

as he could. He used a saucepan on the stove to warm it up, stirring constantly so it wouldn't burn. The soup was Beef, Barley, and Broccoli – probably given to his mom by Mr. Garagan because no one was buying any. It smelled perfectly fine to Adam, even though he wasn't terribly hungry. Being in a hurry, as soon as it was slightly warm he removed the soup from the stove, took it to the table and ate it directly out of the saucepan. Mary had resumed her usual position in the armchair watching TV.

He rinsed the saucepan and spoon in the sink, washed his hands, inspected his clothes and walked out the door. He didn't need to change as his work clothes *were* his everyday clothes.

He checked his pocket and made sure the pin was still there. He didn't know why, but he felt he needed to keep it close.

At the street corner he waited. It didn't take long before Kevin jogged out his long driveway and turned up the gravel road leading to the intersection. It was 4:15 pm, so they had more than enough time to get back to Town Hall before 4:30.

"Did you eat half a cow?" Adam teased as Kevin approached.

"I'm not *late*," replied Kevin. "We've still got plenty of time to get there."

With that, they walked back to Jimmy's house and returned to Town Hall. They were the first ones to arrive.

"We're only 5 minutes early. Where is everyone?" asked Jimmy.

"Well, Gurpreet is probably waiting because Mark is stuffing food in his pockets in case he gets hungry later," said Kevin, "and Marius has 5 kids." Jimmy chuckled and nodded.

"There's Marius," said Adam, pointing up Main Street where a van had just turned the corner.

"And here come the Guptas," said Kevin, pointing up the street to the left.

Mark was still chewing as he and Gurpreet arrived, which caused the other three to chuckle to themselves.

They piled into the van, a lot more comfortably for Kevin and Mark without Karl squeezing in next to them. Once they had all buckled up, Marius headed toward the school.

Adam had been wondering who they would be helping. Needing Marius to drive them meant that whoever it was lived outside of town. Thankfully it wasn't Martha or Aggie that needed the help because Adam couldn't handle listening to all the gossip those two spread.

Marius passed the school and turned south onto the gravel road. Adam figured it out quickly. "We're going to Ms. White's farm, aren't we?"

Gurpreet and Marius looked at each other expressionless. "Yes. I wanted to talk to you all before we got there anyway. You've probably heard that Ms. White likes her privacy."

"I've heard that she's - demanding," said Adam.

"She can be," said Gurpreet, "especially with people she doesn't know. I got to know her because she was friends with my father, so she trusts me. She doesn't know any of you personally, so don't expect much. Also, she doesn't have power or running water, so don't ask to use the bathroom. If you need water, pump some from the well. There's an outhouse I will point out to you, if you need."

Adam thought for a moment. "Is she a member of the League?"

"Yes," said Gurpreet, but continued with his other train of thought. "She's a little old-fashioned, so *if* she wants to meet you, just say 'Pleased to meet you, Ms. White'. Ok?"

Adam didn't find the instructions all that strange after hearing a couple of stories about her from others in town, but especially what he had heard from his mother. The most popular story was how Ms. White fired a shotgun at Mr. Garagan because he didn't honk his horn before coming up the driveway.

They drove in silence for another mile, then over a small hill and down into a valley. At the bottom, they turned into the lane that led up to the yard. Marius gave the horn two quick blasts and one long.

Slowly, he drove up the lane. It was nearly overgrown, and scraped the sides of the van as it moved. Marius winced each time he heard a branch on the paint.

After what seemed like a long drive, the trees opened up to reveal a farm yard nestled into the edge of the valley. It was nothing like Adam had expected. He expected rusty steel machinery with fence wire and half collapsed wooden structures everywhere, but the yard was neat and clean. The buildings were old, but well maintained. Potted flowers were spread all over the yard. It was the complete the opposite of what he had expected.

Marius pulled the van slowly along the lane and stopped at the closest point to the small farm house. Gurpreet stepped out and told the rest to stay put, then walked up to the house. Before he reached it, the door opened, shielding the opener from view. Gurpreet stepped in and the door closed behind him.

"The first time I came out here as an initiate," said Marius, "I had to shovel snow. The wind had made a 10 foot snow bank in front of the barn over there." Marius pointed to the barn. "Ron Nagy had already been out here clearing roads and had cleaned out the lane, but the rest had to be done by hand. I was the only initiate that year, so I spent four hours shovelling. That really sucked. This will be much better."

Adam noticed the garden beside the barn as Marius spoke. It was 4 times the size of the one at Jimmy's house.

The door to the house opened again, and out stepped Gurpreet, alone. He waved for them to get out of the van and follow him to the garden.

The garden was lined in neat rows, and seemed to have everything from potatoes to radish plants. As far as Adam could tell, it had been weeded recently, and the weeds that were left were still small; half the size of the ones in the Jones's garden.

Gurpreet turned over an upside down wheelbarrow at the back of the garden and wheeled it to the side.

"All of the weeds you pick go into the wheelbarrow. When the wheelbarrow gets full, empty it onto the compost pile here," he said, walking up to a mound a few steps from the garden, far enough to not get the smell but close enough to use the compost in the garden. "When you're done, wait out here by the lane. Don't go snooping around."

Adam nodded. After hearing the shotgun story, he wouldn't wander far from the garden.

"It's 4:50 pm now. We'll come back to pick you up at around 6:00, so a little more than an hour. That should be enough time to get finished if you all work reasonably hard."

"Well, let's get at it," said Kevin, grabbing the wheelbarrow and placing it at the edge of the garden.

Gurpreet and Marius smiled. "You are definitely like your dad," said Marius. "Not afraid of a little work."

Kevin smiled at the compliment as the other three stepped into the garden to start working.

Gurpreet and Marius hopped in the van and drove away while Mark watched, looking like a puppy that's been left on the side of the road.

"Get over here and pull some weeds," said Jimmy, "They'll be back."

Mark dragged himself over to the garden and began to work, half-heartedly at first. In a few minutes, he seemed to forget his cares and worked at a steady pace, harder than anyone else expected from him.

They worked in silence for half an hour when Adam signalled for a break. They had finished way more than half of the garden.

"I am honestly impressed," Kevin said to Mark. "I didn't think you could work for that long consistently. Good job!"

Mark was unsure if the comments were sincere or not. "There's a lot you don't know about me," he replied.

"And I'd like to keep it that way, thank you very much," replied Kevin, gaining a laugh from Jimmy.

Adam looked around the yard. It seemed strange. The trees bordering it were so thick that you could only see the sky above them and nothing beyond, except through the small opening to the lane. The trees far to the right of the opening were odd as well. They looked different than any he had ever seen growing around Grayson.

"Did you guys notice those trees?" asked Adam.

"Not until you mentioned it, but now that I'm looking, they do seem strange," said Kevin.

Jimmy said nothing and wandered toward the grove. He saw small bunches hanging from limbs, but didn't recognize them immediately. When he got closer, he called out, "Come here! You have to see this!"

The others jogged down to the trees after Jimmy, and stared in amazement.

"Are those bananas?" said Mark.

"And olives on this one," said Kevin.

"Look at the oranges over here," said Adam, "but none of these should be *here*. We can't grow tropical fruit *here*."

"We can't, but here they are," said Kevin.

A voice called from behind them, "Don't touch the trees please!"

Startled, they turned to see who they assumed was Ms. White. She called to them from behind the screen enclosing her small porch, so they could only make out her shape. *Had she been there watching them the entire time? Was she pointing a gun at them*?

They quickly returned to the garden and resumed weeding, but all thoughts were on the out-of-place fruit trees. How were they able to grow in the northern climate?

Because their minds were occupied with other thoughts, the remaining work went quickly. Kevin emptied the wheelbarrow one last time and returned it to its original spot.

With the job complete they sat at the edge of the weed-less garden.

"What time is it?" asked Jimmy.

"5:49," said Kevin.

They sat quietly; not speaking for fear that Ms. White was watching them, all still wondering about the trees. Jimmy threw a rock down the lane out of boredom.

Adam had calmed his racing mind by telling himself he could ask Gurpreet about the trees once they were in the van and on their way back to town. He scanned the yard, looking for anything else strange, but nothing looked out of place.

In an instant the sunlight dimmed, like a dark cloud passing in front of the sun. At that time of day in the summer, the sun was nowhere near setting yet.

"I hope they come and get us soon," said Mark. "Looks like there's a storm coming."

Adam looked in the direction of Grayson, which was to the right of where the sun had been. Over the trees, he saw the top of a dark mass billowing. It didn't look like clouds, though. It was a thick mist, getting darker and higher as he watched.

Adam's gut tightened as he realized what it was.

"It's the fog! The one that happened at Langenburg!"

CHAPTER TWENTY-ONE

"You boys better come in," Ms. White called from the porch, sounding a lot gentler than the first time they heard her voice.

The boys didn't need any more encouragement than that. They stood up and ran to the house, making Adam step inside the porch first, but Ms. White was no longer there by the time they arrived.

"Come in the house," she said from somewhere further inside. Adam heard an accent that he hadn't noticed earlier.

They stepped just inside the doorway and stayed on the shoe rug, being polite. They squished together with Adam and Jimmy at the front and Kevin and Mark barely inside. The rug lay at the edge of a small living room that was decorated in light pastel colors that reminded Adam of Easter.

"I'm making some lemonade. Please find a spot and sit down. Leave on your shoes," she said from around a corner in a distinctly English accent.

They heard the clinking of glasses and sounds of stirring as each boy found a seat in the living room. There were no photographs in the room, but many pastel paintings of flowers hung tastefully about.

Adam looked around and felt that there was something odd. It wasn't completely dark outside, but the light in the room seemed very pleasant. He remembered that Gurpreet had said Ms. White had no power or water. As he looked up, he realized why he felt strange. The ceiling was glowing like the tunnels, although it was a softer light.

At the same time, Ms. White stepped into the living room. "Who's thirsty?" she asked, holding a tray full of glasses.

All four boys stared at her in silence, unable to speak. She was the woman in the 1910 photograph of Town Hall, not a day older than she looked in the picture!

Adam sat silent, shocked. His mind flipped through scenarios, none of which made sense. Either the lady in front of him was the descendant of the woman in the picture, or she *was* the woman in the picture. If she *was* the woman in the picture, she would have to be well over 100 years old and she didn't even look 40.

"No-one is thirsty? We'll have to drink quickly," she said.

"I'll have some," said Kevin. "Pleased to meet you, ma'am. I'm Kevin Baranov," he said as he remembered his manners.

"Pleased to meet you as well, Kevin," she replied handing him a glass.

The others kept staring at her.

"You're supposed to be old," said Mark.

"I *am* old, Mark," she responded. The fact that she

knew his name surprised him.

"I'm James Jones the Third, ma'am. Pleased to meet you," said Jimmy.

"Pleased to meet you as well. You prefer to be called Jimmy, right?" she asked.

"Yes ma'am," he replied, surprised.

Adam watched as she handed Mark and Jimmy lemonade, then turned to him.

"Hello Adam, nice to see you again," she said.

Again? thought Adam.

"uh...yeah...nice to see you too, Ms. White," he replied.

She smiled and handed him a glass of lemonade. "You won't remember me, but I've known you since you were born. I knew your father well." She looked at each of the boys. "In fact, I know each of your fathers well."

"Sorry, Ms. White?" he replied.

"Don't call me Ms. White. My name is Elianora. Most people call me Nora, but some call me Ellie. Either one is fine." She set the tray on a small table and sat in the chair next to it.

"You're Number 1," said Adam, "That's how you knew my dad."

"Yes," she said without a flinch, "I've heard you are a clever young man."

Adam blushed a little. He wondered who would have told her that he was 'clever'.

"You were here when Grayson was built," he stated.

"Yes, Adam. I was here," she replied.

"How old are you, then?" asked Mark.

She sighed. "Let's just say 'really old', ok?"

"You seem nice," said Mark, "but I've always heard you were an old grouch."

The other boys looked at Mark in disbelief of what he had just said.

Elianora laughed. "Thanks...I think," she replied. "I've kept the appearance of being an 'old grouch' for the sake of all the non-Sentinel League members. It helps maintain my privacy without raising suspicion."

"Did you really shoot at Mr. Garagan when he was delivering groceries?" asked Mark.

Adam and the others were still in disbelief at Mark's questions, even though they wanted to hear the answers.

She smiled at Mark, "No, I didn't. He is a member of the League and we came up with that story to 'discourage' visitors. The story worked a little too well. Now everyone honks on their way in, but I usually know someone is coming long before they get here."

"How do you know when someone is coming?" asked Adam, thinking Elianora must have some interesting science that alerts her in advance.

"It's so quiet here that the sound of cars on the gravel travels a long way," she replied, to Adam's disappointment.

Adam's mind raced through questions he could ask, stopping on the most immediate one. "Is that the same fog out there as the one they found in Langenburg?" he asked.

She frowned and nodded, confirming his suspicion.

"Do you know what's going on?" he asked.

She sighed again. "Yes, I do. It's because of me, actually." She stood up and stepped toward her kitchen. "There's a lot to tell you, and really not much time. If you are done your drink, please follow me."

They chugged their lemonade and followed her through the kitchen, setting their glasses on the countertop as they passed by. She led them through a doorway and down a set of stairs where she opened a familiar sliding door. As she slid her hand on the wall in a slow upward motion, Adam could see lights glow in the room beyond.

They entered and looked around, seeing the room was like a cave, similar to the secret file room at Town Hall, only wider and more brightly lit. One side of the cave held stacks of books and various items, from a curved staff to a top hat and cane. The other side of the cave had shelves filled with jars and bottles of various sizes, shapes and colors. At the far end was a table holding 3 books, each sitting on its own small podium. As they walked toward the books, Adam tried to read the labels on the bottles, but they were written in a script he had never seen before. When he looked at the books on the other wall, there were many different scripts used on their titles, but none that he could read or even recognize.

"I have a story to show you. It will answer a few of your questions," said Elianora, pointing at the books on the table.

"I don't read all that fast," said Kevin, "and you said we were in a hurry."

She smiled at Kevin. "Don't worry. You'll do fine with these books. Gurpreet said he gave you a quick history of the Sentinel League, right?"

They nodded.

She stepped behind the table and moved the middle book to face the boys, then thumbed through the pages. As she flipped through, they saw movement on each page, as if each one was a three-dimensional video screen, the thickness of a paper.

"Here it is," she said stopping at a page, "now watch."

The page began playing a video that looked like a 1920's era silent film. The title screen said 'Larix and the Heartstone' in the same style of script as Adam had seen on other items in the cave, but still in English. Adam looked to Elianora, who smiled and gestured for him to continue with the story. As he looked back to the page, he found the video started from the exact place it stopped when he had looked up.

The page showed a shadow of a man standing on a hill, holding a red glowing object in his hand. Next to him looked like a King wearing a crown of leaves. The shadow man whispered in the King's ear. The King looked down at an army of men who carried spears and weapons that looked to be ancient. The King pointed to a village, toward which the army marched, while the object in the hand of the shadow man glowed. The scene darkened. When it lightened again, the village was burning. Men, women, and children ran from the village. A hail of arrows streaked through the air. The scene went dark again.

They all looked up at Elianora. "Done?" she asked. They nodded, and she turned the page.

The scene began with a group of people coming upon the village. They were dressed in white robes, and their faces could not be seen because of the light streaming from them. They walked through the destroyed village viewing the damage, clearly dismayed. The scene darkened. A new scene began. The shadow man stood alone in a barren plain, facing the white clothed people. They were clearly arguing. The object in the shadow man's hand pulsed brighter as they argued until it exploded into whiteness.

The playback stopped and they all looked to Elianora again. She turned another page.

The next scene began in white, and slowly faded back to where the group had stood. Only the shadow man remained, lying on the ground. None of the people in white were there, clearly destroyed in the explosion. The pulsing object was no longer in the hand of the shadow man. He rolled over and began searching frantically. The scene darkened and Elianora closed the book.

"The dark man's name is Larix. He is the leader of the Decreta - those Teneo who think Mankind should be slaves. Like all of the Teneo, Larix has a special skill set. When he speaks, it is difficult not to be swayed by him. He has used this gift for centuries to cause Mankind to fight amongst themselves."

"Did you say centuries?" asked Jimmy.

"Yes. Things like the Inquisition were started because of him," she replied.

Having learned about the Inquisition in school just the previous year, the group was shocked.

She continued, "The people in white were some of the Teneo who believed in letting Mankind evolve naturally; that they would be capable of great things in time. The object Larix was holding is called the Heartstone, and it gave him great power. Where he found it, we do not know. He used it to destroy our home island, and many good people living there at the time."

"If the Heartstone was that powerful, why didn't he just kill everyone with it?" asked Adam.

"Well, he didn't want to kill everyone as much as he wanted to rule them as a god. As a Teneo, he was small and weaker than most, but he was smart in the ways of deception. With the Heartstone, he gained strength and truly believed he was invincible. He convinced various factions of Mankind that he was a god, and had them do his bidding, which usually meant starting war with other men for his enjoyment.

In the first story you saw, the Emperor was named Titus. He had just become Emperor after the death of his father, Vespasian, in the year 79 AD. We aren't sure if Larix had anything to do with the death of Vespasian, but we know he went to Titus and convinced him that he was a god. By controlling the Emperor of Rome, he controlled almost all of Mankind."

"How could he convince them he was a god?" asked Mark.

"I'm not going to show you that one because it's too long, but since you asked, I'll tell you the quick version. Larix intercepted Titus as he was touring through his southern lands. Larix told Titus to bow down before him because he was a god, but Titus refused. Larix turned to the nearest mountain and, using the power of the Heartstone, he caused it to erupt. That mountain was named Mt. Vesuvius."

All four boys understood what she was saying and were stunned with disbelief.

"Are you saying that this guy - Larix - caused the disaster at Pompeii?" asked Mark.

"Yes. He wiped out an entire city to gain power over the Emperor. That's the kind of thing he enjoyed doing, and that's the power he had with the Heartstone."

"So he lost the Heartstone?" asked Kevin.

Elianora nodded. "Yes, and he's regained it a few times too. It has cost us a lot of lives to recover it each time."

Elianora paused for a moment, almost sad from the memory.

"So, back to the story. In the other scene you saw, a group of Teneo caught up with Larix, intent on bringing him to justice. It was the first time any Teneo had caught up with him since he destroyed our island, and the Teneo had heard stories of Larix's new powers. Something happened that Larix didn't expect, though. The Heartstone went crazy and spent all of its energy in one blast. It killed all of the Teneo present, but spared Larix."

She paused and took a deep breath. "The force of the blast threw the Heartstone a few miles away. It was lost for a while until a shepherd saw it glowing in a field. When the shepherd brought it back to his village, another Teneo was already there. That Teneo's name was Raphia, and he was following his fellow Teneo who had been killed. Raphia had heard stories of the stone Larix carried as well. After hearing the story of the explosion nearby, Raphia assumed the Heartstone had played a part.

The Heartstone seemed to be glowing more and more as time went on, pulsing in a furious manner each time Raphia approached the stone. Each time the shepherd approached it, nothing happened. They realized that the Heartstone reacted to the Teneo but not to normal humans. At the time, they assumed it was recovering from the blast and didn't know how long it would take to recharge. They didn't want to be around when it gained full strength or there would be more unneeded deaths, but they needed to make sure the Heartstone was kept away from Larix. Raphia enlisted the help of the shepherd, and they travelled to meet with the remaining Teneo."

"At the meeting a few days later, the shepherd brought out the Heartstone. As soon as it entered the room with the Teneo, it exploded. Although it was a small explosion, it hurt the shepherd. After helping the shepherd and trying to destroy the Heartstone, the Teneo understood that they couldn't be anywhere near it, so they had to enlist the help of Mankind. Mankind would have to protect it from Larix, under the guidance of the Teneo, in order to ensure the safety of all. That's how the Sentinel League began."

"Why didn't you destroy it?" asked Mark.

"We tried many times, especially after it spent its energy and was weak. Nothing we did had any effect. We even buried it deep in the Arizona desert and hoped it would be gone forever. We had been storing it in a cave for many years without issue, so we didn't foresee any problems. A day later it exploded; leaving a large crater that people still believe was made by a meteor. Luckily, no one was hurt. In the end, too many attempts killed too many good people, so we decided to quit trying. That's when we started constructing locations to hide it, far enough underground that it won't be set off if a Teneo stood directly over it."

"Why not put this Larix guy in jail? Or kill him?" asked Jimmy.

"Well, we aren't that easy to kill, and it goes against all that we believe. We have had him in jail a few times, but he talked his way out more than once."

"So Larix is looking for the Heartstone? He's the reason all of the people are missing in Waldron and Langenburg?" asked Adam.

"Yes," answered Elianora.

"Did the Heartstone cause the explosions at Tunguska and Halifax?" asked Mark, changing the subject.

Elianora nodded. "At Tunguska we retrieved the Heartstone with great difficulty and the loss of many lives. After that explosion, it took a week to find the Heartstone again. Halifax was just an accident while transporting the Heartstone, not explosives as we reported in the story afterward. Luckily, the explosion threw the Heartstone onto the mainland instead of into the ocean. We found it a few days later."

"So you brought it to Grayson after that?" asked Mark.

Elianora smiled. "No. We moved it back overseas into Africa for a while. We thought Larix would hear about the explosion and come to search for the Heartstone here. It didn't come back until much later. In the meantime, we had built sites all over the world to hide it, and we move it around every few years."

"Who knows where it is right now?" asked Mark.

"At the moment - me," she stated. "The fewer people that know, the easier it is to keep secret. I've found that out the hard way too many times."

"Is it here in Grayson?" asked Adam.

"Under normal circumstances, I wouldn't answer that question, but we aren't under normal circumstances. Yes, the Heartstone is nearby. Larix is here to find it in any way possible. I didn't expect him to come for a few more days, though. The fog he is using keeps people out as much as in. It disrupts any electronics, but does more than that. I think they release a gas inside the area. This gas turns people into what you would call 'zombies', stuck in a dream world and half asleep. In that state, he can get answers from them without a lot of effort on his part."

"Are you sure?" asked Adam.

"Pretty sure, but not completely. I know of the gas, but it is a Teneo secret that was leaked or discovered by Larix somewhere else."

"Is there a cure or a vaccination?" asked Mark.

"Yes. I was going to have all the Senior members start taking it tomorrow, but I guess I'm too late."

"So why are you telling us all of this?" asked Adam. "We're just Junior Initiates."

Elianora paused and looked Adam straight in the eyes. "Because I need you to help protect the Heartstone," she said.

The statement shocked the boys.

"Us? Why?" said Adam.

"Because you're young and Larix will overlook you if you're caught," she said in a flat tone.

Adam looked at the others, then back to Elianora. "Is it hidden in the tunnels?"

"No, it's actually hidden outside of town."

They all relaxed a little, relieved that they didn't have to go back into town.

"But the key to finding it is still in town. One of the members knows where the key is hidden, and if Larix finds the key he is one step closer to finding the Heartstone. If you can get the key and bring it back to me, I can keep it away from him and he won't be able to get the Heartstone."

Adam tensed up again. It wasn't going to be easy.

"I'm sorry to have to ask you to do this, but it's the only way I can think of. The member in question was supposed to leave on a holiday tomorrow so he wouldn't be around if something like this happened."

Adam thought for a moment. "Karl," he said.

Elianora nodded. "After your dad died, I chose Karl to move the Heartstone when the time came for it to go somewhere else. He had the right 'skills'. It was meant to move recently, but due to an oversight on my part, it had to stay. Now, I have to make some quick decisions and I have decided to ask you for help. Will you help me?"

The boys looked at each other and Adam nodded for the group.

"Good. The key is hidden in the clock tower at Town Hall. It is the reason the clock hasn't worked for the last ten years. I won't let anyone fix it while the key is there."

"Great," said Mark. "How are we supposed to get back into town without getting caught?"

She smiled kindly at Mark. "Through the tunnels of course. You already know your way around them pretty well, so it should be easy."

Again, Adam was surprised. How did she know they were in the tunnels?

She walked over to the jars and bottles and pulled a jar from the shelf. She opened it and pulled out some leaves. "Eat this and you shouldn't fall asleep if you come in contact with the gas...I'm pretty sure..."

They each took a leaf and hesitated. Adam was the first to put it into his mouth and the others watched him as he began to chew. The look on Adam's face told the others that the leaf was far from pleasant.

"It's extremely bitter," said Elianora.

Jimmy and Kevin popped the leaf into their mouths and started chewing. Mark hesitated, and then finally followed the others lead. He had the worst reaction of all, mainly for dramatic effect.

"Does Larix know about the tunnels?" asked Jimmy after getting over the taste.

"Yes, but not these ones in particular. Each site was built differently, and these tunnels are just a way of moving around easier without being seen. We tried to make these ones confusing, but you seemed to get around in them easy enough. Larix and his men aren't in the tunnels yet, but it won't be long until they are. You'll need to get the key quickly and get back here." She walked over to the other side of the cave and searched through some books. She found a piece of paper and handed it to Adam.

"Study this map carefully. It shows all of the tunnels that are available to use. You haven't gone to the school yet, or into the Fire Hall. If you have to go into the Fire Hall, the key code for the alarm is 2053. As you can see, there is a tunnel from the school to my house. It comes out in my shed. The tunnel that leads to Town Hall is in the barn."

Adam noted the tunnel leading to the school.

"How do we get up to the clock tower?" asked Mark.

Jimmy answered, "As far as I know, the only way is in

Jeff's office. There's a ladder built into the wall that leads up to the attic."

Elianora nodded.

"That's gotta be 15 feet straight up," said Mark, not too happy with the knowledge.

"I don't think we all need to go get the key," said Adam. "I'll go by myself. The less people involved, the less likely we'll get caught."

"I think we should come and at least be lookouts for you," said Kevin.

"I'm fine with staying here," said Mark. Jimmy nodded his head in agreement with Mark.

"Adam is right," said Elianora, "less people equals less chance of being discovered. I do think you need at least one person to keep watch for you, and I am pretty sure Kevin already volunteered."

Kevin smiled and nodded, as did Adam. Mark and Jimmy seemed happy that they could stay where it seemed safe.

"You two won't be sitting here sipping lemonade, though," said Elianora, "I need your help getting ready for when they return."

She walked over and selected another jar from the shelf, then grabbed a paint brush that was tucked behind. "Give me your shoes," she said to Kevin and Adam.

They looked at each other, shrugged, then handed them over. They would have been quieter going barefoot in the tunnels, but it wouldn't have been very comfortable to untrained feet.

Elianora opened the jar, coated the brush in the black substance inside and applied it to the bottom of the shoes. All watched in silence as she grabbed a small spray bottle from the shelf and sprayed a mist on the coating. She fanned her hands over the base of the shoes, then handed them back.

"Put them on," she said, so they did.

"Jump up and down."

They jumped up and down lightly then harder. Whatever coating she put on the shoes cancelled out the sound of their feet hitting the ground. The only sound they made while jumping was the movement of their clothes.

"That's amazing!" said Mark, "Can you do mine?"

Elianora smiled, "It's called sealing. It seals the noises in and won't let them out." She looked to Mark, "Once those two leave I will seal yours and Jimmy's shoes."

She turned to Adam and Kevin. "That will keep you quiet when walking through the tunnels. Just beware of your breathing and clothes. Do you know how to light the tunnels?"

"Yes, but is there a way to turn it on without blinding ourselves," asked Kevin.

"Men - all the same," stated Elianora. "You have to turn the Lumiens on slowly. They are asleep until you start them up, but if you go too fast they send out a mean pulse of light. Just swipe slower in an upward motion. Too slow and they won't respond."

"So they *are* alive?" asked Mark.

"Yes, Mark, so treat them like living creatures. We've had them for a few centuries, although adapting them to this climate was a challenge." She paused, realizing she was getting off topic.

"Anyway, you need to get going. Follow me," she said and brushed past them hurrying toward the entrance.

As Adam turned to follow, he thought he saw a door behind the shelves filled with bottles. He hadn't seen any other tunnels on the map, so he decided it must be a storage area.

Up the stairs and out of the house they jogged, and soon they were at the entrance of the old barn. It was dark outside, like the light of a midday storm. Elianora opened the barn door with little effort and waved the boys through.

"You need to get to back here as soon as you can. Be quiet when you are in the attic. Your footsteps won't give you away, but those old creaking boards might. Go to the front. When you are near the clock mechanism, look up and to the left of the clock face. There's a wooden box there that is out of place. You'll need your dad's lapel pin to open it, just place it on the picture and slide it toward the center. If you slide it too far or not enough it won't open, so it'll take a few tries."

Adam was surprised. "How did you know I had the pin?"

Elianora replied, "Not important right now. You need to go." She pointed at the door. "Make sure you close the sliding doors gently behind you or you'll let everyone know you are there. Oh, and one last thing. When it looks like you are at a dead end in this tunnel, crouch down and use your hands to find the opening. It'll be on your lower right a few paces behind. It'll be the same when you return."

Adam remembered something. "How do we get into Town Hall from this side? The lock doesn't work."

Elianora smiled. "The lock sticks a little. Before you place the pin, pull the door closed tight with the handle."

Adam felt bad because he should have thought of that.

Without another word, she ushered them through the door and slid it shut behind.

CHAPTER TWENTY-TWO

Adam slid his hand slowly up the wall and the Lumiens responded better than the previous times. The light grew brighter without giving them the feeling of burned retinas they had experienced before.

It was strange walking at first, as they made very little sound now that their footsteps were quiet. Soon they figured out how to step with their arms slightly away from their bodies and legs spread apart. They made no sound that either of them could hear above their own heartbeats.

The tunnel wound back and forth in the same fashion as all of the others, and looked as though they were going to hit a dead end at any moment. Elianora's farm was a long way out of town, even if you went straight across country, so they knew they were in for a long walk.

At one point the tunnel led deeper into the earth and stayed that way for a long time. Once it came back up again, Adam thought they must be getting close to the junction, but it still continued for a long distance. They stopped twice to rest, sitting in silence each time before continuing.

As they were feeling like it would never end, Adam

noticed a change and slowed down. "I think we're here, but I want to touch the wall before I'll believe it."

He took a few paces forward and touched the dead end. *Finally*, he thought. He turned and took a step in the opposite direction, crouched and felt the wall for the opening. A few more steps back he found it. He was amazed how well it was hidden, even though it was big enough for them to crawl through.

"I wouldn't believe it if I didn't feel it for myself," said Adam.

He crawled into the opening. It was dark, since there were no Lumiens in the crawlspace. As he looked to the right he saw some light ahead, so he crawled toward it with Kevin close behind. Soon they had crawled out of the other end and stood in the opposite tunnel.

The tunnel they had exited into was a mirror image of the one they had just left. If you didn't know about the crawlspace, it would be easy to mistake the tunnel as incomplete.

They walked away from the dead end and after a few steps they passed the ring tunnel intersection. Their pace quickened, knowing they were nearly there, and within a short time they stood at the file room door.

Adam followed Elianora's instructions and it worked. Moments later he was stepping through the door to the file room. Kevin closed the door behind him without a sound as Adam lowered the drawbridge door. The file room ceiling was lit by the Lumiens as well, which made it easier to find the drawbridge door, but the storage room on the other side was dark except for the light streaming from the opening.

"When we get to the storage room door I'll turn on the

lights for when we come back, but we'll have to stay in the dark on the other side. I think we should leave the basement lights off, just in case. We can follow the wall to the stairs," said Adam.

Kevin nodded his understanding.

Adam wound his way through the box maze and turned on the lights, soon followed by Kevin. The drawbridge door closed behind him, too soon to have been activated by the timer.

"I just pulled up on the door and it closed," said Kevin. "It's a habit, I guess."

Adam smiled at Kevin and opened the door. They slipped through and hugged the wall, shuffling along until they found the corner. By luck or by design, the path along the wall was clear all the way to the stairs. Before reaching them, they saw faint light coming from the stairwell. The lights seemed to be on in Town Hall, which meant there might be people inside.

Adam listened at the stairwell for a few moments. He heard faint voices, but they sounded too far off to be inside. Jeff's office was across the hall from the stairs, so it would be easy for them to cross as long as the building was empty.

Adam crept up the stairs and peeked around the corner, looking down the hallway toward the front doors. The lights were off, but daylight was streaming in from the windows. He found it eerie, since it had been nearly dark at Elianora's.

The voices were coming from outside, and one sounded like a drill sergeant choreographing troop movements.

Adam and Kevin wasted no time getting to Jeff's

office door. Adam turned the handle, but the door was locked.

Oh no, thought Adam as he started to panic. They couldn't break down the door as the noise would alert whoever was outside. Images of capture began to fill his mind.

After he shook off the fear, a thought struck him. He fumbled through his pocket, pulled out the key he had made for the main door and wiggled it in the lock.

It worked.

They slid inside and shut the door with a gentle nudge, locking it behind them. Their hearts pounded as they looked at each other and nodded while taking a calming breath.

Once inside the office, they could see outside through the window. The window looked out the back of the building and they were happy they couldn't see people in that direction. It was bright but hazy outside and the light was almost as eerie as the darkness they had just left at Elianora's.

"Where's the ladder?" asked Adam.

Kevin pointed up to the attic access hole and down the wall beneath it. "It has to be there," he said.

The ladder to the attic was on the outside wall beside the dividing wall to the next room. It had been built out of wall bricks, alternating one recessed with one that was flush. It was difficult to see as it was the same color as the rest of the wall. Both agreed; it didn't look safe.

"I think I know another reason the clock never got fixed," said Kevin.

Adam walked to the ladder and looked up. He really didn't like the thought of climbing it, but knew he had to. He looked at Kevin, shrugged his shoulders and started to climb. When he reached the attic hatch, he tried to lift the cover. It wouldn't even budge. *There must be something heavy on the other side*, he thought. He tried twice more and climbed back down.

"I can't open it. Hopefully you can," Adam said to Kevin.

Kevin looked up, then back at Adam. "Really? ...This is gonna suck," he said, and then climbed the ladder with slow precise movements. At the top, he made sure to secure his feet then pushed hard. He held back none of his power, but had the same luck as Adam. Next, he took a step down and paused while looking up at the hatch. A few seconds later he came back down.

"It has to be locked. There are some scratches on the far side of the hatch, away from the ladder. Do you think it's locked like the door at the monitoring station?" asked Kevin.

Adam mentally kicked himself for not thinking of it while he was up there the first time. It made sense. Up the ladder he climbed, pin in hand so he didn't have to fumble through his pockets at the top. As he climbed, he looked at the attic cover. Once he was halfway up he saw the scratches Kevin had mentioned.

At the top, Adam reached out and slid the pin across the scratches, starting from the outside toward the middle, then pushed up on the hatch. Nothing. He tried the pin again and heard some movement on the other side. Again he pushed up and still couldn't move the hatch. The third time, he tried moving the pin slower while pushing slightly upward at the same time. Once he had moved the pin about an inch, the hatch popped up slightly. Success!

He pushed the hatch open completely and noticed a handle he could grab to pull himself into the attic, so he waved down at Kevin who began climbing. Once he was in the attic, it took a moment for his eyes to adjust to the low amount of light. He then offered a hand to Kevin and helped him up.

"I'm not afraid of heights, but you have to admit – that's a scary climb," said Kevin.

Adam nodded in agreement. "You get to go down first so I'll have something to land on if I fall," he said as he closed the hatch.

There were only three windows in the entire attic, two small ones at the front and one at the back. Thankfully, the one at the back was large and let in a reasonable amount of light. The attic was nearly empty, with only a few boxes scattered about. They could see the clock's mechanical assembly at the front in the center, with a window on either side.

As they took a few steps through the rafters, the rafters creaked and cracked under the weight, sounding as though they wouldn't hold the boys for long.

"And now we know one more reason the clock hasn't been fixed," said Kevin in a hushed voice.

Adam stopped. "I'll go the rest of the way alone. There's less chance of falling through that way. I'll let you know if I need you."

Kevin nodded.

Having less weight on the rafters, Adam could walk slow enough that there were no more creaks.

As he approached the front, he saw the box Elianora spoke about. She didn't tell them that it happened to be located high on the front wall, near the roofline. The closer he stepped to the front, the more Adam realized that he would need to figure out a way to climb up to it, as there was no ladder nearby.

At the front, Adam glanced out the small window. What he saw scared and amazed him. Most of the townspeople stood in a large group facing Town Hall. They stood and swayed together, as if they were snakes hypnotized by a snake charmer. Marius and his family were near the front. The Guptas were near the middle, along with the Chens. Mike and Charity Baranov and the girls were near the back, off to the side, but there was no sign of Kassie. He scanned the crowd, recognizing all of them, but searching out the few he knew best. The Jones family wasn't there yet, so maybe Kassie was with them. His mother was missing as well.

Four men ran up the side of the crowd toward Town Hall. They wore clothes that seemed to blend into the scenery around them. The clothes had made it difficult to see them unless they moved. They carried a large cylinder with a flat plate on the front. A battering ram!

"Open it," sounded a voice directly below where Adam stood. The clock tower was built into the overhanging part of the building jutting out from Town Hall. Adam had forgotten about the design of the building and worried that the voices heard him as he walked to the window. He turned to Kevin and signalled for him to stay still and be quiet.

Bang! They heard the men hit the door with the battering ram, but it still sounded solid. Bang! After the second hit, the blunt noise ended with the sharp splintering sound of wood breaking. A few softer blows, probably kicks, sounded through the building, and the double doors could be heard slamming open.

"It's ready for you sir," Adam heard a slightly muffled voice say directly below him.

"Give me a few minutes and start bringing them in," said the voice that seemed to be in charge. He had a distinct accent, however slight. German or Russian, Adam thought.

"Yes sir," came the reply. Adam watched as the man walked to the front of the crowd, followed by the three other men.

They began lining up the townspeople. Lacey and her family were the first in line, and not far after was Marius and family. Karl was easy to spot near the back. Adam realized the townspeople were being questioned to find the Heartstone, and since Marius knew Elianora, he would point the intruders right to her and the tunnels. They had to act fast.

Adam decided to risk it, so he stepped over to the framework containing the clock mechanism. As he looked at it, he saw that he could use the metal frame and the boards on the wall to climb up to the box. He climbed the structure as fast as he could while still being quiet. When he made it to the box, he couldn't see where the pin could be used to open the box. He examined all exposed sides and the bottom, finally deciding to climb one step higher and look at the top.

There it was; the mark Elianora had spoken about. He took the pin and tried opening the lid, but it was difficult. Trying to work the pin, lift the lid, and hang on without falling took a lot of effort. He kept trying and was getting tired and frustrated. Finally, he pulled up on the lid while he slid the pin, and it worked. The lid popped open, but in the process it launched the pin in the air, bouncing it against the front wall. Adam grabbed for it and fumbled, knocking it into the open box. Luckily, the pin was small enough that it didn't make a lot of noise to alert those outside or below.

He reached into the box and felt the pin on top of something soft. He grabbed the pin and put it in his pocket, then reached back inside the box. Next, he pulled out a small bag with a drawstring on the end and shoved it in his pocket too. His hand searched the box again, and when he was satisfied it was empty, he descended the same way he had climbed up.

Adam stepped carefully back toward Kevin. He motioned for Kevin to move to the attic hatch. He heard the odd small creak as he stepped and hoped no one below heard anything. There hadn't been any talking coming from below which made him concerned.

When he reached the attic hatch where Kevin waited, he stopped, taking a few deep breaths.

"They're inside," he whispered to Kevin.

Kevin nodded, "I guessed that. What did you see?"

"The whole town is lined up outside. I think they're going to question them *here*," said Adam.

"My family..."A horrified look came over Kevin's face.

Adam nodded. Kevin hunched over in sadness for a second then straightened up again, ready to go.

"What do we do?" he asked.

Adam shrugged. He'd been trying to come up with a plan that didn't require an insane amount of luck. "We just have to go down and risk it. I found the key, so now we have to get it to Elianora."

Kevin nodded.

"Let's go," said Adam reaching for the latch.

Before he touched it, a voice on the main level yelled, "Over here."

Adam pulled his fingers away.

Bang! The men below used the battering ram on Jeff's door, shattering it open with the first hit.

Footsteps ran into the room below.

They heard us! We've been caught! thought Adam.

CHAPTER TWENTY-THREE

Adam's heart pounded in his chest and echoed in his head. The sound made it difficult to hear what was happening below as the men seemed to be searching for them in Jeff's office.

"There's the attic," said a voice directly below, causing the boys even more panic.

Adam reached down to the latch mechanism and held it in place.

The hatch jumped a little as someone tried to open it with a hit, then another. "Won't budge," said the voice on the other side of the piece of wood that seemed thinner each moment.

"The whole place has been gassed. Just tell them to come down," came the reply from further below.

A throat cleared on the other side of the hatch. "Whoever is in the attic, come to the hatch and open it," said the closest voice.

The boys looked at each other wide-eyed in fear. It wasn't easy to defy direct orders from an adult, even if they *were* teenage boys. Adam shook his head slightly, telling Kevin that he wasn't opening the hatch for anyone.

The next few seconds of silence stretched on, and it made Adam's mind wander. He pictured the men bringing in a tall ladder and somehow using the battering ram to smash open the hatch. They would take the pin and the key. Adam and Kevin would both be tortured, giving up Elianora's location along with the knowledge of the Heartstone being in Grayson.

"Come down. No one's up there," said the lower voice. "We would've heard them by now. We have other rooms to check."

They don't know we're here, thought Adam, relieved a little, but knowing they were still stuck.

They listened until the footsteps left the room and another door was smashed open before he took his hand off the latch. Adam realized that Elianora's leaves were working, as he and Kevin weren't responding to any commands.

"Anyone in the basement, come up now," they heard a voice say. One of the men was standing at the basement stairs. He would have to move before the boys could attempt climbing down and crossing the hall.

A few more long moments passed. The man by the stairs walked up the hallway saying, "Basement is clear." A few more doors opened and closed followed by another voice saying, "All clear."

Yet another voice spoke from nearby. "The building is clear. Shall we start?"

"Of course," replied the voice of the leader.

Adam realized that the leader was in the boardroom next to Jeff's office. That's why they could hear him so clearly. The attic hatch was in the corner of Jeff's office nearest to the boardroom wall, and the walls were thin.

Adam decided that they would need to stay still until the leader began questioning people and hoped that the leader's concentration on questioning would hide the noise of their escape.

"Come in, sit down," said the leader, but his accent had changed. He now had an English accent like Elianora's. The voice must belong to Larix, Adam decided.

Some feet shuffled closer, and Adam realized that Larix was at the head of the boardroom table closest to the shared wall.

"Tell me about your family, please," said Larix, sounding pleasant.

"I'm Bob Lang, this is my wife Donna and our only child Lacey," said Bob. His voice sounded weak, almost as if he were drunk.

"Good, now tell me something no one else knows," said Larix again.

"We were disappointed for years that Lacey was a girl and we couldn't have a boy. We haven't been able to have any more children."

Adam didn't listen as Bob went on. The time had come to start moving. He opened the hatch and with slow deliberate movements stepped down the ladder. Kevin did the same, closing the hatch behind him.

Adam's mind was torn between what he had heard and escaping. Obviously, the gas made people tell their most intimate secrets. Bob and Donna Lang had always seemed so proud of Lacey.

He pushed the thoughts from his mind as there were more immediate issues to think about. They needed to get to the stairs across the hall.

They crept to the door that was hanging half-open from being broken earlier. Adam listened at the hall and after hearing nothing, he peered up the hallway. It was clear, so he dashed across, stopping near the stair, hidden from the hallway but still visible to Kevin.

Had Adam hesitated a moment longer he would have been seen by the guard leading a group of people in to be questioned. The guard stopped the group in the hallway next to the boardroom door.

Adam heard them walk in but couldn't see who was in the group. He knew Marius and family would be questioned soon. Kevin was trapped and they couldn't risk him blindly jumping across the hall, so Adam would need to think fast.

Again Adam felt trapped. Anything he could think of doing resulted in either he or Kevin being discovered. He pushed his brain, trying to come up with options. Pictures paged through his thoughts, but most were dismissed soon after appearing.

One image appeared in his mind, and it came together making perfect sense. After a moment of reviewing his plan, Adam signalled to Kevin that he should hide behind the door and wait. Kevin looked confused, but shrugged his shoulders and did as Adam asked.

Adam disappeared down the stairs. At the bottom, he followed the wall back into the storage room and hurried back through to the drawbridge door. It seemed to open slower now that he was in a hurry. Across the file room he ran. He opened the sliding door, and once he stepped through, he slid it shut with barely a sound.

Next, Adam jogged through the tunnel until he made it to the first intersection. Remembering the map, he turned left then left again at the second intersection. He ran up the tunnel and soon was faced with the back of another drawbridge door.

I hope this works, he thought.

The door fell open fast revealing another dark room, but Adam had no flashlight. In the light from the tunnel he saw a set of stairs straight across a large empty space. He ran across the empty room and put his foot on the first step before the drawbridge door closed, cutting off the only source of light. That door closed much sooner than the one to the file room.

In the darkness, he climbed until the hand he stretched out front came in contact with something. It had to be a door, he thought, so he felt along the wall for a light switch. He reasoned that there should be one nearby, and he was right.

The door in front of him was nearly new and looked as though it didn't have a lock. He tried the handle, but it wouldn't open. Being a new door, there were no marks to guide his pin placement, so he tried a few locations until he finally heard the lock sliding.

He opened the door and stepped directly into the Fire Hall behind the fire trucks, then waved his hands while doing a sort of dance. If his friends had seen him, they would never have let him live down the odd movements he made.

But Adam's movements were as deliberate as a man doing the Tango, and within a few seconds he heard beeping. He knew he had accomplished what he wanted - he was going to set off the alarm. The alarm panel was giving time for the code to be entered, but if it wasn't entered soon, the alarm would sound.

Adam ran back through the door, making sure it shut behind him. He raced down the stairs and through the drawbridge door again, much quicker having light to see where he was going. He didn't worry about leaving the lights on as there were more important things to worry about. The alarm began to ring loudly and was muffled when the drawbridge door closed.

Back through the tunnels he ran, taking his first right and then the second right again. The file room sliding door was much easier to open since he knew the trick. Again he slid it closed behind him.

He lowered the drawbridge door, and to his surprise the lights were off. Panic set in until he saw Kevin making his way through the box maze. Once Kevin was inside, Adam closed the drawbridge.

"I turned off the light and waited, hoping you were coming back," said Kevin. "I figured I would be able to make it through the boxes with the light from in here, if you opened it up for me."

Adam smiled. "I wouldn't leave you unless I had no other choice."

"Thanks. The alarm sure caused a commotion. They all ran for the Fire Hall, including the main guy."

"Let's not sit here and chat, we have to move," said Adam. He jogged to the sliding door.

Back through the tunnels they ran, careful to take the correct tunnel at the junction. Finding the crawlspace proved difficult again, but soon they had crawled back to the other side. Once through, they slowed down to a strong walk.

"That guy was getting Bob Lang to tell him things you don't want to know and I want to un-hear," said Kevin. "But I did find out that Bob and Donna aren't members of the Sentinel League. They asked him and his wife a bunch of questions about Sentinel League and they didn't have a clue. He left Lacey alone, probably thinking she was too young to know anything."

"I'm glad about Lacey, but I can't believe how easily he made them talk. That's pretty scary. We need to get back to Elianora fast. Marius will be questioned soon and then they'll know about her and the tunnels," said Adam.

The return journey didn't seem any shorter than the first time they had travelled the tunnel, but when they saw the door their spirits lightened. They passed through the door, out of the barn and into the yard, where the eerie dark still hadn't lifted. It felt like passing into a whole different world.

"Where are they?" asked Kevin.

"Let's try the house," said Adam. "Mark will be as close to food as possible."

Kevin laughed, and they jogged over to the house.

Adam knocked. "Hello?"

"Come in, we're in the basement," came a voice from far and deep.

Adam and Kevin didn't waste any time getting through the house and into the basement cave. It felt like it had been days since they had left, even though it had been less than an hour. Mark and Jimmy carried boxes of bottles around the shelves into the door Adam had noticed earlier. Most of the cave was empty.

Elianora smiled as she spotted them. "Did you get it?" she asked.

Adam nodded and pulled the bag from his pocket, offering it to her.

She held up her hand, "You hang on to it for now."

Adam was confused, but put it back in his pocket.

"How did it go?" she asked.

Kevin spoke first, "We almost got caught, and when I was trapped, Adam set off the alarm in the Fire Hall to create a diversion."

"We heard that. We wondered what was going on," said Jimmy.

"Resourceful, just like your dad," Elianora said to Adam.

"They're questioning people in Town Hall. Marius and his family are near the front of the line," said Adam, even though he really wanted to ask her more about Edward.

"Why does Larix's accent change?" he asked instead. The question had been bothering him.

"That's part of his 'special' talent. Some accents make people more trusting, while others are better for intimidating."

Adam nodded, understanding.

"It won't take long for them to figure out where I am, so we need to get out of here quick."

"Where are we going?" asked Mark.

"I need Adam to come with me, but I'm going to send the rest of you back into the tunnels. When Larix's men find the entrance to the tunnels, they will probably take those townspeople that have already been questioned and put them in the meeting hall – that large room you were in once," she said looking at Adam.

Adam felt strange. How did she know they had been in that room, and why did he need to go with her?

"By the time you get there, there should be enough other people in the room that you can pretend to be gassed and sit with them. The guards won't notice you since they aren't concerned with kids," she continued.

"Is that what happened at Langenburg and Waldron? The missing people are in the tunnels?" asked Kevin.

"I am fairly certain, but I haven't been able to confirm. Back to our current problem, though. Once Larix is gone, Jimmy and Mark have some of the leaves I gave you earlier. They will wake everyone up."

Jimmy and Mark nodded.

"What are *we* going to do?" asked Adam.

"I have a place where we can hide and watch the entrance to the Heartstone's location. I'll tell you more once we get there. Now, follow me and we'll get the rest of you going," said Elianora, turning and walking out of the cave.

The group followed her out of the house and over to the shed. The shed was partially built into the hill, the same as the barn. It looked identical to Ben Casey's tool shed. They followed Elianora to the back wall where various gardening tools were hung above a familiar workbench. She pulled up on the workbench and swung it away from the wall revealing another sliding door.

"This one leads to the school. When you get to the basement, you need to go down the hallway to your left in order to find the entrance to the tunnel. Between the two are stairs that lead to the staff room,"

"I always knew there had to be a secret room in the school," said Jimmy. "Mr. Forster would disappear a few times a day. Must have been League business."

"Actually, he just didn't like kids and would hide in the storage room to cope," said Elianora.

They all looked puzzled.

"Why would you become a teacher if you didn't like kids?" asked Kevin.

Elianora shrugged. "You can ask him in the future. Right now, you need to go."

Outside the shed, they heard the approach of galloping horses, quite a few of them by the sound.

"No, they're here already!" she exclaimed. "You have to go, now!" She chased the boys into the tunnel then paused to think.

"You too, Adam." She pushed him into the tunnel with his friends.

Adam looked at her, confused.

"Their gas won't work on me, and neither does Larix's sweet talk, but if they tie me up and search me, I can't have the key. We need to keep it away from Larix, and the best way I can think of is for you to hide with the others and pretend you're gassed until they move on."

"Why don't you tell us where to find the Heartstone? We can get it and run away!" said Adam.

"No. You're too young and it's too much pressure. It drove George nearly insane, and your dad...It's well protected. You go hide with your families and I'll deal with this. Just keep the key away from Larix at any cost." She motioned for them to go, but stopped Adam.

"If something happens to me, go find Brutus in Killaly," she whispered in his ear so the others wouldn't hear.

"We'll do our best," said Adam, nodding to Elianora.

As Adam fumbled for the pin to open the sliding door, a familiar voice yelled from outside.

"Hanelore! Come talk to an old friend."

It was Larix, still in his English accent.

Adam slid the door open and stepped in the tunnel, letting the other three pass by. Elianora slid the workbench shut behind them, but Adam kept the sliding door open. He saw light coming from under the bench, so he bent down to look. There were gaps between the boards where he could see.

Elianora was facing the other way. She straightened her clothes and took a step to the doorway.

"I'm not sure old *friend* describes it correctly," she said stepping to the entrance of the shed.

Adam heard someone dismount from their horse and take a couple of steps forward. He assumed it was Larix.

"Hannelore, Hannelore, lovely as ever," said Larix.

"Elianora now, actually," she responded.

"Of course. You always did fancy a new name after our meetings...like getting a new hair style...Elianora suits you."

Elianora said nothing, creating an awkward silence.

"I've been searching for you," said Larix.

"So I've heard," said Elianora, "but I don't think *I'm* what you're really looking for."

"Come come now, of course I want to see you. You *are* my oldest friend. Besides, we *are* a part of history. The Commons still call us 'Adam and Eve' in their stories, don't they?"

Adam was trying to process what he just heard. *The* Adam and Eve?

"Don't use that word. You know I hate it," Elianora said calmly, but there was a bite to the words.

"Sorry. Old habits. *Mankind* still thinks of you as their mother, even though you're so much more than that."

Elianora brushed off the comments as though she hadn't heard them.

"Last I heard, you were slithering around in the Middle East trying to start a new war," said Elianora.

Larix laughed, "I've forgotten how connected you are. Yes, I did spend some time there trying to create some excitement. It is surprising how people who are so easily angered by the little things are so hard to motivate into taking larger action."

"The last time you did that, it didn't seem to work out for your side now, did it?" said Elianora.

"Well, we didn't expect the overwhelming cooperation against us. Even an elephant can be defeated by enough fire ants...Adolph was a powerful speaker, and I guess we tried for too much too soon. If only he had kept it together we could've turned it back around, but no, the weak Comm...*human* in him gave up and wanted to surrender," said Larix.

"Did you even feel anything when you shot him and Ava?" asked Elianora.

Adolph...Ava? They're talking about Adolph Hitler and Ava Braun! Larix was there? thought Adam.

"Of course I did! How you underestimate me so...I regretted not finding a better spokesman. But that's all history now. I don't have the need to kill the humans anymore or drive fear into their hearts. It's become rather boring. They seem to be bent on destroying themselves anyway. Have you seen what they eat? I mean, really – even I, as a near immortal, wouldn't eat that way. And they've become so lazy that when they have offspring, they let the children make all the decisions! I mean, it shouldn't take more than a couple of generations at this point for them to destroy themselves." He laughed like he had just heard a light hearted joke, and it sounded creepy.

"There's still a lot of good in them. They've come a long way in the last hundred years. It won't take long before they have a better understanding of the sciences than we do, and you know it," said Elianora.

"My dear...Elianora, is it? You always see more in them than they are in reality. Like the 'scholar' who finds hidden meaning in the writings of Nostradamus. You and I both know he was just insane," Larix laughed. "Look at Stonehenge. They're still trying to decipher it all these years after I built it, and think it has some 'hidden meaning' where there is none. I was merely bored! I love to laugh at some of the reasons they dream up!"

"You've always had a twisted sense of humor," said Elianora.

"That depends on your point of view, my dear," said Larix.

Adam listened to the silence. He had the feeling that Elianora and Larix were staring each other down like gunfighters in the old west.

"Well, there's no point in waiting any longer. Where is it?" asked Larix.

"I don't have it," said Elianora.

"I've been talking with a lot of people lately. That's not the stories I've heard."

"I guess people have just found hidden meaning where there is none," Elianora replied.

"I don't want to have to force it out of you. I know it is on this continent. I should have realized it when I heard about the explosion in Halifax years ago. I thought the Heartstone had been destroyed in Tunguska, so you can forgive my lapse."

Silence again.

"I did recently find out that your friend Raphia was on the other ship in Halifax Harbor that day. It had to be the smallest of chances that the ship he was on happened to brush too close to the ship carrying my prize."

More silence.

"It's not like you to be this quiet. You usually like to verbally skewer me for a while...Anyway, I realize you won't talk, even if I kill off every *human* in this town. I mean, if they only knew the danger you put them in! At any moment if you were to mistakenly get too close to the Heartstone, it would explode and wipe the whole place off the planet. Knowing that, they would have been less likely to help you hide it all these years."

"They have understood the dangers the entire time," she said in a firm voice.

"So come then, tell me where to find it," said Larix. His accent was weaker, becoming almost neutral, like the voice of a North American politician.

"It's not here. It was destroyed. End of story."

"I'm not surprised you're sticking to that story, but I have it on good authority that you are lying to me in the boldest way. There are still visions of the Heartstone deep in your old friend George's mind. He was your Number 2 at one point, was he not?"

Larix found George! thought Adam. *I hope George is alright.*

Elianora must have been surprised by that information.

"I was merciful to him; he pointed me here, after all. That, plus what you put him through before me is surprising, especially for you. It's all still in there, buried deep. You'll be happy to hear that I could only read it, not bring it out. How you buried it in his mind I don't know. Maybe you could show me sometime."

"You're the last person I'll show anything to," said Elianora.

"Don't refer to me as a *person. I* am so much more than that," said Larix, the temper flaring in his voice as it changed from an English accent to a slight Austrian one.

"All these years and one little word gets you upset," said Elianora. "Sounds like you could use some sensitivity training."

Larix laughed, but it was a cold and sharp laugh. "You really have spent too much time with these *people*," he spat out the last word as Adam heard him walking closer.

"So, my friend," said Larix, "you really aren't going to tell me where it is, are you."

"I told you. It was destroyed."

"Well then, you leave me no choice," said Larix.

A gunshot sounded.

Adam and his friends jumped at the loud noise that echoed through the small valley.

Elianora slumped over and fell to the ground.

CHAPTER TWENTY-FOUR

Adam watched through the small opening. *They killed her!* he thought.

Elianora was lying on the ground completely still. After a few seconds, to Adam's surprise, she began to move.

"Get up," said Larix.

She wobbled to her feet, swaying as she stood. She grabbed something from her front and dropped it on the ground. It looked like a dart. They didn't shoot her with a bullet, but some kind of needle.

"You've just been given a version of our sleeping gas. The only way it works on us is if we get injected. Now, tell me my dear, where is the Heartstone?" asked Larix.

Elianora continued to sway, "It's...It's..." she seemed to be fighting the chemical in her body. "It's...destroyed," she managed to say.

Another shot sounded in the valley.

"I thought you might need a higher dose. You've always been pretty stubborn," said Larix, still out of Adam's view.

Elianora didn't fall to the ground, but she didn't pull the second dart out either. She stopped swaying, her head hanging forward.

"Quickly now. Tell me where you hid the Heartstone," said Larix.

Elianora kept swaying slightly. In a slow motion, she struggled to raise her arm. It rose and fell, then rose again. Finally, with great effort, she pointed in a direction south-west of their current location and south of town. She muttered a word that Larix understood, but Adam only heard 'ray'-something.

"Much better. It's the first time that you've ever done something I've asked of you. I should've done this years ago," Larix said, sounding almost giddy.

"Knowing you, there are traps and puzzles to get it. What do I need in order to find it?"

She swerved and then spoke in a slow, weak voice, too quiet for Adam to hear.

It was too low for Larix as well. "What was that? Please speak up," he said.

"The key," she said, barely clear enough to understand.

"And where do I get the key?" asked Larix.

Adam could see that she struggled with herself, trying not to say anything, but she lost the battle.

"He has it," she said.

"Who?"

"Adam McTaggart," she said, pointing her finger at the spot he was hiding.

Even though they didn't see Elianora point, the other boys heard enough of the conversation to know what they had to do next.

Run.

Adam started the Lumiens enough that they could see, and they were off. Even Mark wasted no time complaining, as they were running out of fear and necessity.

It would be a long run to the school, judging how long it took to get to Town Hall through the other tunnel. It did the typical winding side to side that the other tunnels did, but sometimes it felt like it almost ran in a circle.

"How far is it?" asked Mark, puffing from the pace. They had slowed down to a jog a few minutes earlier.

"How do *we* know?" replied Kevin, almost angry.

"It shouldn't be too much longer," said Adam, puffing heavily, "but we need to have a plan."

They jogged on a little further, thinking as they moved.

"Let's go hide until they leave," said Mark.

"Where? They'll find us eventually. We don't know if the leaves wear off in time. That, and Elianora will just tell them who we are and they'll use our families as bait to draw us out," said Jimmy.

"Jimmy's exactly right," said Adam. "Give me a minute, I've almost got a plan."

Adam's mind flew though images of all that had happened so far. Town Hall, Elianora's Farm, Ben Casey's house, the Kurling game, the tunnels, the meeting room underground. Non-sequential speech, heard from multiple persons, echoed in the hallway of his mind.

Ahead, a sliding door appeared as they rounded a corner. Adam opened it and they slipped through, sliding it closed behind them and checking to make sure it was locked. They were in the school basement, a place they had only heard about and never seen.

Adam looked around, trying to find something. There weren't many things nearby other than some old wooden school signs against the far wall.

"Grab me that sign." Adam pointed to the one he wanted. It had a picture of the school painted on the front, and was mounted on a thick sheet of plywood.

Kevin brought the sign over to Adam and helped him flip it so the longer sides were up and down. They slipped the wood in between the door handle and the door frame. It was nearly a perfect fit.

No sooner had they fitted the sign and they heard running footsteps coming to the door and the mechanism working. They saw the door move slightly, but the sign held tight.

"It's gonna take them some time to get all the way back to Elianora's and then into town again, thankfully," said Mark.

"Let's not be here when they get here," said Jimmy.

Full of the adrenaline of fear, they made their way to the other door. Once Adam opened it he stopped in the doorway, looking at the mechanism.

"Anyone have any string?" he asked.

The others looked at each other, shrugging their shoulders, obviously not having any. Adam looked at the mechanism again, thinking. After a moment, he had an idea. He removed his shoe, then his sock, and put the shoe back on again.

"What are you going to do with that?" asked Mark.

"I've learned to watch and not question at times like these," said Kevin.

Adam ripped the sock, starting from a small hole at the toe, then tore it again, making a strip. He reached into the mechanism and worked for a moment.

"There. That'll work," he said as he stepped out of the door frame. He slid the door shut then slid it open again without the use of the pin.

"Why didn't you just use your shoelace?" asked Mark.

"If I have to run, I don't want my shoe falling off. I can run without a sock," replied Adam.

"Here's my plan, or as much of it as I can come up with," Adam began. "We need to split up. Jimmy, you go to your house and try to find your mom's pin like this, so we don't all have to stay together," he flashed the pin. "Once you find it, you can go through Town Hall and find Mark in the meeting room. If you can't find the pin at home, come back here and this door will be open so you can get in. Just make sure you leave a door open to the school."

Jimmy nodded.

"Mark, how long will it take to start waking people up? Elianora mentioned that she showed you how," said Adam.

"It can take anywhere from ten minutes to half an hour, she wasn't sure," said Mark.

"Ok, so you'll have to get at it pretty quickly. As soon as Jimmy gets there, he can help you."

"What if there are guards at the meeting room?" asked Mark.

Adam thought for a second. "Just act like you've been gassed. Wobble over to them slowly. They won't think anything of it because you're not 16 yet. They'll just put you in with the rest of the townspeople," he said.

"Just hang your head and moan like you do when your dad tells you he has chores for you," added Jimmy, getting a chuckle out of Kevin.

Mark gave him a look of scorn.

"You can do it, trust me. Start with your dad and other League members. Fill them in on what's happened and hopefully we can hold Larix off long enough that they can come up with a plan. If anyone comes to check on the prisoners, be sure to keep up the act, like Elianora told us to do. If you can't wake them for some reason, just sit with the others until Larix and his men leave, then start waking everyone up." said Adam.

"What are you and Kevin going to do?" asked Jimmy.

"Try and not get caught, that's what," answered Kevin.

Adam chuckled, "Something like that. They are going to be looking for me now that Elianora told them I have the key. Hopefully she doesn't say anything about the rest of you. Regardless, I'm not going to tell you what we're doing exactly."

The others looked at him perplexed.

"I've been thinking about this, and I understand why Elianora wouldn't tell anyone where the Heartstone was hidden. That was the only way to ensure Larix couldn't use a combination of chemicals and his talents to get the answer out of others. If I don't tell you what we're doing and you get caught and forced to talk, you can tell them you honestly don't know where we are or what we're doing."

They understood.

"Get going, and good luck," said Adam, ushering Mark through the sliding door.

"What about the door at the top of the stairs?" asked Jimmy.

"I'm betting you can unlock it from the inside without a key," said Adam, "but we're coming with you to start."

Adam closed the door on Mark, who looked like he was trying to act tough in his situation, then walked over to the stairwell. At the top, he saw that his assumption was right; the lock on the inside of the door didn't need keys. That would keep students (or a teacher) from getting locked down in the basement.

The Teacher's lounge was small and bare, with only a table and chairs next to an old couch and refrigerator. Adam grabbed a roll of clear packing tape from the counter.

"If Mark was here, he'd be raiding that fridge right now," said Kevin.

"Do you miss him already?" kidded Jimmy.

"Not as much as you miss your Barbie Princess Dream House," replied Kevin so fast that he must have been planning that one for a while.

Jimmy and Adam smiled at the jab, even though they were stressed.

They made their way into the dim hallway and then to the main exit door. Adam pushed the last one on the left open, unrolled a strip of tape and tore it with his teeth. He applied the tape to the latch and tested the door. It didn't lock anymore, so he held it open and motioned Jimmy out.

"Good luck," he said to Jimmy.

"Thanks, and be careful," Jimmy replied nodding at them.

Adam closed the door as Jimmy turned and ran.

CHAPTER TWENTY-FIVE

"What now?" asked Kevin.

Adam had a rough plan that again relied more on luck than he preferred.

"Now we go back to Elianora's and then we find the Heartstone," he replied.

Kevin looked surprised. "Are you crazy? Those men are in the tunnel back to Elianora's. Not to mention the fact that we don't know where the Heartstone is hidden and Elianora told us to keep the key away from Larix."

"They'll be trying to find me in town, so I don't think they'll be at Elianora's by the time we get there. We'll have to be quiet so we can be sure."

Kevin didn't look convinced.

"They'll expect us to hide in the tunnels or in town. Us going to get the Heartstone won't be what they expect. It should give us time to get it and get out of town. We can come back after we hear the fog is gone."

Kevin looked slightly more convinced than before. "That *sounds* reasonable. The only problem is we still have no idea where it's hidden."

"I've been thinking about that. I saw the direction Elianora pointed when Larix asked her where it was, and it confirmed my suspicion." Adam told Kevin the location he suspected, and Kevin's face showed enlightenment.

"On top of that, we have the key and they don't," said Adam.

"Speaking of the key, have you looked at it?" said Kevin.

Adam hadn't had a chance to think about the key yet, but now that Kevin mentioned it he thought he should take a look. He had felt a strange lump in the bag when he found it and figured it was probably a unique key, like all the other unique things associated with the Sentinel League. Right then, he had the time and the desire to take a look.

He pulled the bag from his pocket. The knot in the drawstring took a bit of work, but soon he opened the top, reached inside and drew out the key. When he opened his hand, both he and Kevin were surprised.

"It's just a pebble," exclaimed Kevin.

Adam chuckled. "I should have expected that. I knew it wouldn't be a regular key, but this one has me confused."

"Do you think someone found the real key and replaced it with this?" asked Kevin, pointing at the small stone.

"It's a possibility, I guess, but I doubt it. I have no idea how this works as a key, though." Adam's mind was going through possibilities as he spoke. *It could fit in a hole, or maybe it has some property we don't know about, like the aluminum magnet*, he thought.

"Maybe it's a Kurling rock that's easy to control," said Kevin.

"Good idea, I didn't think of that. Whatever it is though, I don't think we should waste time wondering right now. I'm sure we can figure it out when we need to," said Adam, not completely sure he could.

Adam placed the pebble back in the bag, then back in his pocket.

"Man, I hope you're right," said Kevin.

"Onward," exclaimed Adam.

Back through the teacher's lounge they jogged and through the door into the basement.

"I wonder what they tell the teachers about these sliding doors if they aren't part of the Sentinel League?" asked Kevin.

"If we get through this, we'll have to ask someone. I'll bet it's pretty good," said Adam.

He was quiet as he approached the door and listened for sounds on the other side. When he was almost certain it was clear, he removed the plywood sign and opened the door. The Lumiens were on and no-one was waiting to surprise them.

"We should be as quiet as possible on the way. I'll stop and listen every once in a while, just to make sure no-one is in here with us. The chances are that they won't come back down the tunnel, but there's no point risking it," said Adam.

Kevin nodded and they were on their way. They walked at a brisk pace, careful to make as little noise as possible. After a while, Adam stopped and listened for a few seconds. Hearing nothing, they continued at the same pace. That process repeated a number of times until they made it back to the door to Elianora's shed.

Adam listened at the door before opening it. That time he listened for a full minute, but it seemed like ten. The sound of the mechanism was like a fire alarm, at least to ears that were used to the silence. Even the door sliding open sounded like a freight train on rails.

The workbench on the other side of the sliding door was broken away, no longer giving Adam cover. He felt as if he were naked, although he was sure that Larix and his men had left the area. Kevin stayed back a few steps, just in case they had to run again.

Adam stuck his head out a little, like a gopher peeking out of a hole. He listened while he looked, and soon felt slightly safer. He signalled to Kevin, and when Kevin was at the door, Adam motioned for Kevin to hold it open so he could run into the tunnel if he was in trouble. Kevin understood and Adam stepped into the shed.

Although he felt certain no one was outside, Adam had an uneasy feeling in his gut as he peered out the shed door. He stayed still, looking around as meticulous as he could manage, but saw nothing. Then, without much thought, Adam jumped into the doorway and did a strange dance. A moment later he froze and searched the farmyard. If anyone saw him they would be chasing him down, but he saw no-one. He waited there for a full minute until he was sure he saw no movement.

"Come on out. Nobody's home," Adam said to Kevin.

Kevin walked over to Adam. "Why did you do that dance? You have a death wish?"

Adam chucked, "I knew if anyone was in the yard they would have chased me. You would have slammed the door behind me for an easy escape."

Kevin still looked confused. "Yeah, but don't you think it would be tough to run if you got shot by one of those darts they used on Elianora?"

Adam realized how lucky he was at that moment, turning red in the face. "Uh, yeah...I guess you're right. I never thought about that. Sorry."

Kevin brushed it off like it was no big deal, but both boys knew they needed to think before acting.

Adam surveyed the yard. If only there was some type of transportation available to get to their destination. It was a long way to get there, and he would prefer it if they didn't have to walk.

"Let's check the buildings and see if there's something we can drive," said Adam.

Kevin nodded and walked to the barn, while Adam went to the shed next to the garden. Besides the tool shed and the main house, those were the only two other buildings in the yard.

Adam opened the garden shed, and looked around. As he expected of Elianora, the building was tidy and well organized. The only mode of transportation he could see was the riding lawn mower, so he left to see what Kevin found.

Kevin was in one of the stalls, looking through a pile of stuff. The first time they came through the barn they didn't notice much, as their minds were occupied with other things. Now, they saw that Elianora had a lot stored in the barn. Again, in typical Elianora fashion, it all was placed perfectly and looked as though it had just been dusted, even being stored in an old barn. A lot of piles were covered with drop cloths.

"Anything?" asked Kevin.

"Not unless we want to ride the lawnmower," he replied.

"Maybe not. We can walk faster than that, plus it's so quiet out that they might hear it from town," said Kevin.

Kevin resumed looking and Adam went to the other side of the barn to start. It wasn't surprising to see that Elianora had collected many things, considering her age, but what she had stored in the barn would have been amazing to investigate if they had time. Paintings, pottery, goblets, and many statues were hidden under each of the drop cloths. Even to Adam's untrained eye, the quality of the pieces looked amazing. A lot of the art resembled Elianora. He didn't have time to look closely, though, so he kept searching until he met Kevin at the back of the barn.

"Do you think it's worth looking in the loft?" asked Kevin, pointing up at the access hole and the ladder built onto the wall.

"I'll take a peek," said Adam nodding. "If there's nothing, we need to start walking."

Adam climbed the ladder and stuck his head up through the hole. The windows in the loft let in just enough of the dim light from outside that he was able to see. He looked around for a few seconds then climbed into the loft.

"Hey, I thought you were just going to look," exclaimed Kevin.

"Find me a rope," said Adam from the loft. He had seen a bicycle and was looking around for a second one.

The bike he found was an old one, probably from the 70's. Even though it was old, it seemed to be in perfect condition. It was an adult bike with a large banana seat and high handlebars. The entire thing was painted with flowers, and the pedals were petals. Adam guessed that it was an art project of Elianora's and had never been driven.

"Found one," Kevin called up to the loft. "Do you want me to come up, or do you just want me to throw it to you?"

"Just chuck it up," said Adam. He picked up the rope after it landed in a heap on the floor.

"Couldn't you find me a bigger rope," said Adam, teasing Kevin. The rope was about an inch thick and 20 feet long.

"You said 'find me a rope'. I found you a rope. Nowhere in there did you give me specifications," Kevin shot back.

"It'll work perfect," said Adam, hoping Kevin realized he was just teasing. "Go wait under the hay loft door. I'm lowering something down,"

"What is it?"

"You'll see," said Adam. He walked over to the hay loft door and found the latch, opening it to see Kevin already waiting.

There was a pulley on the beam that stuck out above the hay loft door, but there wasn't a rope in it. It was beyond Adam's reach, so he couldn't thread the rope into the pulley. He decided that he would just have to tie the rope to the bike and lower it manually.

"Close your eyes and turn around until I tell you," said Adam.

Kevin gave him a questioning look, followed by a look that questioned Adam's sanity, and finally a look of compliance.

Adam wheeled the bike to the door then tied the rope to the frame.

"Ok, come and get it," said Adam.

Kevin turned and looked at the bike, then laughed.

Adam lowered the bike, and threw the rope down afterward. He closed the hay loft door and soon came out of the barn.

"Where's the one I'm going to ride?" asked Kevin, with a hopeful note in his voice. He was clearly not a fan of the flowery bike in front of him.

Adam shook his head, "This is it. We're going to have to double."

Kevin hung his head. "Really? Are you sure? I could just run."

"This will be the fastest way," said Adam. "It's in perfect shape and the seat is big enough for us both."

Kevin didn't look any happier. "Just promise me you'll never speak about this to anyone."

Adam chuckled. "Hey, I'm not exactly jumping up and down at the thought of riding a flowery girl's bike through the countryside with you, but at least there are no unicorns or streamers on it! I'm definitely not going to be telling this story as part of my 'How I spent my summer vacation' essay when school starts."

Kevin broke a smile, happy that Adam seemed uncomfortable too.

Adam squeezed the tires to check the inflation. Years of checking tires that way had made him a pretty good judge of pressure with only his fingers. He was surprised that they were inflated properly. Even the chain looked like it still had the factory grease on it.

"I'm driving," said Kevin.

Adam nodded. "We can trade off once in a while." He was nervous about being a passenger, as he had always driven and never had been a passenger on a bike.

Adam sat on the bike at the back of the seat, and Kevin sat on the front. It was uncomfortable already as there was nothing for Adam to hold on to. He put his hands on Kevin's sides and said, "Ready."

Kevin shook his head, kicked off and began pedaling. Adam was uncomfortable because he felt so little control on the back of the bike. Having nowhere to rest his feet made every bump vibrate from his butt all the way to his teeth. He couldn't wait for Kevin to tire out so he could have a turn at driving, but he knew Kevin was a workhorse who wouldn't tire easily.

On they rolled down the road, listening to the crunch of the wheels on gravel. Adam was lost in thought as they drove, wondering where he would find the entrance when they arrived. He knew the Heartstone would be underground, but how to get to it was a complete mystery.

Kevin slowed down and finally stopped. "Sorry, I can't do any more. Your turn."

Adam stepped off the bike and Kevin slid backwards. Adam had just noticed that it was now lighter out, as they were out of the shade from the haze surrounding Grayson. The summer sun would be up for a while yet.

Adam stepped back on again. "Ready?" he asked.

Kevin's hands grabbed Adam's sides. "Mark and Jimmy better not ever hear about this. We'd never hear the end," Kevin said.

"If it were them instead of us we wouldn't ever let them live it down, so you know I'll never say a word," replied Adam.

He kicked off and started pedaling. Kevin was surprised by the start and grabbed tight onto Adam's waist.

"Whoa there, you don't need to hang on *that* tight," said Adam.

Kevin relaxed his grip as they reached a steady pace. Adam struggled to keep the same speed as Kevin had maintained. Even though he rode his bike every day that the weather allowed, he felt the extra weight in his legs right away. He didn't know how he could make it very far, but kept pedaling. Thankfully for Adam, the road was flat and straight, unlike the hill Kevin powered up to get out of Elianora's valley. After a while, Adam found a pace a little slower than Kevin's, but he was able to maintain it without much trouble.

The exercise and repetition of the pedals got his mind working overtime. Adam thought about everything he had learned in the recent past, but his mind kept returning to the pebble in his pocket. It was a key, he was sure, but didn't know how.

Adam's pace slowed as he began to get tired, and soon he had stopped. They had made it most of the way to their destination in a short time.

"We're almost there, but I need a rest," said Adam.

"I know what you mean," said Kevin. "It's not that easy to be a passenger on this thing either. When I'm older and have back problems I'll know why."

They stood and stretched for a few moments.

"What if they get there before us?" asked Kevin.

Adam thought for a moment, "They won't. Without the key there's no use coming out here, so we should have plenty of time to get the Heartstone and get away. I think they'll waste a lot of time just searching for me. Hopefully that gives Jimmy and Mark time to wake up Gurpreet and Don. They'll have some plans for defending the town...I hope..."

"There's a lot more luck in that plan than I care for," said Kevin, "but I can't think of anything better. Let's get moving." Kevin pointed to the seat and waited for Adam to get on.

Soon, they neared their destination. The equipment for the weather monitoring station was housed in a giant ball situated in the middle of an empty field. In the distance, it looked like a golf ball on a tee, ready for some giant to strike at any moment.

Adam watched the ball grow steadily as they approached, wondering how much luck they would need to get through what was ahead.

CHAPTER TWENTY-SIX

Kevin managed to pedal the rest of the way to the giant ball without taking another break. He stopped in the parking lot and they hopped off the bike, glad to be finished riding.

The thirty foot white ball sitting on top of a rickety looking stand dominated the area. Even though supporting cables were strung from it to the ground, it looked like it would blow over in the next big wind, like a dandelion that has gone to seed. On one side of the ball sat a small shed. It probably held the lawnmower that was used around the site and maybe some other maintenance tools, Adam thought. On the other side of the ball tower was a small office. The office was nothing more than a small square building with a door on the front between two windows. The yard was gravelled like the road and smelled like dust.

"Do you think they hid it in the ball?" asked Kevin.

"No. Elianora said they put it underground," said Adam, "so I'm betting there's a Sentinel League door around here somewhere. Besides, that thing is way too obvious."

Kevin nodded. "Maybe the pebble opens the secret door," he said.

"Could be," Adam replied. "Let's look around and see what we can find.

They checked the office building first, but nothing stood out indicating the Sentinel League or a secret entrance. They started at the back and searched their way to the front, ending up at the only door.

The door was locked with a regular lock, so they looked in the window. It was almost empty except for a desk and chair. On the desk was a stack of paper, a stapler and a coffee mug filled with pens. Nothing unusual. There were no other doors that could be seen.

"I don't think it's in here," said Adam.

Kevin nodded. "To the shed."

The shed on the other side of the supporting structure was a small steel one with a single door and no windows. The door was unlocked, so they looked inside. A large riding lawnmower sat in the middle, surrounded by shelves packed full of tools and parts. One shelf held some chemicals and oil jugs while another held pulleys and drive belts. Every other shelf was jam packed with various items.

After looking around for a minute, Adam moved the lawnmower to make sure it wasn't hiding a trapdoor. It wasn't, so he pushed it back in place and stepped outside, certain there was no secret entrance in the shed.

"Are you sure this is where she hid it?" asked Kevin.

Adam thought for a moment. "This is where she pointed when Larix asked where the Heartstone was hidden. I guess we need to try the obvious."

"Yep. Maybe being too obvious makes it easier to hide," said Kevin.

"There's only one way to find out. Let's go up," Adam said as he pointed at the ball, far off the ground.

"How about I keep watch down here and *you* go up. Let me know if you find anything," said Kevin.

Adam chuckled and walked to middle of the structure holding the ball in the air. A plaque was attached to the center column. 'Radome' was written on it in big bold letters.

That's what Elianora said – Radome! he thought.

Next to the plaque was a ladder attached to the center column. It was used to access the interior of the Radome through a hatch above. Adam climbed to the top and pushed up on the hatch, but it was locked, probably with the same type of lock as the attic hatch in Town Hall, he guessed. He searched his pocket, found the pin and opened the hatch exactly as he suspected.

He climbed into the Radome and looked around. It was empty. No radar equipment or electronics of any kind were left inside, not even a forgotten wire. At the top of the dome were a few clear panels that let in enough light to see, even though the sun was beginning to fade.

All around the inside of the Radome were small hatches, 4 feet from the floor. Adam opened the nearest one and looked out. He had a perfect view of the rocky field on the west side of the site, and as he brought his focus closer he saw that he was overlooking the shed.

On the opposite side, he looked out a hatch that was already open. He saw the field to the east with its scrub brush trees in the rocky field. Slowly, he brought his gaze closer and closer, seeing nothing much more than the office building.

The Radome had to be Elianora's lookout, he thought, which meant he was in the right spot - but where was the entrance?

"Is the door in there?" Kevin called from below.

"I don't think so," said Adam.

He returned to looking out one of the hatches, but he looked just outside the Radome where the supporting wires attached to the frame. He noticed a middle wire that wasn't anchored at the outer edge of the structure. It ran to a point underneath that he couldn't see because of the curve of the Radome and the position of the hatch. He followed the wire down toward the ground and it disappeared on the far side of the office.

"Hey Kev," Adam called down, "you see the wire that comes up here from the office?"

"Yeah,"

"Does it attach to the office or the ground?"

Through the hatch, Adam watched Kevin walk to the other side of the office.

"It looks like it attaches to the ground, but it really attaches to the office if you look close enough," Kevin called back to Adam.

Adam climbed down the ladder again, pausing to look at the point where that particular cable made contact with the structure. It threaded into a large steel box and disappeared. Normally a person would assume the wire was attached inside the box, but now that Adam was looking closer, that supporting wire looked out of place, not having another one to balance it out on the other side.

As Adam made his way to the side of the office building, he saw the wire anchored to the ground and leading up to the top of the office.

"Look up there where they meet," said Kevin.

Adam could clearly see a separation between the cable coming down from the Radome and the cable coming up from the ground. He started getting excited and began searching around the side of the office until he found a hole in the cement foundation about the size and shape of a small brick. He stuck his hand in the hole and felt around.

"What is it?" asked Kevin.

Adam pulled his hand from the hole and took out the bag carrying the pebble. He held the pebble in his hand and stuck it in the hole, pulling it upward. Nothing happened.

He pulled his hand out and looked at the pebble when another thought stuck him. He put the key pebble in his pocket, instead of the bag he had taken it from, and searched the gravel around the foundation of the office, picking up a small stone similar in size and shape to the key pebble. He put the piece of gravel into the bag, then back in his pocket as well.

Kevin smiled as he understood what Adam was doing.

"Just a little insurance," said Adam.

Next, he took the pin from his pocket.

"Watch this. I have a feeling it's gonna be cool," said Adam smiling.

With the pin face up in his right hand, he reached into the hole and held it to the top edge. A mechanism operated for a couple of seconds and was silent. Adam pulled up and the entire building hinged upwards toward the Radome. Underneath the office foundation was a wide set of stairs leading down into darkness.

Kevin's eyes were wide in wonder. "That's...That's..." he stuttered.

"I told you it would be cool," said Adam, proud of himself for finding the entrance. He had guessed that the wire coming down from the Radome was most likely hooked up to a large weight in the center column of the structure, balancing out the weight of the office building.

Kevin stood still for a moment, looking down into the darkness and Adam could see a thought hit him. Kevin walked to the front of the building and looked in the lower window. "Come see this!" he called to Adam.

Adam walked over and looked through the window. Nothing in the office had moved, not a paper or a pen, let alone the desk or chair.

"It's all fake," exclaimed Kevin.

Adam smiled for a second, but soon his thoughts were back on target.

"We can look at the cool stuff later, I hope. We need to find the Heartstone fast and get out of here."

Kevin agreed. "After you," he said, ushering Adam toward the staircase, more than happy to be going second once more.

Adam led the way to the stairs and took a few steps down. He kept his hand on the wall, thinking he would probably find a touch location to fire up some Lumiens nearby. After feeling all over the wall for a while, he gave up and hoped there would be a panel lower down.

Down the stairs he went, at least 100 steps, when he finally hit the bottom. He hadn't taken his hand off the wall the whole way, but still hadn't found a panel.

"I made it to the bottom. Just wait there and I'll see if I can find a Lumiens panel somewhere.

In the darkness, he ran his fingers over the wall up and down starting at the stairs and moving forward. Eventually, he came to a point where his feet felt an edge. It was probably more stairs, he thought. Deciding not to go down any further without some light, Adam made his way back to the stairs he had already come down and then followed them across to the other wall. He searched in the same way with no success.

"I can't find a way to turn on the lights. What should we do? Keep going down or check the shed for a flashlight?" Adam asked.

Kevin hesitated for a moment. "Let's try the shed. Maybe they didn't put Lumiens in here for a reason." His voice was far up the stairs.

Adam thought about it for a moment and agreed with Kevin's suspicion. Larix had referred to the fact that Elianora most likely had traps around the Heartstone, so they were better off having a light than not.

"Let's make it fast. We wasted a lot of time already," said Adam. He heard Kevin turn and run up the stairs and realized that Kevin wasn't more than halfway down.

Adam trudged up the stairs, glancing up once in a while to see the dimming light at the entrance. He kept a steady pace until he was near the top. Since Kevin had been at the top for a while, Adam hoped he had already found a flashlight in the shed.

Near the top, Adam's pulse dulled his sense of hearing, but between a couple of heartbeats he clearly heard, "Adam, come out."

It was his mother's voice.

Without wondering why she was there, he ran up the stairs and turned in the direction of her voice, only to see her, Elianora and Kevin held by Larix's men.

A man Adam didn't recognize stood beside Mary. In a smooth British accent, he said, "Hello Adam. Please come out of there ... and hand over the Keystone."

CHAPTER TWENTY-SEVEN

Larix didn't look at all like Adam had expected. He was slim in build, average in height, and wasn't as scrawny as the picture Adam had in his mind. Larix's hair was long and blonde, but the most interesting thing about him was his face. Even Adam had to agree – Larix was handsome.

Adam took the last few steps up the stairs and turned to face the group. Elianora and Mary were clearly under the influence of the sleeping gas, and now it looked like Kevin was also. His eyes were glassy and he swayed back and forth just like all the others. Adam was sure that at any moment he would hear a gunshot and he too would be in dreamland. Maybe it wouldn't be so bad.

"You certainly are a resourceful young fellow," said Larix with a laugh. "You made it difficult for us to find you."

"Not difficult enough," said Adam.

Larix smiled. "My dear friend here tells me you have the Keystone," he gestured to Elianora. "You are probably wondering how it works. I can help you with that, if you let me." He reached out a hand toward Adam, sounding sincere.

Adam felt the influence of Larix, but it didn't sway him.

"Why should I?" he asked. "You're just going to make me a zombie like them and put me in the tunnels to die with everyone else."

Larix was still smiling, but Adam saw the evil in his eyes. His voice was so smooth and relaxing.

"Well, if I was going to do that, it would be done already, no?"

Adam thought about it, and Larix wasn't lying. He would have shot Adam full of chemical as soon as he poked his head out of the stairwell.

"Why didn't you then?"

"According to my friend, I need you."

Adam was confused. "What could you possibly need me for?" he asked.

"Bring me the Keystone and I'll tell you."

Adam pulled the bag out of his pocket. He opened the mouth of the bag and drew out the piece of gravel he had placed inside earlier.

"Is this what you want?" asked Adam.

Larix made a lazy gesture that Adam should bring it to him.

"Too bad," said Adam. He turned and threw the pebble as hard as he could toward the rocky field, where it would be nearly impossible to find.

Larix immediately punched Mary across the face. She fell to the ground whimpering, still in her dreamy state.

"No!" cried Adam.

Larix smiled, but it was a cruel smile. Somehow he managed to look kindly an instant later.

"Now, let's try this again. Bring me the Keystone from your pocket."

Adam couldn't believe what he heard. Larix knew that the pebble Adam had thrown wasn't really the Keystone, but he still punched Mary in the face without a moment of hesitation.

There was nothing else Adam could do, so he pulled the Keystone from his pocket and handed it to Larix.

"Ahh, an Impression Stone. Rare and unique. There are only a handful that have ever been found. You've outdone yourself this time Elianora," said Larix.

"How does *that* work as a key?" asked Adam, still full of anger but also curious, "and how come you need me?"

"I didn't expect your *common* mind to figure this out, no matter how easy it is," Larix commented, smoothness in his voice. "You've learned that boring game they call Kurling, right?"

Adam nodded.

"You see, some of *us* and the odd Common have the ability to connect with rocks much deeper than others. Most connections are associated with a feeling of happiness but some are much stronger. Skilled individuals will see themselves falling into the middle of the stone. Someone as skilled as Elianora here can actually place things in that stone, like instructions. That's why this is the Keystone – it should have instructions on how to get to my prize."

"I should have just dropped it then," said Adam.

291

Larix breathed as if he were frustrated, like explaining the movements of the solar system to a 4 year old. "That wouldn't work, boy. If you put a message in a regular stone and it hits the ground, the message is lost - the same way that a Kurling rock loses connection when it touches the ground. An Impression Stone won't ever lose the message and the connection remains until you connect with another stone."

"Why do you need me then? Just take Elianora. She can lead you through them," said Adam.

"The Heartstone will sense her and *expend* itself. Elianora assures me that it is buried deep enough that if it does explode it will be buried forever."

Adam thought that was a pretty good reason.

"But how am I supposed to help? Just read the stone yourself."

Larix's smile faltered, and his accent became unrecognizable. "I can't," he stated simply with a clenched jaw. "and neither can anyone else in this wretched flatland...but Elianora thinks *you* may be able to read the Impression Stone."

Adam remembered his connections in the Kurling game where he had seen himself falling to the center of each stone.

"Why would she think that?"

"Because your father was able to read them," said Larix, his British accent returning.

Adam thought about his father for a moment. He remembered Karl saying that Edward made strong connections with the Kurling rocks, so Larix's story sounded possible.

"So, then, let us make a deal. If you lead me to my prize, I will promise to leave this town without hurting anyone else - If not," he looked down at Mary, sitting on the ground with blood streaming from her nose.

Adam understood fully what would happen. He also didn't believe that Larix would keep his end of the bargain.

"My guards will have found your other two friends already, so you are out of options. Do we have a deal?"

Adam's heart sank at the news of Mark and Jimmy.

"Deal," he said.

Larix handed the Keystone back to Adam. "Get on with it."

Adam cupped the stone in his hands and held it to his forehead. Being angry and scared, it took him a few moments to start a connection with the stone. When he did, his mind felt that the stone was deep. He travelled much further to the center than the other rocks he had connected with in the past.

At the center, it felt as if he was floating, but he had no body that he could see. He tried to wave his hands in front of his face, but nothing appeared. It was an odd feeling.

Something appeared in the distance, getting closer. It looked like a book. It floated closer and closer until it stopped in perfect view. The pages opened and revealed some pictures, giving instruction how to proceed. After playing once, it slammed shut and disappeared. The moment it disappeared, he snapped back to reality.

Adam was confused. The images he saw didn't make sense, and drifted out of his mind. He tried to focus on any of them, but it felt like trying to grab a cloud. He had a strong feeling that the images would only come into focus once he was down the stairway.

"Are you ready to proceed?" asked Larix

"I...I...think so," said Adam, unsure. Images were still coming and going in his mind. He placed the Keystone back in his pocket and headed toward the stairway.

Larix pointed to two of his men. "You and you, come with us." He pointed to the other two men. "You two, guard our 'friends'. If he comes out without me," he pointed to Adam, "shoot him then shoot the others."

The guards loaded the guns they held. Those guns weren't filled with tranquilizer darts.

The other two guards made their way behind Adam, and Larix fell in line last.

At the entrance to the stairwell, one of the guards clicked on a flashlight and pointed it into the darkness. The light disappeared as if it were pointed into a bottomless pit where there was nothing to reflect it back.

"Your flashlights won't work here," said Adam, surprised that somehow he knew. "We need to feel the stairs with our feet and stop at the landing about a hundred steps down."

He started down the stairs and disappeared into the darkness.

CHAPTER TWENTY-EIGHT

Adam stepped slowly down the stairs. The first time he made that trip he hadn't read the Keystone. The information was in his head, but it all seemed out of reach. All he knew was that he needed to stop at the landing before going any further.

His mind ran through images of everything that just happened, trying to find a way out and escaping from Larix. All of the scenarios ended up with Larix holding the Heartstone and everyone else locked in the tunnels with no food or water until...

Adam shook his head to wake from the daydream. How many steps was that? Last count was over fifty, but how many more to the landing?

Step after step, he dropped further into the earth, feeling the wall on his right side the entire way. It had led him to the landing the first time, so it was the safest thing to do again. Twenty three steps later, he reached his destination.

The instant both feet touched down, an image appeared in his mind. It was as though the lights had been turned on for a second giving him a view of the entire staircase ahead. Straight in front of him was a large hole where he earlier thought there were more stairs. If he had continued on his way the first time, he would have fallen into the hole, never to be seen again. The image sent a chill up his spine.

Adam spoke to the others behind him, "There's a landing here, and beyond it is a large hole. You need to go to the left side. There are stairs on the left, about two feet wide. I don't know how far down they go."

He shuffled his way across the landing using the bottom step as a guide, feeling relieved the moment he touched the left wall. With great care, he shuffled ahead until his foot found the edge of the stairs, then started down another long staircase. He knew it would be long as well, but just how long wasn't revealed to him at the landing.

Adam guessed that he would only be given instruction by the Keystone as it was needed. The glance he had been shown of the open pit had only been a flash, just enough for him to understand where the danger was. He hoped that in the future the instructions would get clearer.

"Are you all still with me," Adam called back to the others, hoping at least one had silently fallen. He could still hear footsteps, much to his disappointment, and they were closer than he preferred.

The two guards gave an arrogant chuckle, silently stating they wouldn't be that easy to lose. Larix said nothing.

On Adam went, step by step, further and further down. The air was stale and humid, and the deeper they stepped the colder it felt. The walls were almost slick with the hint of condensation forming as the temperature dropped. Adam wondered if the coating Elianora applied to his shoes helped with grip on the slippery stairs or if they would actually make it worse.

Adam's foot jarred onto another landing, and an image of a Lumiens panel appeared in his mind. He reached to the left, sliding his hand in a smooth motion upward as it found the panel. The Lumiens glowed in reply.

Once the light was at its brightest, a warm yellow glow filled the large cave, and Adam could hardly believe his eyes. The cave was at least the size of a football stadium. A few steps forward, the landing opened the entire width of the cave, but straight ahead it dropped off a sharp edge into a cavern.

Adam took careful steps to the edge and looked down. He saw the wall going down for a few feet, then disappearing into darkness like the stairs under the office. If he had a stone, he would have dropped it just to hear it hit the bottom – if there *was* a bottom.

He stepped back from the edge as the others came near.

"What now?" asked the guard with the slimmer build.

"I don't know yet," said Adam.

"Hurry it up," said the thicker built guard, hitting Adam with the butt of his gun and laughing.

"Relax," said Larix placing a hand on the guard's shoulder.

Larix looked at Adam. "Walk around until you trigger more information."

Adam rubbed his shoulder where the guard had hit him, then looked around. They were in the middle of the expanse, and the cave was wider than it was long. The cavern in front of them ran the length of the cave and was at least fifty feet across. There was another landing on the other side that looked identical to the one they were standing on, with a doorway in the middle. Adam couldn't see any way across from where he stood, so he walked to the right, looking around as he stepped. The others stayed where they were.

Adam reached the right side of the cave. The moment he touched the wall it triggered another image. It showed him bridges on the right and left side of the cave. The bridge on the right only went a short distance and dropped off into the cavern. The bridge on the left went over the entire span, but somewhere before halfway he saw a break in the bridge, marked on both sides by something on the wall. It also showed him the break was covered by something, but it didn't show him what it was.

Adam looked where the bridge should be, near where he stood, but there wasn't one. Confused, he turned and walked toward the opposite side of the cave.

"We need to get to the landing on the other side. There's supposed to be a bridge across the cavern on that wall," said Adam pointing, "But somewhere around halfway it looks like there is a break we'll have to jump over. There's some kind of marker near the break."

He walked over to the other wall, and as soon as he touched it, the same information played in his mind again. Differing from the first one, he saw the break was closer to a third of the way over the cavern, but still could not tell what or where the marker was on the wall.

"Hang on, Adam," said Larix, as Adam approached the edge of the cavern. "This good fellow is going to go first."

Larix tapped one of the guards on the shoulder, and the guard stepped in front of Adam. It was the guard who hit Adam with his gun.

As far as Adam could see, there was no bridge, just a drop off to the bottomless pit below. The guard in front of him must have seen the same, because he wasn't moving.

"It's an illusion," said Larix, "The bridge is painted to hide it from viewing in this direction. Take a few steps forward and look back; then you will understand."

The guard felt ahead with his foot. When he seemed satisfied that there was solid support, he stepped ahead with the other foot. Being cautious, he stepped a few more times, then turned around and laughed as he looked down.

"I can see the bridge. It's only about two feet wide, so stay close to the wall," he informed the others.

Adam watched as it looked like the guard was air walking across the cavern. It was an odd sight. The guard seemed to be getting more confident in his steps, moving a little faster while scanning the wall as he went.

The scanning triggered Adam's memory of the direction markers in the tunnels. Those markers couldn't be seen but had to be felt. Panic set in.

"Feel the w..." is all Adam could say before the guard disappeared, as if he were sitting in a dunk-tank at the fair and someone hit the target.

They heard him scream for a moment, then complete silence. Adam's stomach churned. Even though the guard had just hit Adam, Adam didn't think it was right to wish that fate on him.

Larix sighed, "Stupid Common," he muttered to himself. "And that is why I asked him to go first," Larix said to Adam.

He turned to the remaining guard. "Your turn, my friend," he said, as though he were letting the guard onto a carnival ride rather than sending him into danger.

"Feel the wall," said Adam. "You won't see the marker; you'll have to feel it."

The guard nodded and stepped forward as though he were a hunter in the woods stalking his prey. His hands began searching the wall at the second step, and he made sure to feel every inch.

"I feel something," the guard called back after making it near the point where they had last seen the other, "It feels like a checkmark."

"Stay there," said Larix. He ushered Adam toward the unseen bridge. "After you," he said; his voice full of kindness.

The more Adam was around Larix, the more he understood how dangerous Larix was. Just his voice began to send chills up and down Adam's back.

Adam stepped ahead with great caution. Even though he had seen two others do so already, it was hard for his mind to believe there was a bridge supporting him. If only there was some dirt or sand he could throw on the bridge to stop the illusion, he thought, but he had nothing. After a few steps he looked back and immediately the illusion stopped, being made for anyone moving forward, not backward. Every few steps he would turn and look back, just to get a mental break.

"It is quite impressive, and disturbing," said Larix as Adam looked back. Larix was quite a few steps behind.

Adam turned forward and kept moving without saying anything in return. After a few more steps, he made it to the point where the other guard had stopped.

"Right here," the guard showed Adam, and Adam put his hand on the spot.

More instruction popped into his mind. It showed a trapdoor immediately in front of them. A view of the bridge from the side showed a figure starting from a point behind them and running over the trapdoor, which was now shown to be too large to jump.

Adam snapped back to reality again. "We need to back up and run over the trapdoor. It's too big to jump and it's on a timer that starts as soon as it senses a footstep. If you don't run fast enough, it'll open before you make it across. If you make it across, it won't open at all. The timer resets itself automatically."

The guard looked at Adam then to Larix.

"Yes, you can go first," said Larix.

I don't think that's what he was thinking, thought Adam.

Larix backed up a few steps to make room as Adam and the guard retreated down the bridge.

"Get on with it," said Larix as the guard paused for a bit too long.

The guard took in a few deep breaths then sprinted forward, slowing down a little as the arc of the bridge started going downwards, but he didn't stop until he made it to the landing on the other side.

"Your turn," Larix said to Adam. "I'll be right behind you, so you better run fast."

The thought was no comfort to Adam. He did the same as the guard before him and took a couple of deep breaths, then broke into a sprint. Adrenaline fuelled him as he felt the angle of the bridge change. He slowed slightly, but it felt as though Larix was breathing in his ear and that made him speed up again. He nearly tripped on the last few strides and fell into the stomach of the guard on the other side.

"Sorry," said Adam.

"No problem," the guard replied in a gruff voice.

"Well now, that was *fun*," exclaimed Larix, laughing as though he really did have fun.

Not by a long shot, thought Adam, his heart still racing and his body full of the adrenaline of fear.

"On to the next adventure," said Larix in a cheery voice.

Adam wished Larix had gone over the bridge first.

CHAPTER TWENTY-NINE

How am I going to get out of this without dying or getting everyone else killed, thought Adam. He hoped there weren't any more traps ahead, but knew that it was a false hope. The best he could wish for was that whatever was ahead would take Larix and not himself.

Adam looked around, and in the middle of the landing was a doorway. Even though he was certain they needed to go through it, he needed to see if there were more information trigger points so he didn't miss something important, possibly fatal. He started at the wall near the bridge they had just come over, and felt his way along, following the wall until he was near the doorway, stopping when he found another trigger. It showed nothing more than a figure walking into the doorway.

Back to reality, Adam continued along the wall to the right of the doorway, triggering the same information he had seen on the other side. When it finished, he continued walking, feeling the wall until he made it to the edge of the cliff on the far end of the landing. Nothing triggered, so he walked back to the doorway.

Adam waved for the other two to follow and stepped

in. He found a Lumiens panel inside and started them glowing, only to reveal a long narrow corridor. The corridor was only wide enough for one person at a time, and would be trouble for the guard, as he was over 6 feet tall and it wasn't. It looked like a dead end from the point where Adam stood.

They walked along the corridor, Adam first and Larix last. The guard in the middle grumbled, as he walked hunched over the entire way. At the end of the corridor, the floor dropped into a long set of stairs, but the ceiling stayed at the same height, meeting a wall far ahead. The room widened and there had to be a hundred more stairs to the bottom, in Adam's opinion.

As they descended the stairs, Adam saw a doorway at the bottom. The wall from the doorway went straight up and met the ceiling that had continued out from the top of the stairs. *It must have taken years to build this place,* he thought, remembering the area they had just passed through and seeing the current area that was so clearly man-made.

Looking ahead he noticed an opening straight above the doorway, halfway up the tall wall in front of him. He wondered how anyone would be able to reach it, and decided there must be a way from the other side. It must be for ventilation of some kind.

At the bottom near the doorway, Adam touched the wall again and was instructed to continue through. The others followed, and after walking down a short hallway Adam came out in another cave. It was high, as high as the ceiling on the other side of the hallway they had just come through. It was shaped like a 'V' with the top much wider than the bottom, but not at enough of an angle to be able to climb the walls. There was a doorway straight ahead, so Adam walked toward it.

A few paces from the door Adam felt his foot sink an inch followed by a click. Next, he heard loud noises in front of him and behind. Huge rocks closed off both doorways.

Uh-oh, he thought.

Another loud click echoed in the cave, followed by the sound of rushing water. It sounded like a dam bursting in the movies, but loud in the echo of the chamber. In seconds the water was waist deep and rising fast.

"What do we do?" the guard yelled in a panic.

"I...I don't know," Adam yelled in reply. "I think we should just let it fill up..."

They were quickly treading water, but the water seemed different. It was easy to stay floating at the surface, unlike regular water that took some effort.

The guard looked stressed, but Larix was still wearing a smile.

"I hate this," said the guard. "This is my worst fear."

"Relax," said Larix. "There will be a way out. Our friend here will figure it out."

Adam looked around. The Lumiens on the ceiling lit the chamber dimly, but as it reached half full, Adam saw a landing at the top that wasn't visible from lower down.

"Look," he said to the guard, hoping to calm him down. The guard saw it and swam so he could get on the landing once the water level rose enough.

Adam and Larix swam toward the landing as well, but the guard scrambled onto it before they could get there. He seemed relieved to be standing on something solid.

The water level rose slower, and Adam made it to the

landing. As he touched it, instructions filled his mind again.

As he snapped out of it, he shouted "Stop!"

The guard, being relieved to be on solid ground, had gone to the back wall to lean against it for a break. Instead of leaning on solid rock, he fell through the wall. It was another illusion. Again, Adam heard only a short scream and then silence. At least it was quick.

Larix pulled himself up on the landing, feet still in the water. He was smiling. "I should have brought more Commons with me. They're great entertainment," he exclaimed, laughing a horrible laugh.

"So, my little guide, we are going to have to be a lot more careful with you from now on...what do we do next?"

Adam was still trying to get over how easily Larix brushed off the death that just happened.

"If what I saw is right, this isn't normal water. We're supposed to be able to breathe in this water," said Adam.

Larix just nodded, like he wasn't surprised.

"We swim down to the doorway that we should have walked through. It's open now. Then, we swim for a long way until it goes up. Past that, I don't know.

Larix nodded and dived into the water, like a teenager at a pool. His head popped out a few seconds later.

"Elianora didn't know that I've done this before," he said in a soothing voice, although it wasn't soothing to Adam. "I used to have a phobia about water, but that was long ago. Now, I am as natural in it as a fish."

Adam couldn't help but notice the similarity between

Jeff's speeches and the one Larix had just given.

"Hold on to the landing and lower yourself into the water as far as you can," said Larix. "Exhale all of the air from your lungs and inhale fast and deep. The less air you have in your lungs and the faster you inhale, the less likely you are to cough."

Adam wasn't sure how much he could trust Larix, but realized that Larix needed him alive. He lowered himself as far as he could, exhaling all the way, but he was afraid to take the water into his lungs. It went against every instinct he had, but because he exhaled on the way down he needed to take a breath soon.

It was excruciating trying to override everything he had learned about being in water his entire life. His logical brain fought against his subconscious, and so far the subconscious was winning. He felt himself getting dizzy from lack of oxygen, and in that moment his subconscious gave up just enough that he was able to open his mouth and suck in some water.

It immediately burned all the way into his lungs. He tried to cough but couldn't because his entire airway was full. The rush of water and oxygen began to clear his dizziness and he was able to exhale and inhale again. He was breathing the water, and it felt wrong, but yet it felt good.

Larix appeared in front of him, a large grin on his face. He had been watching Adam struggle with water breathing and enjoyed every second. After he realized there wouldn't be any more struggling, he pointed in the direction of the doorway.

Adam swam down. It wasn't as difficult to swim down as he thought it would be, probably because he had no air in his lungs so it made him sink easier. There were pockets of Lumiens all over the walls now, leading him deeper and deeper, and finally to the doorway. He would much rather have walked to the doorway than swam.

The doorway led to a long narrow hallway, dimly lit all along. Adam bumped his hands on the walls numerous times as he swam through. He didn't glance back at Larix; he had no doubt Larix was still behind, enjoying himself all the way.

There had to be a way to beat Larix. He was arrogant, that was true, but for his age he didn't seem to have much wisdom. He was quite full of himself, almost in the same way as Jeff Wyndum. Maybe that was something he could use.

The hallway turned upward and Adam swam into the wall because it was so sudden. After he recovered, he saw a ladder built into the wall so someone could climb if the entire thing wasn't filled with water.

Adam kicked and swam upward. At first he couldn't see anything but the scattered spots of Lumiens on the walls. Slowly he saw what he thought was the end of the water. As soon as he was sure, he swam faster, and soon his head broke out of the water.

The first breath he tried to take didn't work too well. He realized he still had lungs full of water too late. He exhaled and tried to inhale again, but it only brought on intense full-body coughing. He fought to climb out as he kept coughing the water from his lungs, ending up on all fours, heaving heavily.

Larix popped up beside him, breathing out a large amount of water and laughing.

"The first time's always the worst," he said. "You needed to exhale as hard as possible again before taking the first breath of air. I forgot to mention that." He laughed while Adam kept coughing, enjoying the show. "Hurry it up, we don't have all day."

Adam coughed with all his strength and struggled to his feet.

"You have some *spirit*," said Larix. "I've seen countless other Commons who would have lost their minds just at the thought of *breathing* water, let alone the confined spaces. Those that would have made it this far would still be shuddering in fright at the waters edge, but here you are, standing and ready to move on. I *like* you. I *may* keep you."

The thought was no comfort to Adam. He struggled to push it from his mind and keep on the task at hand. There will be a way to trap Larix somehow, he kept telling himself, using it as motivation to continue.

He wiped his eyes and looked around. They had surfaced in another cave, dimly lit in the same way as the other ones. It was a large cave, although only a quarter the size of the first one, about the size of a hockey rink. In the middle was an island surrounded by a deep pit with no visible bridge to cross. The island was small, only 10 feet wide at most. In the middle of the island stood a pillar.

Adam decided to walk around and find another trigger. As he reached the edge of the pit, blue green fire roared up around the island. As soon as he took a step back it stopped.

"That rules out extending a ladder across," Larix laughed.

Adam barely heard the comment as he was intent on finding a trigger. Finally, he touched a spot on the right side wall that showed him a short series of images. He wasn't happy with what he saw.

"It's impossible," he said to Larix. "I have to land the Keystone in a little hole on top of that pillar," said Adam, pointing. The pillar was at least three times the distance from them as the button was from the hack in a game of Kurling.

"Obviously it isn't impossible. How do you intend to do it?" asked Larix, sounding like a teacher forcing the student to come up with the answer they already knew.

"I don't know. I can't make that shot. I thought you might have an idea," said Adam.

Larix sighed after a deep breath. "You Commons don't see what's right in front of you. Don't you remember what I told you about the Keystone?" he asked.

"Just that it's rare and doesn't lose its information when it hits the ground."

"Not just the information, it doesn't lose its connection. You can throw that pebble a hundred times and still pull it back for another try. I may not be able to connect with them, but I understand how they work."

Adam remembered hearing Larix talk about the Impression Stones, but only then fully realized what he meant.

"Well, go on," said Larix.

Adam fished the Keystone out of his pocket. He stepped toward the edge of the pit, but not so close that he would set off the fire. Strangely, he could still feel the connection to the Keystone as he held it.

His first throw was terrible and completely missed the target, but when he concentrated and pulled the pebble back, it landed in his hand fast enough to sting, surprising him.

The second throw was much closer as he remembered that he had control over the pebble and could change its direction in the air. The Impression Stone changed direction much easier than any of the Kurling stones he had thrown.

The third throw hit the mark, although slightly to the side. It fell off the pillar nearly a foot before Adam pulled it back.

The fourth throw was textbook. It landed flat on top of the pillar, and Adam had enough control over it to not only stop it on the pillar, but slide it back slightly and drop it in the small hole. The pillar rose up a few feet, and a loud clanging sound bounced around the cave. Up from the depths rose a narrow bridge leading to the island.

"Well done! You *are* a natural," said Larix. "Now, scurry over there and bring me my prize."

Adam felt as though he was a rat in a maze getting cheese for the entertainment of its master.

"You're not coming with me?" asked Adam.

"You don't get to my age by taking stupid risks," said Larix. "That's why I brought you. I just wish I had brought a few more *Commons*." He spit out the last word.

Adam stepped to the bridge, making sure the flames didn't flare up as he reached the edge. When he was somewhat satisfied he might not be burned alive, he took cautious steps across.

Feeling relieved, he stepped onto the island and looked at the pillar, now standing taller than himself. He couldn't see anything unusual about it, so he touched it, hoping it would trigger more information.

Nothing.

Adam continued to look around. Nothing stood out, and no instructions, came to mind. He walked around, touching things and trying to find a trigger, but nothing happened.

"What's taking so long?" Larix called to Adam.

"I can't figure out where it's hidden."

Adam saw that Larix was getting upset, even across the bridge.

"I honestly thought you were smarter than that," Larix called back, obviously frustrated. "but I can't wait anymore. Take that lapel pin from your pocket and place it on top of the pillar. The pillar will drop away and you will find a small drawstring bag in the hole."

Adam was shocked. "How do you know that?" he asked.

Larix laughed, and it was frightening. "Elianora told me exactly what protection she had built here. Didn't you realize that I've known about each of the traps the entire time?" he laughed again.

Adam couldn't believe it. Larix had sent the first guard across the bridge, fully realizing the guard would fall to his death. The thought sickened Adam.

He dug the pin from his pocket and placed it on top of the pillar. The pillar slowly dropped until it stopped a foot below the surface of the island. At the same time, the bridge dropped away and the blue flames returned, hiding Adam from Larix's view.

Adam looked into the hole made by the pillar sinking.

Tucked away in a little hollow was a drawstring bag.

As Adam reached for the bag, another instruction triggered in his mind.

The instruction was different from all the others. It was short, and to the point, but seemed to be poorly done, like looking at a child's drawing compared the Mona Lisa.

The instruction was clear, though. Connect with the stone in the bag.

CHAPTER THIRTY

The blue-green flames roared around the island, providing enough cover so that Adam could take his time. He reached in and pulled out the bag, then untied the elaborate knot in the drawstring.

Opening the bag, he pulled out the stone and looked at it. It was beautiful. It was a deep red color, and although it wasn't transparent, it had depth while seeming to shimmer. It wasn't large, just big enough to fit comfortably in the palm of his hand.

Then Adam remembered the instruction. Connect with the stone. He cupped it in his hands and brought it to his forehead but was nervous to start. The stories of its power made him worry that connecting with it might not be a good idea, but the instruction he received told him otherwise, and so far it hadn't been wrong. He took a deep breath and concentrated on making a connection.

Into the stone he fell, but not as far as he was expecting. He reached the center and once again floated limbless inside. Instead of a book, a small scroll came forward, filled with writing. Once it was close enough, Adam read:

To whoever is connected with this stone: this is not the Heartstone you are looking for, it is a copy. The real Heartstone has been taken away without the knowledge of Elianora or any others in the Sentinel League, in the hopes of keeping it safe.

We know our locations have been compromised. Elianora was unwilling to believe, so we have taken over.

A strange symbol appeared at the bottom of the scroll before Adam was thrown back to reality.

Larix is not going to be happy with this, he thought.

He put the copy of the Heartstone back into the bag and tied it up as it was before. He thought for a moment, formulating a plan. Once again it relied on luck more than skill, as his plan was basically to run.

"Have you found it yet?" yelled Larix over the roar of the flames.

"Yeah, I just have to get the bridge back," Adam shouted in reply.

He grabbed the pin and the pillar rose again. The flames died, and the bridge came back once more.

I have to get out of here, thought Adam.

He walked across the bridge, watching Larix beaming with joy on the other side. Adam knew his joy would be short-lived when he figured it out.

"My prize. It's been away for too long," said Larix, reaching his hands out toward Adam.

Hoping to buy some time, Adam threw the bag against the far wall and ran for the hole they swam out of initially.

Larix laughed as he sauntered over to the bag. "Run, boy, run. I don't need you anymore."

Adam exhaled as hard as he could and dived into the water. He inhaled, and that time had no trouble breathing the water right away.

He was nearly at the bottom, where it turned into the hallway leading to the chamber, when a scream sounded through the water, even as far down as he had already swam. The sound of it scared him, and he swam as fast as he was able, hoping he didn't waste time finding the exit in the next room.

He felt a pressure wave hit the water. *Larix is chasing me, and he's angry! Swim!*

His legs and arms ached from the effort. His hands knocked the walls again and again, but the fear in him hid the pain. Once he was through the doorway, he swam up toward the landing they had been at before. Seeing the edge of the water ahead, he took in a deep breath of water, popped his head out and exhaled with all the power he had in his chest. The first breath of air burned all the way down, but he fought the instinct to cough and grabbed the landing.

As he touched the landing he triggered another image. On the far wall was a hidden platform and exit.

Adam pushed off and swam as fast as he could manage. As soon as he reached the wall he felt for the hidden platform. He found it exactly where the image in his mind showed it to be, then climbed out of the water and ran through the connected zigzag passageway.

He stopped at the exit. It led to the room with the high ceiling and long stairwell. It had been filled halfway with water. Adam realized he was standing in the opening he had seen above the doorway into the chamber.

He dove into the water and swam for the stairs, staying above the water as he didn't want to go through the change from breathing liquid back to air again.

As he reached the stairs, he heard a familiar yell behind him.

"Get back here now, you filthy Common bug! Bring me my prize," Larix screamed in an unrecognizable accent, almost hysterical.

Adam ran up the stairs, not stopping. There was no way he was going back to Larix. Fear filled and fuelled him.

"You have it, don't you?" Larix screamed as he came through the same opening Adam had just left. "All of you planned to give me that *trinket* just to laugh at me. I'll show you!"

Adam kept climbing, his legs burning, but once again adrenaline was carrying a lot of the load. Soon he made it to the top of the stairs and ran down the long hallway.

Back at the large cave, Adam ran to the right. As he approached, he saw how the entire bridge was visible from that direction. He ran over the bridge and sped up when he neared the trapdoor area. He flew over the trapdoor then slowed his pace on the other side, and soon he was at the base of the bridge, his side in pain from all the effort.

Larix stepped through the hallway opening on the other side, walking like he was strolling through a park. He had brought his temper under control, stopped and looked at Adam across the cavern.

"No need to run. You have nowhere to go anyway,"

said Larix. "Just give me my prize, and I'll keep you around like I said before. You made me angry, but you can make it up to me. Just hand it over." Larix sounded like a child begging for a toy.

Adam had almost caught his breath again. "I don't have it," he called back to Larix.

Even from across the cavern, Adam saw Larix's face curl up in anger.

"Why do you have to *lie to me,*" he shouted back at Adam, running toward the bridge.

Adam ran to the stairs, the fear back again. He took a moment to make sure he was on the right side stairs instead of the left, so he wouldn't fall into the hole, then climbed into the darkness.

Please forget which side the hole is on, he wished to himself.

He heard footsteps approaching the stairs below him then starting up the stairs at a quick pace. He was amazed at how fast the footsteps sounded.

"You just keep running. I'm in great condition and I'll catch you soon. Then I'll teach you not to lie to me!"

Adam kept going as fast as he could, but Larix was gaining ground. He made it to the first landing and saw dim light at the entrance above, reflecting off the bottom of the office building. It had to be yard lights, as it was past dusk.

What to do? Larix was catching up to him, and Larix's men were still at the top.

Adam decided to run for it. Dive out of the stairwell and try to get behind the office or Radome. Maybe he could even make it into the Radome. It was the only plan he could think of as he climbed the stairs.

Larix's footsteps sounded on the landing much sooner than Adam anticipated. He was gaining on Adam, and unless Adam sped up, Larix would catch him before he reached the top. At that moment, Adam would rather have faced the bullets than the wrath of Larix.

"You really think you can beat me?" he laughed, then started climbing the stairs at an impressive pace.

Adam concentrated on his task, although he was already exhausted both physically and mentally. He had to try. He couldn't give up. For Elianora. For Kevin. For his mom. Somehow he managed to sprint the last length of stairs.

"Shoot him when he comes up then shoot everyone but Elianora," yelled Larix, right behind Adam as he neared the top.

The last steps were agonizing as Adam thought he felt Larix's fingers grasping at his pant legs. Near the top, he jumped out with all the strength he had left and rolled.

Two gunshots sounded in the darkness.

Adam stopped rolling and lay still. Was he dead, or just asleep? Is this what it feels like to be dead?

He felt himself all over and didn't find any blood or darts.

His thoughts were interrupted by a gruff voice. "Get up."

Adam looked toward the voice. In the dim light streaming from the Radome he saw Ben Casey.

CHAPTER THIRTY-ONE

If you had told him a week ago that he would be excited to see Ben Casey, Adam would have laughed out loud, but at that moment Ben was a beautiful sight.

Ben stood in the spot where Adam had last seen Kevin, Elianora, and his mom. But where were they now?

Two figures ran over to Adam, and he recognized them instantly by their movement. It was Jimmy and Mark.

"You're one lucky man," said Jimmy. "If you hadn't come out of there when you did Ben was going to blow the whole thing up.

"I guess that does make me lucky," said Adam, not realizing until that moment how hoarse his voice had gotten. The water breathing and running had taken a toll.

"I'm not the only lucky one. You two aren't zombies, and you're not dead. I want to hear what happened, but where are Kevin, Elianora and Mom?"

Jimmy stepped aside and pointed a few feet behind Ben. Adam saw Marius, Gurpreet, and Don hunched over three lumps on the ground.

"They'll be ok. They're just getting the antidote. It'll take a few minutes for them to recover," said Jimmy.

Adam noticed that the men who were guarding his mom, Elianora, and Kevin were lying on the ground a few feet from the group.

"As for those guys, I'll tell you about that after Mark tells his story. It's short and sweet – like him." Jimmy joked.

Mark gave Jimmy an angry look, then sighed and began telling his story.

"Well, when you locked me in the tunnels, I started making my way to the junction nice and quiet. When I made it to ring tunnel, I went left because I though it would be a shortcut...and I sort-of got lost. Those tunnels get confusing," said Mark.

"All you had to do was walk to the junction, go straight across and take the first one to the left," said Adam, "or feel for the 9:00 marker."

"I didn't know that!" Mark replied, indignant.

"You saw the map. You followed us through the tunnels, how come you didn't know?" asked Adam.

"*I* wasn't watching. *You* were leading. I just followed."

Adam put his face in his palm. "Go on," he said.

"I was only a little bit lost, and after walking a long way down a tunnel, I knew I was in the wrong place, so I just turned around and walked straight for the junction. I heard a noise and started walking like one of the sleepers when a guard stepped into the junction. I made a groan to get his attention, and he pointed his gun at me. It really scared me and I nearly dropped the act and ran - "

"- but that would involve running," Jimmy interrupted.

"Ha ha ha," said Mark, "anyway, my acting worked. He grabbed me by the arm and led me straight to the meeting room. He took me to the back and sat me down behind Jimmy's parents then left, but there was another guard at the door watching over all of us. A little while later, the first guard came back and dragged me out of the meeting room. He knew I was still awake and asked me where Jimmy was. I told him we split up and I didn't know. He tied me up at the front desk in Town Hall and said Larix would get answers out of me later. I was pretty worried, but Ben and Jimmy showed up a while later."

"I guess it's your turn," Adam said to Jimmy.

"Now you get the interesting story," said Jimmy, elbowing Mark lightly.

Mark elbowed him back hard, making Jimmy wince.

"When I left the school I knew I didn't want to walk straight down the middle of the road. I ran across the street and behind the church hall. After that, I followed the back alleys all the way home, taking my time before I crossed every street - like a ninja, only better."

Mark rolled his eyes at Jimmy.

"That coating on our shoes is amazing! I made no sound, even on the gravel. I was sure my breathing was going to give me away at some point because that was the only thing I could hear. Anyway, when I reached home, I had already figured out where Mom would have hidden her pin. She has a purse that she only takes to work, then hides it when she gets home. She thinks we don't know where it is, but we do. I'm not telling you, though."

Adam nodded, indicating that it was alright.

"Thankfully it's Sunday and Mom didn't have to work, or she would have had it with her when they put her in the tunnels. I dumped everything out on the bed, and when I couldn't see it, I felt the purse. I found it, of course. It was in a hidden compartment. Where else would it be? But I figured it out." Jimmy's chest bulged during the last sentence.

"Please Jeff, go on..." said Mark, which made Adam break out in a hearty laugh. Jimmy's chest fell. He looked as if he were going to refuse telling the rest of his story, but must have decided that it made him look good enough to continue.

"When I left my house, I knew they would have guards around Town Hall, so I didn't want to go there. I was kind-of tired from running, so I decided to try going up the back alley to Ben's house, and if I couldn't get in the shed I would see if the bar was open. The only problem with that is I had to cross Main Street, straight up from Town Hall.

When I got there, I peeked out from behind a building and saw a guard out front. He was pacing back and forth kind-of strange, so I decided to watch him for a minute and decide if I was going to run for it or not. Right away I found out why he was pacing. He ran to the side of the building and unzipped his pants. I guess he really had to go! The second I realized what he was doing, I ran for it. He didn't see me and he sure wouldn't have heard me."

Mark was about to open his mouth to insult Jimmy, but Adam held up his hand to stop him.

"Thanks," Jimmy said to Adam. "I got to the shed and it was closed, but I used the pin and got down to the jail cell. Ben was in the cell in a daze. They even tied his hands and feet and laid him down. I was lucky that the way they laid him down I could still reach his head, so I gave him some of the antidote. You know how they say not to wake an angry bear? I just witnessed it when he came around. You think he swears a lot normally, wait until you hear him when he's mad!"

They all looked to Ben, who was in the middle of tying Larix's hands. Ben heard the comments.

"If you don't like it, don't come to my house if the Roughriders are losing!"

"Have no fear, I'll stay far away during football season," said Jimmy. "Anyway, Ben told me how to open the cell and get him untied. After that, I just followed along. He had a jar of the stuff we had on our shoes, but he coated the insides of his pants and his arms with the stuff too. He literally made no sound when he moved. It was strange to see an overweight old bald guy moving like he did - no offence," Jimmy added as he looked to Ben.

Ben grunted in response.

"From then on, it was the Ben show. Let me just say, you *do not* want to make him angry. I saw him do things to those guards that they've never even thought of in the movies. He didn't kill them, but they'll have a hard time walking from now on."

Ben laughed loudly, "They'll be fine. With a good chiropractor and a month of bed-rest they should be able to feed themselves again."

It was the first time they heard Ben laugh, and they didn't want to hear that ever again.

"So, these two took out the guards," said Mark, pointing at Jimmy and Ben, "then Jimmy and I started by waking up Marius, Dad, and Don. We told them what happened after feeding more of the antidote to other

Sentinel League members. The men discussed a plan, and we showed my mom and Karl how to wake everyone."

"They tried to leave without us, but I convinced them that we might know something they needed, so they brought us along," said Jimmy, proud of himself again.

Mark nodded, "Ben had snuck away without us noticing, so we followed the other men out to Elianora's. You know the basement room where we hid all her books and stuff? It has a secret tunnel that comes out in the trees near here. By the time we got close enough, we could see Ben standing here with the guards on the ground."

Adam was listening intently, taking it all in.

Mark continued. "Dad and the others started talking about their options while they laid the three down to give them the antidote. Ben said they had agreed to blow up the whole thing in this situation. Soon after, we heard Larix yelling at you. Ben already had a tranquilizer gun, but he gave a real one to my dad and told him to shoot Larix if he didn't go down from whatever was in the dart. You popped out, Ben dropped Larix with two shots, and you know the rest."

"Adam!" came a shout from behind Jimmy. Mary had woken up and ran toward Adam, grabbing him in a big hug as soon as she was close enough.

"Are you alright? Did he hurt you?" She examined him, full of concern. It felt strange, as Adam couldn't remember Mary ever being concerned about him that much.

"I'm okay," said Adam, fidgeting in her arms.

"Are you sure?"

"Yes, Mom. Are you?"

Mary felt her nose and winced. "I'll be fine, thanks."

The awkwardness was broken when they heard someone clear their throat. Kevin stood nearby looking tired and sheepish. Adam broke out of his mom's grip.

"Sorry I told them about the pebble being in your pocket instead of the bag," he said. "I couldn't help myself."

"That's ok," said Adam.

"No, it's not. I feel terrible. All he asked was 'where is the Keystone' and I couldn't stop. I pointed and said, 'In Adam's pocket. The one in the bag is just a piece of gravel.'" Kevin's face showed genuine disappointment in himself.

"Don't beat yourself up over it. You heard what other people told him. No big deal. I'm safe, he's caught and we're all ok. Nobody died," said Adam, although that wasn't true. He thought of the two guards down below.

Kevin smiled a little. "Thanks," he said, slightly louder than a whisper.

"You look terrible," said Adam.

"You don't look like you just came from the spa either," said Kevin.

"I could go for some of Kevin's coffee right now," said Elianora, startling the boys.

They turned and looked at her. "How..." Kevin started.

She held up a hand to silence him. "Thank you. All four of you. Your quick thinking saved us all. But where is the Heartstone? I assume it is still hidden?"

"It was a fake," said Adam.

"Are you sure?" asked Elianora, shocked at the news.

"As soon as I gave it to Larix, he knew it was fake too. He thought I had the real one and was trying to escape with it."

Elianora looked concerned.

"What are you going to do with him?" asked Adam.

"He'll be shipped to a special prison made just for him. Hopefully he will be there for a long time. It is soundproof, so he won't be able to talk his way out."

"And the rest of the men that followed him?"

"First, we send them to our prison. We will interview all of them and find out which ones are genuine criminals and which are just under *his* influence. A committee will decide what happens to them from there."

Adam was almost afraid to tell, "There are two guards down there." He pointed down the stairs. "Will someone get their bodies?"

Ben laughed. "I doubt they're dead, son. We don't kill anyone, unless we absolutely have to."

Elianora nodded. "They will be fine, although being in a dark soundproof echoless room can play with your mind a little."

Adam felt a lot better at the news, but another question popped up.

"Larix said that his men had captured 'the other two', but Jimmy was never caught. I'm confused."

"That is typical Larix. He found out about the other two while questioning me. He used that knowledge and a lie to make sure you felt helpless and out of options. That way, you would tell him everything you knew."

Adam now understood and felt like he had been fooled, although in the end everything seemed to work out.

"I need to speak to Adam," Elianora said as she pulled Adam aside, indicating she wanted privacy.

They walked to the other side of the shed and stopped.

"Tell me everything that happened, including all of the images you triggered along the way," she said.

Adam told the story, step by step, shuddering when he thought about breathing underwater. Elianora listened and absorbed every word. Twice she made Adam tell her the instruction he triggered while grabbing the fake Heartstone, and twice more what he read from it. Her face looked concerned the entire time.

"You don't know who took it, do you?" said Adam.

Elianora shook her head. "I thought it was here. It's the first time in many years that I don't know where it is, and I don't even know how long it's been gone."

"What do we do now?" asked Adam after a long pause.

"Well, we continue living the way we have. Larix will be safely imprisoned for a long time, and *you* will be safe. We will keep teaching the ways of the Sentinel League because there are still many things Mankind isn't ready to know."

"But what about the Heartstone?" asked Adam.

"Larix will be locked away so it doesn't matter where the Heartstone is. For me it's almost a relief not to be worried about it constantly." Her eyes showed that she spoke the truth.

Adam nodded in agreement.

With that, they rejoined the group.

CHAPTER THIRTY-TWO

Another sunny summer day shone on the town of Grayson.

It had been a week since the fog surrounded the town, and when it left it brought change.

The Sentinel League members were happy that their long-time foe was on his way to prison, never to be let out again. Special members came to transport Larix at the request of Elianora. Only she would know the status of the Elite Transport Team, and she would inform everyone once Larix was secure in his new home.

Since the incident, the whole community knew about the Sentinel League, and all residents were invited to join as initiates. The missing residents of Waldron were found, still in perfect health. The residents of Langenburg weren't so lucky. A few of the sick and elderly passed away due to their extended time locked underground.

Adam sat in front of the store as he had done the day he had first heard about Langenburg.

Aggie and Martha walked past, deep in conversation, once again ignoring Adam. They discussed their gardens and talked about how the bugs were eating their potato plants. It made Adam remember how clueless he was those few weeks ago.

In mid-sentence, both ladies stopped. Aggie didn't move a muscle for half a minute, followed by a strange full-body shake. After she recovered, she turned around and walked straight toward Adam.

"You need to stay safe," she said, looking him in the eyes and pointing at his chest.

She caught Adam off guard. It didn't seem like one of her usual stories that were so easily ignored. It felt the same as when she had warned Jimmy about his shoelaces long before he had tripped on them in the tunnels.

"Why? Larix is gone," said Adam.

"No. Larix is about to escape. He thinks it was your fault he was captured and that you know where the real Heartstone is. He *will* come for you, but I can't see when. You need to stay safe."

She stopped speaking and her whole body shook again. When she stopped, Adam could tell she had changed somehow.

A confused look came over Aggie's face. She turned and walked back to Martha. "Like I was saying, I'm sure those potato bugs were living in the potato sacks when we bought them." They continued on with their prior conversation as if Aggie hadn't said a word to Adam.

How does she know that Larix is about to escape? he wondered.

The hair stood on the back of his neck.

About the Author

Scott Gelowitz grew up in Grayson, Saskatchewan, and now lives in Regina, Saskatchewan, with his wife Jennifer and their four children.

Grayson is used as the setting for this novel, and most of the places are real. The people, however, are completely fictional.

The Book of Adam – Town Secrets is Scott's first novel, as well as the first book in the series.

For contact information, or information on other books in ***The Book of Adam*** series, please visit:

www.scottgelowitz.com

CPSIA information can be obtained at www.ICGtesting.com
Printed in the USA
LVOW04s2130210215

427736LV00033B/1550/P